**Brighten your world with *Sunday Times*
bestseller Libby Page . . .**

'A testament to ki̶̶̶̶̶̶̶̶̶̶̶̶ip'
all ̶̶̶̶̶̶

'Tender, thought-provoking and uplifting'
Daily Mail

'Such a warm and wise story about female friendship
and vintage fashion. A joy to read!'
Alex Brown

'A heart that shines from every page'
AJ Pearce

'Heartwarming and uplifting'
Sun on Sunday

'I simply adored this gloriously uplifting story
about friendship and fashion'
Kate Eberlen

'Full of heart'
Lucy Diamond

'This wholesome book will make perfect reading for a chilly day'
Prima

'Brimming with charm and compassion . . .
a feel-good celebration of community'
Daily Express

'A joyful celebration of community'
Observer

'Heartwarming'
Good Housekeeping

'Like a warm hug'
The Sun

'Heartwa̶̶̶̶̶̶̶̶̶̶̶̶̶̶̶̶

'Feel-good̶̶̶̶̶̶̶̶
Da̶̶̶̶̶̶

Libby Page is the *Sunday Times* bestselling author of *The Lido*, *The 24-Hour Café* and *The Island Home*. *The Vintage Shop* is her fourth novel. Before becoming an author, she worked in journalism and marketing. She is a keen outdoor swimmer and lives in Somerset with her husband and young son.

Follow Libby on social:
@libbypagewrites
🐦 @libbypagewrites
📷www.libbypage.co.uk

Also by Libby Page

The Lido
The 24-Hour Café
The Island Home

THE
VINTAGE
SHOP

LIBBY PAGE

ORION

First published in Great Britain in 2023 by Orion Fiction,
This paperback edition published in 2023 by Orion Fiction,
an imprint of The Orion Publishing Group Ltd
Carmelite House, 50 Victoria Embankment
London EC4Y 0DZ

An Hachette UK Company

1 3 5 7 9 10 8 6 4 2

A CIP catalogue record for this book
is available from the British Library.

ISBN (Paperback) 978 1 4091 8833 9
ISBN (eBook) 978 1 4091 8834 6
ISBN (Audio) 978 1 4091 8835 3

Typeset by Deltatype Ltd, Birkenhead, Merseyside

Printed in Great Britain by Clays Ltd,
Elcograf, S.p.A.

MIX
Paper from
responsible sources
FSC® C104740

www.orionbooks.co.uk

For
Sally Page
and
Sally Lane

Who taught me how to live life colourfully

PROLOGUE

THE SHOP

Two women stand side by side behind a shop counter. Sunlight streams in through the freshly cleaned windows and catches on the fabric of the dresses that hang neatly on the rails. There are clothes in every colour of the rainbow, from poppy-red to pale sage-green, to pinks so bright they make your mouth water and blues so blue you can't help but think of the glittering sea on a hot day.

For now, the shop is empty of customers, the clock above the door telling the women that it is nearly time to open up. The floor has been swept and the curtain in the changing room pulled back to reveal a glistening mirror, ready and waiting to greet the customers who will wander inside later today, on the hunt for something particular or instead drawn inside by the wink of a dress that they simply can't resist.

The two women behind the counter look around, checking everything is ready for the day. They have both spent countless hours preparing for this moment, the shop a manifestation of both their passion and hard work. Once they are satisfied that everything is as it should be, they glance at one another and share a smile. It's a smile that speaks of all the things they have been through together and everything that has led them to this point. It's a smile built on tears, secrets and pain, as well as the shared love, laughter and friendship that has pulled them both out from those dark moments.

Eventually the clock above the door hits ten and they nod to one another.

'Do you want to open the door?' says one of the women, holding out a key.

The woman at her side shakes her head and reaches for her arm. 'Let's do it together.'

It's time to open the shop and welcome their customers. But it's so much more than that too. For both women, it's time for a second chance.

LOU

The new shop at the top of the hill in the small Somerset town of Frome is worth the walk up the steep cobbled street. At least that's what its owner Lou tries to tell herself as she stands alone behind the counter, the autumn sun shining through the window and onto her face, neatly made up as usual in her 1950s-style make-up. *We've only been open a couple of weeks*, she reminds herself, *they'll come*. And when they do, how could they not want to rummage through the racks of colour, her collection of vintage clothes and accessories lovingly hoarded over the years and now steamed and hanging neatly on wooden hangers.

She's made the most of every space. Suspended from the ceiling is a wire birdcage looped with scarves so the customers can easily touch them (an important part of the shopping process, in Lou's mind) and try them in front of one of the antique mirrors dotted around the shop. All the rails of clothes look vibrant and enticing. Lou remembers finding every single item and has dreamed up stories about the history of each piece before they came into her life. It's one of the reasons she loves vintage so much. As she stands in her shop, she feels as though she is not alone but instead surrounded by hundreds of lives. Those lives are woven into the threads of each and every piece, the memories of unknown people left behind like a trace of old perfume.

She glances at the wall behind the counter, where a black-and-white photo of her mum hangs in a gold frame beside another of both her parents on their wedding day. She likes to think of them both watching her as she works. It was her mum who encouraged her to open the shop. Lou always dreamed about having her own place where she could share her passion for vintage, but never quite managed to find the confidence to leave her stable job in recruitment and set out on her own. But when her mum died six months ago after a long battle with ovarian cancer, Lou finally found the motivation to turn her dream into a reality. Life, she had painfully learned, was short. She didn't want to keep putting off her dreams any more.

Lou decided to open the shop in her hometown in Somerset. She may have left when she was a teenager, spending many years in London, then Brighton, but when her mother received her diagnosis, she moved back to care for her. Lou's father had passed away ten years ago, not long after Lou graduated from university, and Lou hated the thought of her mother facing her illness alone. As her mum grew sicker and sicker, Lou was there to look after her, the two of them back together in the house where Lou had grown up. After her mother's death, it seemed fitting to remember both her parents by starting her business in the place they had lived for most of their lives, a place that Lou may have been eager to swap for a busier city when she was younger.

The day after her mother's funeral, Lou started work on the shop, researching premises and organising viewings. She decided to sell the family house that was left to her in the will; it felt too painful to continue living there once both her parents were gone. The house held too many sad memories and what Lou needed was a fresh start.

She eventually settled on this building at the top of Catherine Hill, the charming cobbled street lined with independent shops and cafés. The shop had been empty for a while and needed renovation, something Lou took on herself, the sanding and painting and hanging of rails proving a welcome distraction from her grief. The flat above the shop was a different story; it had been used as a storage space for years and had fallen into more substantial disrepair that needed working on by a professional. For now, home for Lou is a room in the town's Premier Inn. Plenty of Lou's parents' old friends had offered for her to stay until the work was completed on her flat, but Lou couldn't bear the thought of their kindness. She knew they would keep asking her if she was OK and she couldn't stand the thought of having to keep lying.

Blinking quickly, she looks away from the photographs and back around her shop. It still makes her proud to think that it's really hers. It's exactly how she pictured it when she used to daydream in her old office job, right down to the colour of the walls and the carefully handwritten tags that hang from each item. She worked hard to get to this point, spending long days and nights doing DIY and decorating and sorting all her stock. Now everything about it is perfect. All she needs is customers.

DONNA

Donna doesn't like surprises. She doesn't like change either, which is why she has lived her whole life in Cold Spring, a small village that hugs the edge of the Hudson River in Upstate New York like a limpet. For sixty years, she has never dreamed of going anywhere else. Each day, she does the same walk along Main Street with her dog Luna, taking in the same clapboard houses with their wraparound porches and painted mailboxes and looking across at the same view over to the forest on the opposite side of the river where the colours turn from green to gold to fire-tinged red with the seasons. The changing seasons are the only kind of change she does like, it being a transformation that can be predicted and plotted on a calendar.

Each morning, she eats the same thing for breakfast (half a grapefruit, a black coffee and a bowl of Cheerios) and puts on the same outfit (a pair of indigo jeans and a plain sweatshirt that she owns in multiple shades of blue) and goes to work

7

in the office at the Sycamore Inn, the family business where she first started as a teenager and which she later took over with her husband when her parents retired. Her husband and their long-standing manager take care of the messy business of interacting with guests, while Donna deals with the accounts, admin and managing the online booking system. For the most part, her days form a pattern as neat and as easy to follow as a perfectly written recipe.

So, when her elderly father, who lives just down the road and isn't scheduled to see her until a family dinner the next day, rings her at 11 a.m. one Tuesday, she feels a shiver run up her spine.

'Dad? What is it?' she asks anxiously, picking up straight away.

'Is John with you?' her father replies in a shaking voice.

Donna looks up from her desk where she had been engrossed in sorting through that month's expenses and sees her husband in the doorway, perhaps alerted by the sound of her phone or maybe simply drawn to her when she needs him the most, as he so often has been over the years.

'I know you hate shocks,' her father continues, 'but I'm afraid we've had one. It's your mom.'

Donna has boiled the kettle fourteen times already and it's not even midday. There has been a steady stream of visitors to her parents' home ever since her mother returned from hospital after what turned out to be a minor stroke, or a TIA as the doctor called it. She only had to stay for one night, but it is a small town and somehow word has spread with the speed of a bad cold making its way around an elementary school. Donna can hear John and her father talking with a group of well-wishers in the living room as she fills the kettle again in the kitchen.

'We were so worried when we heard, weren't we, Don? Our cousin Jean had a stroke last year too and she hasn't been the same since.'

'The doctors say she's doing OK though?'

'Here, I've brought some of my jam, just a little something, you know.'

'Oh, how kind of you,' she hears John replying, 'and home-made you say? Delicious. I'm sure Shirley will be delighted. I'll make sure to show her when she's awake.'

And that's why Donna has spent the whole morning making coffee, leaving the greeting of visitors to John. She just doesn't have it in her to pretend to be thankful for yet another pot of jam.

These particular visitors don't stay long and once she has heard them say their goodbyes, Donna leaves her hiding place and joins her family. Her daughter, Brooke, has caught the train from Manhattan to be there, leaving her toddler, Chloe, with her husband, Tom, for the day. It unnerves Donna to see her daughter in a tracksuit and hoody and with a bare face, instead of in the smart clothes and meticulous make-up she usually wears to work in the city. She has always been close to her grandmother, the two of them having more in common, in some ways, than Donna and Brooke do.

'If anyone brings another pot of jam, we might have to open a shop,' Donna grumbles.

Brooke smiles weakly. 'They're just trying to be kind, Mom.'

'If they wanted to be kind, I'd rather they stayed at home!' she says, trying not to raise her voice. 'Your grandmother needs to rest, and so do we. I just don't understand what possesses people to think that the very day when a family member arrives back from hospital is the time to pay a social call.'

'You're right,' says her father, Ken, 'but I guess it's just what people do.'

'What would you do if a friend had just come out of hospital?' asks John.

Donna thinks about it. 'Well, if they'd only been in there a short amount of time, I would walk their dog. If it had been longer, I'd probably clean their car.'

'And why's that?' Brooke asks, raising an eyebrow.

'Well, if they're just back from hospital they're not going to be thinking about cleaning their car, but at this time of year you know how much of a mess the leaves can make. If we get any rain, the leaves form a mulch that glues itself to your car windscreen. If you don't clear the car regularly, it can become a total nightmare. The last thing they'd want to think about when they're trying to recover.'

To Donna's surprise, Brooke reaches out and pulls her into a hug, squeezing her tightly.

'I love you, Mom.'

Donna blinks quickly.

'I love you too.'

The sound of stirring upstairs causes them all to look upwards.

'Shall we go and check on her?' suggests Ken and in silence

the family follow Donna's father up to her parents' room, where her mother is propped up in bed. Her skin is pale and her typically blow-dried white hair lies flat against her head, making her grey eyes seem larger than usual as she looks up at them all.

Donna glances away, still not used to seeing her mother like this. Shirley may be eighty-five, but she is still a member of nearly every organisation in the town, including the walking club that arranges regular hikes through the Hudson Highlands. Donna knows logically that given her mother's age she is lucky to have lived such an active life up until now and that a health scare like this was always going to happen eventually. But although logic might usually be Donna's friend, it can't help her now. Faced with the image of her elderly mother propped up in bed, she doesn't feel like a sixty-year-old looking at an eighty-five-year-old, but like a child looking at their parent and wishing them to be invincible.

'Oh good, you're all here,' her mother says, her voice faltering slightly. 'Now we're all together there's something I need to tell you all. Well, something I need to tell *you*, Donna.'

The tone of her mother's voice makes Donna panic.

'Did the doctors tell you something else? Are there complications?'

But her mother shakes her head rapidly. 'It's not that. Although, of course, I do have to be careful and watch what I eat and keep taking my medication. But this whole thing has given me a scare. It's made me realise I just have to tell you something. It's something I really should have told you years ago.'

'We both thought about it so many times,' chips in Donna's father, who is now standing beside his wife holding her hand. 'But we never managed to find the right words or the right moment. And then the longer we left it, the more difficult it became. Until it felt impossible.'

Donna looks rapidly around the room, taking in the expressions of each member of her family. The furtive glances shared between her parents, the furrowed brow of her husband and the way Brooke keeps looking over at Donna as though checking she is OK while still clearly being troubled herself too.

'What is it, Mom?' Donna asks, struggling to force the words around the boulder that has formed in her throat.

On the bed, Shirley bows her head, tears filling her eyes.

'This scare has reminded me that I'm old. And she is too, if she's still alive.'

'Who is?'

But her mother continues as though she hasn't heard Donna's question, the tears dripping into the deep lines on her face. 'I've left it long enough as it is. It might already be too late. But I have to finally tell you. Or perhaps it might be easier to *show* you.'

And she reaches into her bedside drawer and pulls out an envelope and from within it a photograph.

'Her name is Eleanor,' she says, passing it across to Donna, who reaches for the photo and holds it with the edge of her fingertips, John and Brooke gathering close to look at it too.

The image wears the faded, painterly style of a photo from another era. In it is the blurred figure of a woman, her features unclear apart from a broad smile. She looks as though she is

12

spinning, and the movement creates ripples in the skirt of her bright yellow dress, a dress covered in tiny embroidered flowers.

'At least, that's what we were told,' adds Donna's mother. 'We don't know much else. But I kept this photo, always planning to one day show you. I'm just so sorry it's taken me so long.'

'Who is she?' asks Donna, doing her best not to shout, her blood thumping loudly in her ears.

But her mother is crying too hard now to speak, so instead it's her father who looks up at her and in a soft voice tells her the truth.

'She's your mother. Your birth mother.'

There are as many kinds of dresses as there are types of people. A high-necked black dress that seems shy at first until the wearer turns round to reveal a low back and the curve of a shoulder blade; a show-off kind of a dress covered in ruffles; a hard-working pinafore dress. And then there is a yellow dress, a dress made for dancing.

In certain lights, the dress looks like freshly churned butter, but as a shaft of sunlight slants in through the kitchen window, the fabric glows like the inside of a buttercup. Two women lean over the dress, a Singer sewing machine between them on the kitchen table, cleared for the afternoon of its vegetable peelings and dustings of flour. One of the women is young, her dark hair pulled back today in a pink dotted headscarf, her neat eyebrows creased as she concentrates on her work. The other woman is not young but has a face that reminds you nonetheless of youth, of a time before war, children and endless laundry carved lines

15

into her pale skin. Beyond the pair, the scullery door is open, letting in a humid breeze and the sound of children playing in the dusty Islington streets. The wireless chatters in the background, but no one listens.

'And you're sure they said it was just regular cotton?' mumbles the older woman through a mouthful of pins.

'Of course, Mother,' replies the younger woman, her attention on a delphinium-blue thread that she pulls carefully through the yellow fabric, adding another stitch to her embroidery. 'The pattern called for six yards. I'd have to work for a year at the store to afford that much silk.'

'You could have chosen a simpler style. This big skirt – are you planning on hiding a circus under there?' The older woman sniffs and adjusts the fabric on her lap, her plain blue housecoat covering a simple straight skirt and cream blouse, the buttons resewn countless times.

'But rationing's over now, Ma. And think how wonderful it will be to dance in.'

The young woman's mother doesn't say that it's been a long time since she went dancing, so long in fact that she can't quite remember what it feels like to sway to music or rest her cheek against a warm chest, listening to a heart beating. Instead, she continues pinning the hem of the skirt as her daughter adds more stitches to the embroidery that adorns the nearly finished dress. In the absence of silk, the embroidery is an attempt to make the day dress into something fit for a dance hall. Both women's fingers are stiff from the effort.

'Shall we see how it's looking?' the younger woman asks her mother.

Together they stand, holding the dress in front of them.

The top half of the dress is neat and fitted with a collared V-neck, the waist slim and decorated with a row of shiny buttons. After the neat waist, the skirt billows out in folds of sunshine. The entire dress is covered in flowers, all rendered in miniature by multicoloured threads. Roses with tiny green leaves, poppies in bright lipstick-red, sunflowers and cornflowers and tiny white daisies. It is as if a wildflower meadow is growing out of the fabric itself, each leaf and petal picked out in delicate thread.

The young woman and her mother exchange a rare smile as they hold up the dress, admiring their work. And for a moment everything else falls away: the pain in their backs and their fingers, the chores that still need to be done, the endless worries about money, the one empty chair at the table and all the arguments that have been and all those that are still to come. In their small kitchen, with a golden dress nearly ready to be worn, it feels for a second as though magic is in the room.

That afternoon, the yellow dress that started as an idea has been finally realised, a pile of fabric and a tangle of threads transformed into something else, something with a life of its own. After all the hours of strain and stitching, it feels like an end point. But, of course, for the dress and the people who will come to love it, it is only the beginning.

LOU

The shop bell rings and Lou looks up as a grey-haired woman dressed head-to-toe in black steps inside. Without meaning to, she takes in every detail of the woman's outfit, reading the story that is written there. The black that this woman wears isn't like the bold statement of the sixties minidress that hangs on one side of the shop, or the luxurious confidence of the sequinned ballgown from the 1980s on the other. This black is a kind of cloak, loose-fitting and plain enough to hide behind, the kind of outfit put together by someone who wears clothes as a necessity rather than a joy. The sartorial equivalent of a tasteless ready meal.

Lou can't help but notice the difference from her own outfit – her high-waisted fitted dungarees and bold floral blouse, the flash of red lipstick and the crystal earrings shaped like parrots that hang from her ears, the green of the feathers matching the colour of her eyes. She wonders, as she sometimes does, if she looks ridiculous. But over the years, the bright and the bold have become her own version of a uniform.

'That yellow dress,' the older woman says, her voice cracking slightly as she speaks, 'how much is it?'

Lou follows the woman's gaze to the dress that hangs on the wall above the counter. The fabric is a shade of yellow that Lou struggles to aptly pinpoint. Is it the shade of a primrose or the citrus tone of sun-warmed lemons? It depends completely on the light. Right now, it looks like the petals of a sunflower. Lou's favourite thing about the dress is the embroidered flowers that cover the entire material, starting in delicate, widely spaced-out blooms near the top and becoming a dense meadow at the bottom.

'I'm really sorry, but that dress isn't for sale.' It's the only piece in the shop that isn't.

'Oh,' replies the woman, her face falling. 'It just caught my eye from the street. It's so happy-looking. I could do with a dress like that today.'

'We have plenty of other yellow dresses though,' continues Lou. 'Oh, and a scarf that would look wonderful on you. I can show you if you like?'

But as Lou comes out from behind the counter, the older woman steps back, shaking her head and rubbing her tired-looking eyes.

'No, no,' she says quickly, 'it was a silly idea. Yellow really isn't my colour.' And before Lou has a chance to say anything else, the woman has hurried outside, shoulders slumped and head bent as she disappears down the hill in a bundle of black.

*

19

It is another relatively slow day, but Lou at least feels cheered by the enthusiasm of the few customers who do step inside. Two friends, a little younger than Lou, visit in the afternoon, pushing prams. Both women immediately spot an indigo dress with an off-the-shoulder velvet bodice and a full satin skirt that shimmers in the light, exclaiming that it looks exactly like a dress one of them wore to their school prom when they were teenagers. Both friends take it in turns to try on the dress, Lou offering to watch the sleeping babies in their prams while they do.

'I feel like I'm sixteen again,' says the first woman.

'It's nice to wear something not covered in sick for a change,' says the other.

Lou feels as though she has just seen them transform from busy mothers to carefree teenagers. In the end, neither buys the dress – they admit they have no occasion to wear it – but they do leave with matching dungarees. They are still talking about the prom when they step outside, their babies starting to stir in their prams.

Then there's the teenager with the blue streaks in her hair who comes in with an older woman Lou assumes is her mother. They browse for a long time, the girl eventually deciding on a selection of patterned silk scarves.

'They're just like something Gran would wear, don't you think?' she says to her mother. 'I think I'll take them next time we visit. Maybe seeing them will get her to tell us one of her stories.'

As they pay, the older woman explains to Lou that her mother has dementia. 'But there's still so much she remembers about her past. Sometimes it helps to show her something to prompt her – a photo or a piece of clothing. She doesn't always remember who we are, but the stories she tells us …' The customer tries to smile, but it doesn't quite work. Lou smiles back, trying to communicate in that smile, that she understands what it's like to see someone you love slipping away.

It might not have been a big day in terms of sales, but the enthusiasm of her customers makes Lou think she must be doing something right. Her shop is somewhere that, once inside, people want to explore. She just needs to get more customers through the doors in the first place.

After locking up at the end of the day, she makes a detour up to the flat above the shop.

'Hello, it's me!' she calls over the sound of whirring power tools, peering through the archway where a door should be. Except instead of a door there is a gaping hole, rusted hinges hanging loose. Through it she can see bare floorboards, electrical wires hanging from the high ceilings, and tall windows, the glass smeared with grime. And among the chaos is the builder, Pete, who is currently cutting something with a circular saw, pieces of dust flying up into the air.

He stops what he's doing and looks up with a smile, brushing a strand of chin-length hair out of his face, sawdust catching in his beard.

'Hi, boss,' he says cheerfully.

'I just thought I'd check in to see how things are going.'

'It's going OK. I'm just finishing up for the day actually,' replies Pete in his thick Somerset accent.

They went to school together, not that Lou thinks he

remembers her. He was much cooler than she ever was, one of those breezily confident boys who everyone fancied, but unlike the others it didn't seem to go to his head. He was too down-to-earth to ever seem to notice the adoring glances that followed him around. He's never indicated they know each other and she's too embarrassed to bring it up herself in case he confirms her fears – that as the quiet girl she was before she developed the confidence to throw herself into the world of vintage, she was deeply forgettable.

She wonders how many other people she might know who have moved back here in recent years. When she came home, Lou's mum kept encouraging her to get out more. 'I promise not to die while you're at the pub, you need to spend time with people your own age,' she used to joke. But to Lou it was far from a joke.

'Great,' she says now, fighting hard to push away the memory, 'so how long do you think it will be until I can move in?' The hotel room may have its appeal, but there are limits. The wardrobe isn't nearly large enough for all her clothes for starters.

'Ah, the big question. You know it's against the code of my profession to give you a definite answer.' Pete laughs and, despite it all, Lou finds herself smiling back. 'But I'd say a few weeks.'

Her smile disappears.

'Oh, right. That might be a problem. I definitely can't afford to keep living in a hotel for a few weeks. I've already gone over budget fitting out the shop – I wanted it to be perfect. But it means things are pretty tight.' She tucks a rogue curl back inside her headscarf and rubs her forehead. 'Oh God, I'm going to be one of those people whose business closes within a few months because they had no idea what they were doing, aren't I?'

This was exactly why it took her so long to turn her dream of running her own business into a reality. She has never been a risk-taker. Now it hits her how much she has poured into this venture – all the time, money and hard work. Her shop *has* to be a success.

'Hey, it's going to be OK,' Pete replies. 'And if you need somewhere to stay, a mate of mine's mother-in-law is looking for lodgers. She has this big house, but it's just her on her own. Séb asked me if I knew of anyone. I imagine lodging for a few weeks would be cheaper than a hotel?'

'Oh, that's really kind of you,' she says, trying not to sound too taken aback, 'but …'

She trails off for a moment, thinking about what it would be like to move in with a total stranger. The idea overwhelms her, and yet the thought of throwing away even more money on the hotel feels even worse. If she really wants her shop to be a success, maybe she can't be too picky about where she lives.

'Actually, maybe I will give her a call after all. There can't be any harm in meeting her. Perhaps you can give me the details?'

'Sure!'

Lou hands him a piece of paper torn from a notebook she keeps in her bag, along with a pen, and he scribbles the name and number.

'Thanks,' she says. 'Right, I'm heading off now, are you coming too?'

'I'll just tidy up here,' he replies, gesturing around him.

'OK, see you tomorrow. And thanks for this.' She holds the scrap of paper in the air. 'Hopefully this woman can help and this whole venture won't be a total disaster.'

MAGGY

'At least you got the house.'

As Maggy stands outside her front door, the words of her friends ring loud in her head. She had messaged them earlier to let them know the news – that after nearly fifty years of marriage and a year of separation, today the final paperwork landed on her doormat. She is officially divorced.

Maggy knew that things would be finalised this week but didn't want to make a fuss by planning anything particular to mark the occasion. It had been a while since Alan left, after all. And yet, when the papers arrived and their separation was made final, it still hit her hard and made her feel off-kilter, so off-kilter that she spent the day doing things that were very unlike her, like arriving five minutes late to collect her grandsons from school and even trying to buy a yellow dress from the new vintage shop in town, a dress that would have stood out like a neon sign in her wardrobe of black and grey. She knew as soon as the woman working in the shop told her the dress wasn't for sale that she'd made a mistake anyway. She was not a yellow kind of person. Not anymore.

She knows her friends are right – all things considered, her solicitor did a good job – and yet, as she turns the key in the lock of the front door, she pauses briefly and takes a deep breath before stepping inside.

The tiled hallway used to feel cramped, filled as it was with bicycles and discarded shoes and school bags when the children were growing up. Now, as Maggy hangs her coat on the other- wise mostly empty coat rack, the space stretches around her. Her eyes land on the thick envelope containing the divorce papers, resting on the table by the front door where she left it this morning. She shakes her head, still not quite believing it all.

Maggy always imagined these years of her life would be calm and predictable, spent alongside the husband who was as known to her as her own reflection. That's what she thought she had signed up for when she chose to marry a man like Alan. He was the kind of person who liked to go back to the same hotel year after year on their family holiday, who kept all his important documents in a neatly organised folder labelled 'important documents' and who bought her the same Christmas gift (a small bottle of her second-favourite perfume and a box of chocolates) every year.

They may have run out of things to say to each other a long time ago, but she thought that's just what marriage was after a certain point. What they had felt like enough. Yes, since their children, Nick and Charlotte, had left home their lives had be- come quiet and somewhat separate, her throwing herself into her role as a grandmother and spending time with her friends while he played golf and pottered in the garden. But her life felt like it fitted her, like a comfortable pair of jeans softened and shaped to her over time. She pictured family gatherings, the two of them hosting Christmases and birthdays for the grand-children. Maybe the occasional holiday together. Perhaps they could even try something new and take dancing lessons.

And then Alan surprised her by suddenly wanting more. He announced one day, not long after his seventieth birthday, that he was leaving. He'd met someone, a woman called Tracy who worked at his golf club. The first thing Maggy thought when he told her was, *No wonder he's been spending so much time there. He's terrible at golf.* And the second thing was, *What on earth am I going to do now?*

Maggy tucks the solicitor's envelope under a pile of magazines and then heads down to the back of the house, the place that was always the heart of the home when her family still lived here. A large slate-floored kitchen opens out onto an expansive living room, filled with two cream sofas and a teal armchair clustered around a large coffee table, a TV and a fireplace, the mantlepiece topped with photos of her children and grand-children.

She doesn't bother to turn all the lamps on, just the overhead kitchen lights, the rest of the living room still in gloom. That way, she can ignore the dust that creates shadows on all the surfaces and the tiles and floorboards that need a good scrub. She just hasn't found the time or energy lately for cleaning, especially as there is such a lot of house to clean.

A rumbling in her stomach reminds her that she hasn't eaten since lunch. She may have prepared a snack earlier for her grandsons, Luke and Otis, while she looked after them until her son and daughter-in-law arrived home from work, but she was too busy doing a quick whip around with the hoover (just to help out, given she was there) to think about eating too.

Maggy hates to admit it, but she's tired after today's baby-sitting stint. When did it happen? When did her energy start leaking away like air slowly escaping from a punctured tyre? For years she has tried to ignore the fact that she is getting older. But this past year she has felt it more than ever. Not that she would ever admit that to her children when they ask if she'll help out with childcare. She is still useful to them. And when she no longer has that, what does she have besides an empty house?

The sound of her mobile ringing breaks the silence, making her jump.

'Is this Maggy?' comes a female voice in reply when she picks up.

'It is …'

'Oh, hello,' the woman continues. 'I got your number from a friend – he tells me you're looking for a lodger?'

Maggy had nearly forgotten about the advert she put up on a few community noticeboards around town last week. She did it on something of a whim. Maybe a lodger could help to fill some of the space around her. But she hasn't heard anything since, so the thought had slipped to the back of her mind.

'Yes, I am …' she replies hesitantly.

'Is tomorrow morning too soon to come and view the room? I could come over before work, if that's not too early?'

Maggy takes in the unwashed dishes in the sink, the dust on the shelves and the odd jobs that need doing but that she just hasn't found the time or enthusiasm to begin. Perhaps she should put off this woman's visit and clean the place up a bit? Or abandon the idea of a lodger altogether? But then maybe it is just what she needs. Since Alan left her life has been frozen, as though she has pressed the pause button and then lost the remote. Something has to change.

'Tomorrow morning is perfect,' she says.

DONNA

Donna hasn't talked to her mother in days. Not since she showed her the photograph of the woman in the yellow dress and everything Donna thought she knew about her life changed forever.

'I understand you're upset,' says John one morning as they are having breakfast, 'but don't you think you should at least let her tell you her side of things? Let her explain why they never told you that you're adopted?'

Donna's daughter, Brooke, has tried to persuade her too, emphasising the fact that her grandmother is still unwell and the stress of the rift could be bad for her. But Donna has been insistent.

'There's nothing to tell!' she says crossly, attacking her morning grapefruit vigorously with a fork. 'She's been lying to me my whole life.' With her other hand, she straightens her coffee spoon so that it lines up exactly with the edge of the table mat.

'But what has *really* changed?' John says gently, pouring them both their morning coffee. 'It doesn't change the years you've spent together.'

Donna stands up suddenly, her legs so jittery that she is unable to stay seated. The room feels as though it is growing smaller, pressing in on her. It's how she has felt ever since she found out. Every now and then, she lets herself forget, focusing on organising the inn's calendar or filing receipts or walking Luna and taking in the colours as the season puts on its new outfit of orange and yellow around her. But then she remembers and a feeling of panic rises in her chest.

'*Everything* has changed! I thought I was from Cold Spring. I'm not. I thought I was my mother's daughter. I'm not. And what does that mean about my life? Everyone I grew up with left and lived big lives. And I stayed here. I thought it made sense, because this is where my family are from, it's where I'm from. But now I'm not so sure. I don't know who I am any more.'

'Oh Donna, I'm sorry.' John stands up and pulls her into a hug. She is stiff at first, but then lets herself be hugged back, breathing in the familiar smell of him: washing detergent, mint shower gel, coffee and that extra, indescribable him-ness. It makes her feel less like she might spin up and away.

She pulls back after a moment, brushing a thread off her blue sweatshirt and then looking up at his familiar blue eyes.

'I might not know who I am, but I'm going to find out,' she says.

'What do you mean?'

Donna looks around the kitchen, at the same fruit-print

31

blinds that have hung there for decades, the alphabetically arranged spice rack, the black metal scales that were a wedding present from her parents, and at all the other accumulated debris of a life. Just like the rest of her home and the inn where she grew up and has worked for most of her life, it all looks different now.

She reaches inside the book she has been reading, resting on the kitchen countertop, and pulls out the photograph of the young woman in the yellow dress that has been marking the page.

'I've decided,' Donna says firmly, pointing at the photograph. 'I'm going to find her.'

The first time she wears the yellow dress is to go dancing. It was why she made it, after all. She gets ready after work, smiling into the mirror as she applies a bright red lipstick and pinches her cheeks, two circles blooming there like flowers. Next, a spritz of her birthday perfume on the inside of each wrist. She doesn't believe in saving things for 'best', even if she knows her mother would chide her for being frivolous. Money has been tight since Father died. Her life revolves around her job at the department store and helping her mother with the household chores that never seem to end.

That will all change one day. She opens her dressing-table drawer and glances at the slim pile of magazines in there – another expense she knows her mother wouldn't like, which is why she hides them in here, purchased with the little money she has left after handing most of her wages over for housekeeping.

She picks up the issue on the top of the pile and flicks it open, *her eyes meeting the steady gaze of the women on the pages, modelling designer clothes that she dreams of owning rather than having to make reproductions of herself. In the mirror, she practises her steady smile.*

'One day, that will be me.'

She stands up, the yellow dress falling to just below her knee, and walks up and down, imagining herself on a runway. She is so busy trying to keep her head held high that she bumps into the spare bed. She rubs her knee and laughs at herself.

'Maybe I need a bit more practice,' she mumbles.

The sound of the doorbell downstairs makes her stop, putting the magazines away and smoothing the fabric of her dress.

'Right, time to go.'

Her boyfriend, Percy, is waiting for her in the hallway. He is a pale-faced young man with bright white-blond hair, who is an inch shorter than her, which is why she always wears flat shoes for their dates. Tonight, he is dressed in a grey suit and is gripping a bunch of chrysanthemums, which he hands over to the young woman's mother, who wipes her hands on her apron and takes them.

'Oh, well aren't you a gentleman. Thank you, Percy.'

On the stairs, the young woman rolls her eyes. The floorboard creaks and Percy and her mother turn and look up. Her mother's face softens and Percy rubs at the neck of his shirt as though it's too tight. He coughs.

'You look lovely tonight.'

'It looks even better on,' admits her mother, her voice softer than usual. 'Let me take a photo before you go.'

The camera belonged to the young woman's father and was

his pride and joy. They don't often use it. Just as her mother presses the button down, the young woman in the yellow dress twirls, the skirt and her hair floating out around her.

'Oh, you've ruined it now!'

'No, I haven't. It's a dress made for dancing. I had to be dancing in the photo.'

'Well, I suppose that will have to do,' her mother says reluctantly as Percy reaches out for his date's arm. 'Have a good time, don't be too late back.'

As soon as she leaves her home behind her, the young woman feels buoyed up by a sense of freedom. She and Percy head to the local dance hall, where they meet up with a group of friends, the girls all complimenting her on her new yellow dress. But after a couple of dances she tells Percy she isn't feeling well and is going to head home.

'Let me walk you back,' he says.

'No, no,' she replies hastily. 'You stay with everyone here. I'll be fine!'

Before he can object or follow her, she dashes off in a whirlwind of yellow.

Outside, she takes a deep breath of the summer air, the London street busy with people out for the evening and enjoying the longer days. Then she turns quickly away in the opposite direction to home, her heart racing with excitement. It's time for her real evening plans to begin.

MAGGY

'Oh, it's you!'

When Maggy opens the door to greet the potential lodger, it surprises her that she recognises the woman standing on her doorstep immediately. With her Christmas-red lipstick and vibrant outfit, the woman from the new vintage shop in town is not someone you forget in a hurry. This morning, she is dressed in a full-skirted dress in candy stripes of pink and white, worn with a denim jacket covered in colourful embroidered patches and a pair of lace-up boots and chunky-knit socks. Maggy quickly looks down at her own grey drawstring trousers and black jumper.

'Oh, hello,' says the woman on the step, adjusting her hair, carefully styled in 1940s rolls. 'You came into my shop, didn't you? My name's Lou. Thanks so much for letting me come and view the room.'

Maggy guesses the woman is in her mid to late thirties,

around the same age as her daughter Charlotte. Her outfit and make-up may be impeccable, but there's a paleness to her cheeks and under her eyes that gives Maggy the impression of someone who hasn't slept through the night in quite a long time. Although she doesn't know this woman, the part of her heart that grew and stretched for each of her children gives a little squeeze.

'I'm Maggy, come on in.'

'Shall I take my shoes off?'

She is already leaning to unlace her boots, but Maggy waves a hand.

'Please, don't worry. You'll see for yourself that the house isn't exactly a show home.'

But as Maggy shows her around, Lou makes many compliments, seeming particularly drawn to the old paintings Maggy inherited from her parents, the slightly rusting but nonetheless elegant clawfoot bath in the main bathroom and the William Morris curtains in the dining room – a room Maggy never uses herself unless the family are visiting.

It feels strange to try to see her home through the younger woman's eyes as though for the first time. They pause on the second-floor landing, where in-built bookshelves are tucked underneath the staircase that leads up to the next floor. There are more stacks of books piled on the floor too, their covers grey with dust.

'What a wonderful collection,' says Lou, crouching slightly to inspect some of the titles.

'A lot of them belong to my children. They say they don't have space for them at their own homes but couldn't bear for me to throw them away. I must admit, you'll easily spot the ones that are mine – I'm afraid I can't claim any of the classics, mine are the well-thumbed whodunits.'

Lou smiles, reaching a hand out to lightly touch the spine of an Agatha Christie.

'My mum loves those kinds of books too,' Lou says. But then the smile drops from her face. 'I mean *loved*.'

There's a brief pause, but before Maggy can say anything, Lou adds, 'She always used to pride herself on guessing who committed the crime.'

'And was she right?'

'Oh, every time.'

'Then your mother must have been a fair deal smarter than me.'

They share a half-smile and Maggy feels a rush of warmth towards this woman she has only just met, the woman who is dressed like a sweet shop and who owns the most colourful shop in the town but whose sadness is like the grey sky behind a rainbow.

'Let me show you your room. Or rather the room that would be yours if you decided you wanted it.'

The attic bedroom is painted ballet-pump pink, the double bed covered in pink and green sheets and cushions in a mismatch of floral, gingham and polka-dot prints.

Maggy watches as Lou runs a hand gently over the bedspread and then pulls back.

'It's lovely. The whole house is lovely. But I'm not sure if I can afford it. Starting the business has been more costly than

I expected. I should have known it would be …' She trails off. 'And I'm only looking for something temporary.'

'I'm not looking for much,' Maggy replies quickly. 'If I'm honest, I'm after the company as much as anything else.'

Lou looks up and, as their eyes meet, Maggy gets the instant feeling that this woman knows what it's like to wake up in a house alone.

'And temporary works for me too,' she adds. 'We can just see how it goes.'

'Well, if you're sure that works for you,' Lou says hesitantly. Then, more firmly, she adds, 'Then yes, I'd love to stay here, Maggy. Thank you.'

They say goodbye, agreeing that Lou will move her things in the next day before going to work.

After she leaves, Maggy feels so energised at the thought of having some company in the house that she even does some dusting.

'It should be with the boxes on the left-hand side behind the old rocking horse,' Maggy calls up into the attic, where she can hear her daughter, Charlotte, walking about. She is steadying the ladder on the floor below. It's been decades since she went up there herself. That was always Alan's job.

'Sorry to do this,' Charlotte had said when she turned up on Maggy's doorstep earlier, not long after Lou left, 'but Dad called asking if I'd bring a box of books he thought he left here when we go to visit him next week.'

The mention of her ex-husband had made Maggy flinch.

But then she gave herself a talking-to. *He's their father, after all, and the little ones' grandfather. He always will be.*

After a few moments, some more footsteps and a dragging noise of boxes being shifted, Charlotte reappears at the top of the ladder. She climbs down carefully, balancing two boxes under her arm.

As she reaches the landing beside her mother, she places both boxes down.

'Mum,' she says, laughter in her voice, 'what on *earth* are these?'

Out of the smaller box, she pulls a pair of yellow boots. They are sunshine-bright and as shiny as rain-slick marble. There are zips around the ankles and Maggy knows if she were to put them on again they would come up to mid-calf and would feel stiff but comfortable. But Maggy hasn't worn those boots in more than fifty years.

Her daughter looks from the boots to her mother and back again.

'They're mine,' Maggy replies simply.

'When and *where* did you wear these, Mum? I don't think I've ever seen a pair of boots that are less *you* in all my life.'

Her daughter's words sting, but Maggy knows she shouldn't be surprised by them. She sees herself through Charlotte's eyes – the practical, plain clothes she has worn ever since becoming a mother and that have somehow become more and more sombre over the years. Then another image enters her mind – a memory she hasn't thought about in years. A young woman standing on a street in Kensington, a miniskirt brushing against her thighs as she walks with purpose, a bag swinging from her arm containing a brand-new pair of bright yellow boots. It's hard to believe that the woman in the memory was her.

'Oh, you know, a long time ago,' she says vaguely, waving a hand in the air. 'Did you find the books your dad was after?'

'Yes, I've got them here,' Charlotte says, gesturing to the box at her feet. Then she bites down on her bottom lip – an expression that Maggy recognises from when her daughter was a child and had done something naughty or was trying to keep a secret. 'Mum, I've got something to tell you.'

'Are you OK?' Maggy says anxiously, her skin turning warm. 'And Séb and Fleur?'

But Charlotte nods her head. 'It's not that, we're all fine. It's Dad. I wanted to let you know that he's getting married again.'

A prickle tingles the back of her neck. For a second, her daughter disappears from view and Maggy is totally alone.

'Mum? Mum? Are you OK?'

Maggy inhales deeply and then waves a hand in the air as though wafting smoke. 'Yes, I'm fine. I suppose it shouldn't come as a total surprise. He's been with Tracy a while now, hasn't he?'

'I said he should have told you himself, but I think he didn't know if you'd want to hear from him.' A buzz makes Charlotte glance down at her phone. 'Oh God, I'm really sorry, Mum, but I've got a meeting to get to. Are you going to be all right?'

Maggy reaches out to brush a cobweb from the attic from her daughter's shoulder. 'Don't worry about me, darling, I'm absolutely fine. You have a good day.'

Charlotte's eyebrows are still crumpled in a frown, but after a moment's pause she kisses her mother's cheek and lifts up the book box, the yellow boots now lying abandoned on the landing.

Once Maggy has followed her daughter downstairs and waved her goodbye at the door, a smile frozen on her face, she shuts it firmly. And then she sinks down onto the doormat, leans back against the door and wraps her arms around her knees. She stays there for a long time.

LOU

The day that Lou moves in to her new temporary home is one of those grey days when it feels like the sky is a low ceiling and at any moment you might knock your head against the heavy grey clouds. It's a short journey from the hotel to Maggy's house, but it takes Lou longer, what with dragging her suitcase up the hill and over the uneven paving stones that give the town its charm but are not easy to navigate in heeled brogues and with luggage. She arrives out of breath and feeling flustered. Standing on the doorstep looking up at the navy front door with its large brass knocker and the panels of stained glass in shades of red and blue, she wonders if she is making a mistake. She may have warmed to Maggy instantly, but she is essentially a stranger. What will it be like living with a woman she hardly knows and who must be twice her age?

Before she has time to further question her decision, the front door swings open, making her jump.

'Sorry,' says Maggy, 'I didn't mean to startle you. But I spotted you from the window and thought you might like a hand with your things.'

'Oh, that's kind, thank you.'

'Welcome, come on in,' Maggy says, reaching for one of Lou's bags. 'It's so lovely to have you here.'

Any uncertainty that Lou might have felt falls away at the warmth of Maggy's welcome. As she follows her inside, she notices that the house seems a little tidier than the day before. She spots fresh flowers in a jug on the kitchen table and she sniffs the air appreciatively.

'Something smells delicious!'

'Oh, it's just a banana loaf that's finished baking. It might be too early for cake, but maybe you'd like to take a slice to work with you for later?'

'It's never too early for cake! I hope you didn't go to all that trouble just for me, though.'

'I had some bananas that needed using up,' says Maggy dismissively. 'It takes two minutes to throw together. It's a recipe I've been making since my children were small. It's one of my grandchildren's favourites now.'

I think I'm going to like living here, Lou thinks to herself.

'That would be lovely, thank you.'

The room is even cosier than Lou remembers and Maggy has added an extra rail for her clothes alongside the substantial oak wardrobe that stands in the corner. On the bedside table, she spots a small pile of Agatha Christie books that she swears weren't there before. She can't help but smile.

'Thanks so much for helping with my things,' she says to

Maggy, who is standing in the doorway, having just placed a pile of towels on the end of Lou's bed. 'But I should be getting to work now.'

'Of course, don't let me keep you.'

Lou follows Maggy out onto the landing, but before heading downstairs, something catches her eye that she hadn't noticed on the way up, lumbered as she was with all her belongings.

'Oh my God!' she exclaims, her eyes honing in on the flash of yellow on the floor just below the hatch leading up to the attic. 'Are those ... No! I can't believe it. Are those *Mary Quant* boots?'

The older woman beside her flushes slightly.

'Yes, they are,' she replies somewhat sheepishly.

'Can I ... Do you mind if I take a look?'

'Of course. Help yourself.'

Lou lifts up one boot as gently as if it were a baby bird fallen from a nest. With her other hand, she traces a finger over the gold zips that wrap around the ankle and continue up the sides.

'The Daddy Long Legs boots,' she says in a hushed voice. 'I've only ever seen photos of these. These zips! I just love that you could wear them as either ankle boots or knee boots, it's such a brilliant idea. And that colour! Doesn't it just make your heart happy looking at them?'

She glances at her new landlady, who is looking at the boots with a faraway expression on her face. Lou can't believe she's actually holding a true vintage gem from one of the most famous fashion designers of the 1960s. And she also can't believe that they belong to the woman in front of her, the woman who is dressed head to toe in shades of black and grey.

Maybe there's more to Maggy than meets the eye, Lou thinks to herself.

'Well, yes, they do actually,' Maggy replies. 'That's why I bought them. But of course, that was a very, very long time ago.'

'I'd love to know the story behind them,' Lou says eagerly. 'When you bought them, where you wore them … It's why I love vintage clothing so much. All the stories. If you don't mind sharing, that is?'

A jittery sense of excitement fills Lou's body, the same kind of excitement she gets whenever she finds something really special at a car boot sale and that she felt when she opened her shop door for the first time.

Maggy tilts her head to one side, looking lost in thought.

'Those boots belong to a different time and a very different Maggy. I've never told anyone about that part of my life before …' She pauses for a moment and Lou can sense her weighing up how much to reveal. 'But if you'd like, I can tell you. It's a story to be told with a glass of wine, though. How about I tell you later tonight when you finish work?'

Before opening up, Lou stops in at the café next door to her shop for her morning coffee. The café's owner, Beth, had popped in on Lou's opening day with cake, a gesture which caught Lou totally off guard. Lou has made a point of buying all her coffees from there since.

'I meant to tell you, Lou,' Beth says now as she prepares Lou's daily cappuccino, 'I'm the head of the town's local small business network and we have our monthly meeting next week at the Three Swans. It's less formal than it sounds, I promise – it's really just a chance to share experiences about how things are going for us all. It's good fun too. You should come.'

Lou bites down on her bottom lip, trying to think of a polite way to say no.

'Thanks, I'll try to make it,' she replies, knowing that she probably won't. She doesn't mean to be rude. But the truth is, she hasn't been to a pub in a long time. After the year that she's had, she doesn't really feel up to being in a room surrounded with happy, laughing people. 'I hope you have a good day.'

'You too,' Beth replies. 'Let's hope the weather brightens up.'

Lou waves goodbye, grateful for Beth's kindness but also happy to get back behind the counter of her shop. When she's there she feels safe and in control, everything else pushed aside.

It's another quiet day, the grey weather and a few sudden downpours keeping customers away. Lou uses the time to rearrange the window display and to do some research on her laptop into new stock. She already has a few bargains found on eBay on their way to her, but she bookmarks some upcoming local auctions and flea markets that she'd like to check out. It would mean having to close the shop for a day, but her business relies on finding new pieces, as well as selling the ones she has. For now, the shop is still well-stocked though, a thought that brings a mix of emotions. It means she doesn't need to rush out to find new things just yet, but it's also a reminder of her worries about the future of the business.

In quiet moments throughout the day, she finds herself thinking about her new landlady and wondering about the story behind her yellow boots. Every now and then, Lou's eyes fall on the yellow dress that hangs behind her own shop counter. It's a dress that means so much to her and yet, just like the yellow boots she found in her landlady's home, its true story is still a mystery. She wishes she knew more about it. But deep down, she knows it's too late for that.

In the early hours of the morning, a young woman in a yellow dress pauses on the corner of her street, a man's arm held firmly around her waist. He pulls her closer, the fabric of her skirt rumpled between them as he leans down and kisses her.

The street is quiet, the windows in the terraced houses black. The two figures huddle together in the semi-darkness, holding one another tightly.

Earlier that evening, the young woman's mother had glanced anxiously at her watch as she got ready for bed before remembering that her daughter was out with sensible, reliable Percy. They'd be home soon enough. There was no harm in shutting her eyes for a moment.

On the street corner, the young woman pulls away, tucking a loose strand of hair back in place as she steps out of the shadows slightly and under the glow of the street lamp. Despite the hour, there is still warmth in the air and her skin feels prickly and damp.

'That really is some dress,' the man says softly, running a finger up the row of shiny buttons on the front. 'Nearly as beautiful as the woman underneath.'

She is grateful for the dim light to hide the flush of her cheeks.

'Shhh,' she says quietly and then pushes him gently away, glancing over her shoulder. 'I hate having to do this,' she adds, a frown appearing across her pale skin.

'Not long now,' he replies, kissing her on the forehead.

'I should go,' she sighs, straightening her skirt and adjusting her hair again. But he pulls her back towards him for one final kiss.

At the window where the young woman sleeps, the curtain moves slightly, but down on the street below, the young woman in the yellow dress is too preoccupied with falling in love to notice.

DONNA

'I suppose I must be the oldest person who's ever come in asking about their past?'

Donna shuffles on the uncomfortable chair as she speaks. The adoption agency's office is filled with filing cabinets and as she looks at them she feels overwhelmed suddenly by the thought of all the lives documented in those folders. Is her story in there too?

'You'd be surprised,' says the woman behind the desk, tucking her dark hair behind her ears and pushing her glasses slightly up the bridge of her nose. The glasses are smeared with fingerprints that catch the light; Donna noticed the dirty marks as soon as the woman greeted her earlier and led her from the airy reception area into this cramped office. She wonders how the woman can see anything at all through them.

'Would you like a tissue?'

The woman looks startled. 'Excuse me?'

'For your glasses,' says Donna, reaching into her bag and handing the woman one.

The woman holds it limply before placing it down on the table. A slight cough, then she continues her previous train of thought.

'Yes, a lot of people choose to find out about their birth parents when they're in their twenties, but not everyone. It's complicated and totally personal. We had someone in recently who was in their late seventies and wanted to find out about their birth family for the first time.'

'I would have found out earlier if I'd known,' Donna says quickly. 'My mother – my adoptive mother – only just told me. We're not speaking, but I got her to give me the details of this agency via my daughter.'

'I see,' says the woman, looking more startled than Donna thinks she ought to. Perhaps she used to have a different career and is new to the business of other people's lives.

'Well, thank you for coming in today,' the woman continues after a slight pause. 'I'm afraid we're going through a bit of an archiving process here at the moment, sorting through all our old files and moving them from a previous storage location into this new office. There wasn't much I could dig out for you, but I do have some things to share with you.'

The woman pulls an envelope out of the desk drawer and places it on the table, patting it lightly. Donna's hands fidget at her sides. She suddenly wishes she'd agreed to let John or Brooke come with her to the meeting. They had offered, but it was something she wanted to do by herself.

'Eleanor Morris,' says the woman behind the desk. 'That's your biological mother's name.'

The agent looks down at the paperwork in her hand, then frowns.

'There should be more in here – there should be a whole sheet with information, like her date of birth and where she was living when she came to us. But I'm afraid it's not here. As I said, we're reorganising at the moment and while we pride ourselves on the efficiency and security of our new systems, unfortunately for some of our older files, well …'

'I'm not that old!' Donna snaps.

The woman jumps. 'No, no, of course not. There are a couple of photographs here though.'

She hands them over and Donna takes them quickly, holding them carefully at the edges so as not to smudge them.

Unlike the blurred image that her parents gave her, these are both crisp and clear. The first is a simple head and shoulder shot in black-and-white of a young woman. Donna swallows quickly, her heart pounding. The young woman in the photograph looks just like her daughter Brooke. They have the same full lips, high cheekbones and slender physique. She is smiling, but with her lips closed and her chin lifted slightly.

Eleanor, Donna says to herself. The next thought settles in her throat and the spaces between her ribs. *That's my mother*.

The second photograph is not of Eleanor but of a newborn baby, swaddled tightly in a blanket and wearing a tiny pink hat. It takes Donna a moment to realise the baby must be her.

'Again, I'm really sorry we couldn't give you anything more,' says the woman behind the desk.

But Donna is barely listening. Clutching the photographs, she stands up and walks out, the people in the office flashing past and making her feel dizzy. Once she is outside, she crosses the road to her car and sits in the driver's seat, staring for a long time at the two photos held in her hands.

'What happened to you?' she says quietly, directing the question to the young woman with the defiant smile, but also to the tiny baby in the pink hat.

MAGGY

'I may never have left Somerset if it wasn't for my cousin Audrey.'

Maggy and Lou are sitting in the living room together, the lamps glowing cosily as the light fades outside. They have just finished dinner, a spag bol Maggy cooked for them both while Lou worked her way around the house doing bits of DIY that Maggy had been putting off for months. Maggy had been halfway up a ladder when Lou returned from work, trying to hang a picture that had been leant against the wall for so long that it had started to wind her up. Lou had looked at the hammer in Maggy's hand and the brick dust sprinkled on her clothes and kindly told her that she needed to use a wall plug instead of a pin.

'Do you have a drill?' Lou had asked, rolling up the sleeves of her candy-striped dress.

'I do, but I don't really know how to use it,' Maggy had

confessed. 'I know it's not very feminist of me to admit it, but my ex-husband always did all the DIY – he enjoyed it, so I just left him to it.' She knows that she is perfectly capable of learning, of course. But that doesn't mean she wants to.

'That's OK,' Lou had replied, 'I can do it. If you just show me where the drill is.'

Maggy's new lodger had turned out to be highly proficient with a drill and a screwdriver and by the time the spaghetti was cooked had hung three pictures, put up a shelf, fixed the wobbly banister and assembled a flat-pack coffee table, the box for which was covered in a thick coating of dust.

Maybe I should have got a lodger months ago, Maggy had thought to herself as she served up the food, Lou pouring them each a glass of wine from the bottle she'd bought on her way home.

Now, Lou rests an elbow on the arm of the sofa, her chin in her hand as she leans forward, ready to hear Maggy's story. It's a story that Maggy has been thinking about ever since Charlotte stumbled across the yellow boots in the attic. When she moved back to Somerset after her brief spell in London all those years ago, the yellow boots were stored in the attic and replaced with practical shoes for pushing prams up and down the small town's many hills, and clothes that would hide baby sick and her changed body. The children grew up, but then came the grandchildren and Maggy moved smoothly from her role as mother to grandmother. Sometimes even she forgets that she is not just 'Mum' or 'Granny' but 'Maggy' too.

But as the young woman on the sofa in front of her leans eagerly forward, ready to hear the story that Maggy has never shared before, she feels for a moment like that young woman again. Lou's eagerness makes Maggy forget that they don't really know one another. It is nice to be listened to.

'I grew up in a village not far from here,' she continues. 'We lived on a farm, which I always found terribly dull. The height of excitement were the dances held in the local village hall. It's where I met my husband, Alan. My ex-husband, I mean.'

Lou smiles gently but, to Maggy's relief, doesn't press her for details. Instead, she just nods slightly and waits.

'He was from town, but he still existed in the same world as me. He was going to stay in Somerset and take over his family's accounting business, just like my parents wanted me to start helping with the admin on the farm, before getting married, of course. We started dating when I was sixteen. I'd never been out with a boy before that.'

Maggy pictures Alan as he was when they were teenagers. He may only have been a year older than her, but he seemed like a true grown-up, somehow. He always wore the exact perfect thing for the weather, unlike Maggy, who often forgot her hat or her raincoat. He was already knowledgeable in accounting, having watched his father from a young age, and he liked to read biographies and historical books, rather than the novels she preferred. Her parents loved him.

'And then Audrey moved to London,' Maggy continues. 'I didn't have any siblings, but my older cousin was like a sister to me. She lived in the next village, but she never seemed to fit in there. She was an artist, a real whirlwind of light and energy. I was bereft when she left for art school in London. But we kept in touch. She would write to me and her letters

57

were just full of London, London, London. It all sounded so wonderful and so different from anything I'd ever known. The parties, the galleries, the friends, the clothes … Her parents were better off than ours – my aunt had married into money – and they were more open-minded too, I think. They supported her dream of becoming an artist and even bought her a tiny flat in Kensington. And whenever Audrey wrote, or whenever we spoke on the phone, she would ask me to come.

'It took some work to convince my parents, but when I turned nineteen they agreed that I could go and stay with Audrey for the summer. I asked Alan to come with me, but if I'm honest, I never expected him to say yes. He hated cities, and London in particular, although he'd never actually been. So I went alone, promising to call and to come back when I could at weekends.

'Oh, I still remember arriving for the first time! The crowds, the traffic, the music pouring out from the open doors of shops and bars. Can you believe at that point I'd never heard The Beatles before? And then there was Audrey's flat – tiny but wonderful, packed with records and canvases and clothes. Her kitchen sink was always full of paints, some art project pegged up on the curtain pole to dry.

'When Audrey greeted me at the station that first day, I nearly didn't recognise her with her tiny skirt and sharp bob. The first thing she did was take me to a salon to cut off what she called my "farm-girl locks". "*You're not in the village any more*," I remember her telling me. And I wasn't.'

Even now, Maggy's heart races to remember the excitement of that summer.

'Audrey sounds like a character,' Lou says.

'She was.'

Tears spring unexpectedly to Maggy's eyes. Even after all this time, she still misses her. She died in a car accident in her forties. Sometimes it catches Maggy off guard that she isn't around, that someone so full of life and spark could be gone when she is still here, living in the same house she has lived in since she was twenty. What would Audrey make of the woman she has become?

'The yellow boots?' says Lou gently, easing Maggy out from her more painful thoughts.

'Ah, the yellow boots. I bought them with my first pay cheque. Audrey helped set me up with the job – one of her friends from art school worked at a new store where they were looking for staff. She said they were less interested in experience than in finding people with the right look who could help their customers feel like they were shopping with friends. Audrey helped me with that too. She let me raid her wardrobe so that when I turned up at Biba on Kensington Church Street, I looked the part, even if I didn't feel it.'

'You worked at Biba?' Lou says excitedly, her eyes widening. 'It's one of my favourite vintage labels. I remember the first Biba I bought – an emerald-green velvet skirt that I found in a charity shop of all places. It's for sale in my shop! I almost didn't want to part with it, but the thought of someone else having that same feeling of spotting it and falling in love with it too makes it worth it. And then to think where they might wear it and all the memories they will associate with it …

Sorry, I'm getting carried away. Tell me, what was it like to work there?'

Maggy looks over at the younger woman, noticing how different she seems to the person who turned up on her doorstep earlier. Her green eyes sparkle with enthusiasm. When was the last time Maggy experienced that kind of passion? Her family and friends bring her joy, but what does she really have in her life that's just for her and that makes her light up the way Lou is lighting up right now? The thought makes her uncomfortable, so she returns instead to the past.

'It was wonderful. The shop was unlike anything I'd ever seen. It didn't even really seem like a shop, more like an extravagant woman's dressing room. There were plants all over the place and this beautifully ornate art nouveau wallpaper on the walls. And the clothes were just everywhere, clothes that were so different to the outfits the women I knew wore. All those stripes and checks, the little Peter Pan collars, the pockets, the short skirts, the smart narrow trousers, the *hats*. I loved helping customers find things – they were mostly normal girls like me who had saved up their money and wanted something special. I loved seeing them transform when they tried them on.'

'Yes!' says Lou. 'That's exactly what I love about my shop. Seeing someone walk in as one person and leave as another, or just leave with a slightly different way of walking and holding themselves. It's wonderful.'

'And I felt transformed too,' nods Maggy. 'By Audrey, by Biba, by London … I never would have had the confidence to approach Simon otherwise.'

His name slips out before she can stop herself. And it might have been over fifty years since she last saw him, but his face appears as clear as a photograph in her mind – the brown eyes framed by long lashes, the curly chestnut hair, that smile.

'Simon?' Lou says questioningly, raising an eyebrow.

Maggy has never told anyone about Simon. Audrey knew about him, but she was good at keeping secrets. And yet this young woman doesn't know Maggy, or Alan, or the children. And she is listening so attentively that Maggy feels that she can speak without judgement. So, like the pair of boots pulled down from the attic, she unboxes the memories she once worked so hard to shut away.

'I met him at one of Audrey's parties. The flat was absolutely packed with people, everyone dancing and chatting and smoking out the windows. I felt out of place – they were all older than me and seemed so exciting. I felt certain that despite having the right clothes and the right hair they could see through it all and see that I didn't belong there. And then I saw him.'

She can almost smell the cigarette smoke in the air and hear the records playing as she remembers meeting his eye for the first time. How he looked back and didn't look away.

'He was in the middle of a group of people and was laughing, his face so open and warm and alive. There was something about him that was so inviting, so irresistibly *attractive*, in the truest sense of the word – I felt myself being pulled towards him as though I had no control over my movements. And he looked at me as though he knew me, as though it was totally natural that I had just walked over and joined him and this group of people I didn't know. He pulled me into their conversation with such ease that it made me feel totally calm, while at the same time my heart was racing. At some point, there came a pause in the conversation and he turned and looked me straight in the eye and asked if I wanted to go for a walk. We left the party together and walked all around the Kensington streets. It was the middle of the night by then and quiet, apart from the odd winding-down bar and the sound of our conversation.'

'What did you talk about?'

'Oh, everything. I told him about life in Somerset, he told me about his dream to become an actor. He worked in a restaurant to pay his way, but acting was his true passion. I loved hearing him talk with such enthusiasm, especially as I had nothing like that in my own life, not that sense of purpose and direction anyway. Eventually, he walked me back to the flat – everyone had left by then – and kissed me goodnight. "I'll pick you up tomorrow evening, there's a film I just have to show you," he said. It didn't occur to me to say no. It sounds awful when I say it now – I had a steady boyfriend back at home. But my whole life there felt so far away. And I don't think I could have turned him down even if I'd wanted to. I just couldn't have made the words form in my mouth. I absolutely had to see him again. I'd never felt that way before in my life.'

What she had with Alan was so different. Over the course of their marriage, they built something that she is sure was a type of love – it felt solid and comfortable and became her life. But it wasn't *that*. That rush, that sense of a momentum she was as unable to control as the weather.

'I bought the yellow boots the day after meeting Simon. I

62

was out on a walk and saw them in the window of the Mary Quant shop – a shop I'd always wanted to step inside. They caught my eye and they were so luminous – they matched my mood perfectly.'

The morning after the party, she woke early, Audrey still snoring in bed. The sun peeked through the makeshift curtains and there was a buzzing energy in Maggy's limbs. She dressed quietly and left the flat, the cool air kissing her face.

Without realising it, her footsteps took her out of Kensington and into Knightsbridge, passing along crescents and down streets of tall white town houses, skirting the edges of private gardens, where trees grew behind black iron fences. Eventually, she emerged onto the King's Road, the street still quiet but just starting to get busier as shops opened their shutters and customers stepped inside cafés and bakeries for their morning dose of coffee and bread. Before long, she found herself in front of Bazaar, the Mary Quant store she'd only ever stood outside before, gazing longingly inside.

The windows were decorated with large daisy stickers, the mannequins inside striking jaunty poses, dressed in colour-block pinafore dresses, miniskirts, roll-neck tops and opaque white tights. And then she saw the boots. They shone in the morning sunshine, a yellow so yellow that it seemed to radiate light and joy. As Maggy looked in through the window, her mind still filled with the night before and the sound of Simon's laugh and the feeling of his hand in hers as they walked, she suddenly understood the meaning of the colour yellow. She felt it in her bones, in the racing of her heart, in the warmth of the sun shining down on her on that London street. She was nineteen years old and life felt in that moment as yellow as the sun. She had to have those boots.

Resurfacing from the memory, it is almost a surprise to see that Lou is still there on the sofa, a smile on her face.

'So what happened next?'

Maggy glances towards the window. It is dark now, her reflection staring back at her in the glass. She rubs her arms.

'Do you have a boyfriend, Lou?' she asks. 'Or girlfriend?'

'No.' Then Lou hesitates, letting out a small sigh. 'I had a boyfriend, but we broke up a while ago, just before I moved back to Somerset. Well, he broke up with me. He didn't want to relocate when I had to move back to take care of my mum.'

'That doesn't sound fair.'

'I guess I understood that it was a big thing to ask of him, but we were pretty serious. I'll be honest – I had hoped that he would be there for me.'

'Of course,' replies Maggy. 'Life is the bad bits as well as the good. He should have supported you. But it's his loss.'

'Thanks,' Lou says, almost smiling. 'I still miss him some-times, though.'

'That's loneliness talking.'

'I suppose you're right.'

A silence descends.

'It's getting late,' Maggy says. 'Why don't I tell you the rest of the story another time?'

'Of course,' replies Lou, pulling herself up from the sofa. 'I hadn't noticed the time. I should get to bed. Thanks again for dinner.'

She heads for the door, but pauses at the last minute, turning back to Maggy, who is still sitting on the sofa.

'This has been the nicest evening I've had in a long time,' she says. 'Thank you.'

'Same here,' Maggy replies, realising how true it is as she says it. As she watches her new lodger head upstairs, it hits Maggy that for the first time in a while she won't be going to sleep in an empty house.

LOU

Lou only moved in just under a week ago, but she already feels at home in Maggy's cosy attic room. It might only be temporary, but after the impersonality of the hotel room, it makes a nice change to be in a home again, but a home that isn't full of all the painful memories of her own childhood house. And there's something about Maggy that makes Lou feel immediately at ease. She has welcomed her so warmly, with endless cups of tea and thoughtful questions about her day in the evenings.

It's a kindness that she has watched extended to Maggy's own family; by now Lou has crossed paths with both of Maggy's children, as well as all three grandchildren, who seem to spend a large amount of time being looked after by their grandmother after school. Lou has noticed how much Maggy's family depend on her for free childcare. Maggy clearly adores her grandchildren, and her children, but Lou can't help but think they might occasionally take advantage of Maggy's good nature. She holds back from saying anything though, not wanting to overstep the line. And it's been a nice distraction to be surrounded by the chat and noise of a family.

In return for Maggy's kindness and the extremely comfortable room, Lou has tried to help out as much as possible, making sure to keep the wine rack stocked with Maggy's favourite wine, cooking dinner for them both and doing more odd jobs around the house. Having been initially worried about how they would get on as housemates, Lou now looks forward to getting back from work each evening, knowing that Maggy will be there.

Tonight, when she arrives home after shutting up the shop (four cosy jumpers and two winter coats sold, thanks to the chilly spell), Maggy is in the kitchen pouring a glass of wine. Spotting Lou, she reaches for a second glass. Her hair looks freshly washed and Lou notices a tiny sparkle of stud earrings – she's never seen her in jewellery before.

'I was thinking of meeting some friends at the Three Swans,' Maggy says. 'If you don't have plans, would you like to join us?'

Lou takes a sip of wine and decides to tell the truth.

'Actually, there's a meet-up happening there tonight for a group of local business owners. I've been invited, but I'm not sure if I'll go …'

Beth had mentioned it again that morning when Lou went in for her usual coffee. By now the other staff there know her order too and always say hello when she pops in.

'That sounds great,' says Maggy enthusiastically. 'I can only imagine how challenging it must be running your own business. It could be nice to meet some other people in the same position?'

'I know you're probably right,' Lou replies, rubbing her forehead. 'And Beth, who invited me, is really nice. But it's been a long time since I've been out, honestly. Not since before Mum died. I'm not sure if I'm up to it.'

Lou had told Maggy about her mum and how she found herself back in Somerset earlier in the week, and to her relief she has been nothing but understanding since.

'That's hard,' Maggy says now. 'I haven't been out much since my husband left either. I used to meet up regularly with the gang I'm seeing tonight. But after the divorce it all felt a bit too much. I couldn't stand all the questions, or worse, the pity.'

'Yes!' Lou replies. 'That's exactly it. I couldn't bear it.'

When she left Brighton, she drifted apart from her old friends, not just because they had been part of her life with her ex-boyfriend Richard and keeping in touch felt too painful. It was also that no one understood what she was going through – no one she knew had lost one parent, let alone two. Some of them tried to be understanding, but how could they possibly understand? It felt exhausting to think about having to articulate her grief, rather than have anyone just *get it* without having to be told.

'But you know,' adds Maggy softly, 'I do think there comes a time when you just have to get out there, even if it feels hard. I remember the first time I went out with friends after my cousin Audrey died. My children were still small then, so I was exhausted as well as grieving. But I was just absolutely sick of staying at home all the time. I went out for a meal with a couple of other mum friends. And I cried in the middle of dinner because one of Audrey's favourite songs came on in the restaurant. But do you know what? It was actually OK. I was OK. I got through it.'

Watching the emotion on Maggy's face, Lou thinks that's probably another reason why she has become so close to her new landlady so quickly – because she's been open with her and it's made Lou want to be open at last too.

'You're probably right,' she replies, feeling tears catch in her throat. 'I'm just not sure I'm ever going to get through this.'

During the day, Lou is mostly able to push her grief aside, focusing on the shop and her customers. But every now and then it catches her totally off guard.

Maggy crosses the kitchen, places a hand on her shoulder and looks her straight in the eye.

'But you *are*. It might not feel like it, but just by getting up each day you are doing it. Sometimes just being *in it* and still keeping going is enough.'

Lou takes a sharp inhale.

'Come on,' Maggy continues gently, rubbing Lou's arm. 'Let's go out together. And then if at any point it gets too much, you can just come and find me and I'll take you home, OK?'

Steeling herself, Lou finds herself nodding and saying, 'OK then, let's go.' Since opening her business, she has surprised herself by the things she has learnt how to do. If she can manage that, surely she can manage a trip to the pub?

Despite her earlier determination, as she stands outside the entrance to the Three Swans, the thought of stepping alone into a bar for the first time in over a year fills Lou with dread. But as she pushes on the door, the warmth and sound of voices spilling out into the chilly October air, she is not alone. Maggy is at her side, dressed in her usual black and grey but with a faint shine of blush pink lipstick on her lips. They share a smile as together they leave the street behind and walk into the noise and cheer of a Friday evening in one of the town's favourite pubs.

Lou scans the crowded room, her eyes eventually finding Beth, sitting in the middle of a large group gathered around a long table. She is talking and laughing, a beer in one hand, and as Lou looks over, she waves warmly.

'Ah, too late now,' Maggy says quietly beside her, a smile in her voice, 'you've been spotted. Oh look, and there are my friends too.' She lifts her hand in greeting towards a small group of women of a similar age in an adjoining room on the opposite side of the open bar. 'I'll be just over there if it gets too much, OK?'

Come on, Lou tells herself, adjusting her outfit – a fitted red jumper worn with high-waisted, wide-leg checked trousers – and smoothing the red-and-white spotted scarf tied around her hair, *you are the owner of your own business, you built most of the interior yourself and you are wearing a cracking outfit. You can do this.*

'Thank you, Maggy. I'm so glad I found out about your advert for the room. It's been really wonderful to meet you.'

Maggy beams. 'You too, love. Now go on.'

'Hi, everyone,' Lou says as she joins the group, trying to make her voice sound more confident than she feels. 'I'm Lou.'

'Lou!' says Beth, standing up and pulling her into a quick embrace. 'I'm so glad you came.'

The others in the group smile at her warmly and Lou smiles back.

'I'm just going to grab a drink and I'll be back. Can I get anyone anything?'

The others shake their heads, raising full or nearly full glasses.

'We're all good,' adds Beth. 'See you in a minute and then I'll introduce you to everyone.'

The warm welcome buoys her, making her feel a little more confident as she orders a glass of wine at the bar. As she waits, a familiar voice from further along the bar catches her attention. It takes her a moment to recognise Pete, dressed as he is in dark jeans and a pale blue shirt instead of the dusty work clothes she is used to seeing him in. He is with a small group, the faces sparking something in Lou's mind. She is just trying to work out whether she knows them when he spots her and smiles.

'Hi there, boss.'

'Hi, Pete, good to see you.'

He shuffles up to make room for her at the crowded bar.

'Do you remember Will and Josh from school?' says Pete, gesturing to the two smiling men beside him, who Lou realises she does recognise. 'And these are their wives, Laura and Mel.'

They say their hellos and then Lou turns to Pete again. She takes a big sip from her glass, the red wine emboldening her.

'So, you do remember that we went to school together!'

Pete laughs. 'Of course I do! I just wasn't sure that you did. I sort of hoped you didn't – I was a right bellend back then.'

'I can vouch for that,' chips in Josh.

'Yeah, mate, but so were we,' adds Will.

'Not much has changed then,' jokes his wife, Mel, planting an extravagant kiss on his cheek.

'I don't remember it that way,' Lou says, thinking back to the teenager she once knew. 'You all played rugby together, didn't you? I remember you seeming like a tight group, it was nice to see, especially for a group of boys.'

'I suppose we were tight, so tight that we're still stuck to one another. You, meanwhile,' says Pete, 'were one of those people you just knew were going places.'

She feels her cheeks growing warm, not just because of the wine.

'I don't know about that.' She always felt so out of place at school. At home she spent her time rifling through her mother's wardrobe and exploring vintage-collectors' forums and blogs, but then each morning she had to put on her grey uniform and it felt like having to turn off a light that she sometimes felt was inside her. At school she couldn't be herself, she was just another girl in another grey uniform. And despite her passion for vintage clothing, she never thought she could make a career out of it. She did well academically and was naturally cautious, which is how she ended up doing a 'sensible' job in recruitment for so long before opening her shop.

'And besides,' Lou adds, 'I'm back here now, aren't I?'

'Ah, it's not so bad here. And you're running your own business!' Pete turns now to his friends. 'Lou's shop is great – you should check it out. And the flat above it will be great too when I finish. Which I will, I promise.'

He grins. Lou thinks again how different he looks not in his work clothes. His smile is the same, but his chin-length hair is free from dust and loose now, instead of pulled back at the nape of his neck. The blue shirt matches his eyes. He looks good.

'Anyway, we shouldn't keep you from your friends,' he says, gesturing to the corner.

Suddenly she finds herself not wanting to go, preferring to stay with Pete and his friends. But remembering why she came here she says a somewhat reluctant goodbye and heads towards the huddle of people in the corner.

'Right, Lou,' says Beth as Lou joins them, squeezing in at the end of a bench seat, 'let me introduce you.'

There's a redheaded woman Lou recognises from the café who Beth introduces as Danie, her partner. 'Business and life,' she adds with a laugh. A man called Joe, in a shearling jacket and with a thick, well-groomed beard, runs a new barber's shop. Gemma, dressed in a jumper stamped with the words 'read more books', unsurprisingly runs the local bookshop. Two young women, friends called Flic and Latika, own a popular refill store where customers can bring their own containers to stock up on dried goods and household products.

'I love your outfit!' says a woman who Lou guesses is in her forties, with long blonde hair tied back in a plait, dressed in jeans and wellies. 'I'm Zara, I run the flower shop.'

'Oh, it's such a lovely shop,' says Lou, picturing the buckets filled with flowers that adorn the street outside.

'Thanks,' replies Zara. 'I love it too. I've always loved flowers. My dad was a gardener and taught me all about plants. It's

73

a challenge keeping it going though. But of course, you must know what that's like.'

As Lou nods, it strikes her that she has never really talked with anyone about her business before – the good and bad bits of working for yourself. When she made her business plan and designed the shop layout and organised her stock, she was in the thick of grief and it was a welcome distraction. But she did it all alone. Now she wonders whether the shop would be doing better if she'd taken the time to get some advice, or at least to talk things through with a friend.

The group welcome Lou in warmly, looping her in to their conversations about difficult customers, slow business weeks, but also family, town gossip and everything in between. They talk about how the town has changed over recent years, the independent market that takes over the streets once a month, bringing new visitors and a sense of optimism among the shopkeepers.

'It's always our busiest day of the month,' says Flic.

'Us too,' adds Gemma. 'It always gives me hope that perhaps books, and indie bookshops, aren't a dying breed when the shop is heaving like that.'

'I haven't been to one yet,' admits Lou. She had heard about the market, but for the last one she didn't think she could handle the crowds, so closed the shop for the day, knowing it didn't make business sense but simply not feeling up to it.

'It's just wonderful,' Beth enthuses. 'The town really comes alive. It's such a great atmosphere. And good for business too.'

'The town never used to be like this when I was young,' Lou says, remembering how desperate she was to leave Somerset when she was a teenager, eager for somewhere with more going on. 'And I must admit that since moving back I haven't really been out and about that much.'

'So you're a local?' asks Joe, the others looking at her with interest.

Somehow, Lou gets through the story about how she ended up back here without crying. Her voice shakes when she tells them about her mum, but she manages to get the words out.

'I'm so sorry,' says Beth, reaching for her arm. 'That must have been awful.'

'It was. But I'm glad to have had my shop to throw myself into these past couple of months. It was my mum who really inspired me to open it. But honestly, things have been a little slow since opening day.'

All Lou's worries return in a flash. She has started running some online ads, as well as placing a notice about the shop in the local paper. Footfall has increased a little and she had her best day so far last week, but it's still a long way off what she'd hoped for.

'I've got an idea,' says Latika enthusiastically. 'Why don't you use the upcoming independent market to have a bit of a relaunch? You could decorate the shop, maybe have some music ...'

Lou can suddenly picture it all so clearly. Bunting in the window, little cups of Prosecco, old-fashioned scones and cakes ... Perhaps she could hire live musicians – a swing band to match the style of the shop.

'That's a great idea! Thanks, Latika, I think I might do it.'

Ideas buzz excitedly in her head. It will be something to pour her energy into, a way to give the shop a boost and herself too.

'If there's anything we can do to help,' chips in Beth, 'you only have to ask.'

'Thank you,' Lou says. 'I will.' And for the first time in a long time, she means it.

MAGGY

After their trip to the pub, Maggy and Lou end up back at Maggy's house side by side on the living room sofa, sharing a pot of tea.

'That wasn't so bad after all then, was it?' Maggy says with a smile, passing Lou the plate of biscuits. Lou takes a Hobnob and settles herself against the sofa cushions.

'It was actually nice. Nicer than I was expecting,' Lou replies. 'It sounds like you had a good time too.'

Maggy smiles to herself. It had been so good to see the girls again. Well, they are all grandmothers by now, but she still thinks of her old friends that she made back when the children were young as 'the girls'. She hasn't seen them that much recently, not for their lack of trying. Tonight, they had lovingly chided her about going AWOL and she had promised to be better at staying in touch.

'Yes, I need to see the old gang more often. I tell myself there isn't time, what with looking after the grandchildren as often as I do, but maybe I just need to make time.'

'You deserve some time to yourself, Maggy.'

Time alone is something she came to fear after Alan left. It's maybe why she has made herself so available to her children to help out with babysitting. But increasingly Maggy is starting to wonder if she needs to find a better balance. Since Lou has moved in, she no longer dreads coming back to an empty house. And she's loved hearing more about Lou's business. She knows owning the shop must come with so many challenges, but hearing Lou speak with such passion about what she does has sparked a glimmer of envy in Maggy. She found a sense of fulfilment in being a stay-at-home mother, but now that her children are grown and her husband has left, she can't help but wonder if she missed out by not having a career of her own.

'However nice it was to be out,' she says, pushing away the thoughts for now, 'it's nice to be back here too.'

'Now, Maggy,' says Lou, 'you still haven't told me the rest of your story and what happened between you and Simon. I keep thinking about it all.'

Maggy's face clouds as she brushes biscuit crumbs from her fingers and leans back slightly against the sofa cushions.

'Ah, Simon,' she says softly. 'You know, I hadn't thought about him in years, but ever since talking to you, I must admit I've been thinking about him and that time more and more.'

Earlier in the week when she had been looking after Fleur, Simon's face came suddenly into her mind. As she watched her beloved granddaughter playing in her overgrown garden, it struck Maggy how close she nearly came to ending up with a different man from this girl's grandfather. Her marriage, which over the years came to seem the defining feature of her life – her home, her children and her daily existence built around it – so nearly didn't happen.

'I wore the yellow boots on our first proper date,' she confides. 'As soon as Simon saw me, he grinned. "*Hello, Yellow*," I remember him saying. He called me Yellow after that. I know it's impossible to imagine it now. It probably seems silly that I even kept the boots at all. They're not something I would ever wear now.'

She looks down self-consciously at her black jumper.

'It's not silly,' says Lou. 'Do you know, I still have a pair of dungarees from when I was ten years old? They were my absolute favourites – my mum made them for me out of this amazing purple corduroy fabric and I wore them all the time. When I grew out of them, I wouldn't let her throw them away. I've kept them ever since, carrying them with me through every house move, every new wardrobe. They just make me think about being ten once more. Not long ago, I was looking at them again and I found a twig in one of the pockets, could you believe it? I remember wearing them to climb the tree in the garden, although I'd usually get stuck and Dad would have to help me down again.'

She trails off now, her expression serious.

'Back to London,' she says. And realising that Lou would prefer to sink back into someone else's story rather than dwell on her own, Maggy continues.

'After that first night, we started seeing each other most evenings. Sometimes we'd go to the cinema together and he'd spend the journey home talking passionately about the director and the actors. I just loved listening to him. Other times, I would go to the Italian restaurant where he worked, sitting in the corner and watching him move around the room and talk to customers. He was so brilliant with people, making them laugh, making them feel welcome. I felt so lucky that, of all the people who seemed charmed by him, I was the one who would be going home with him at the end of the night.'

Her cheeks grow hot now and she clears her throat.

'I feel I should say that we never slept together. I did still feel some sense of loyalty to Alan. But it really did feel like he was part of a totally different life. The things Simon and I talked about – films and music and books and travel – I never would have talked about with Alan. And *I* felt different. "London Maggy" was nothing like "Somerset Maggy". In a way, it felt like both men were seeing two totally different women. At least that's probably how I tried to justify things to myself – that and holding back from going to bed with him, however much I might have wanted to. I may not have slept with him, but I did fall for him, which is probably much worse.'

'You can't help who you fall in love with, though,' says Lou. 'Trying not to fall in love is like trying not to sneeze.'

'I suppose you're right.'

'And did he fall in love with you too?' Lou asks.

'I thought so. He knew about Alan, but he didn't seem to mind. I suppose because when I was with him, I was so with him. I hung on his every word. We would talk for hours, we felt so close, so in sync. It got to the point where I even started thinking about a future with him. He dreamed of moving to Los

80

Angeles to pursue his acting career. Things weren't working out for him in London and he became convinced that he'd have better luck in America. I started saving up money from my job at the shop, thinking I might go with him. I imagined myself getting a job as a nanny, us getting an apartment together ...'

She trails off, looking around the room in the home she has lived in for more than fifty years. Her eyes fall on the spot on the mantlepiece where her wedding photos used to stand before being replaced with pictures of the grandchildren.

'And then one day Alan turned up in London. I couldn't believe it when someone buzzed up to Audrey's flat that day and it was him. He'd never been to visit me before. I was thankfully alone. "*Is this really where you live?*" he asked and for the first time I saw it as he must have seen it – the mattress on the floor where I slept, the dirty dishes, the laundry hanging everywhere. Then he gave me this whole speech – I felt certain he must have practised it on the train – about how I'd had my fun but that I couldn't live like this forever. It was time to return home and to begin our lives together. And then he asked me to marry him.'

Lou's eyes widen. 'Oh wow!'

Maggy pictures herself back in that flat, Alan clutching his A–Z and looking so incongruous among the detritus of her London life.

'I felt so conflicted. Because I couldn't deny that it was good to see him again. I had known him for years and felt a great sense of affection for him. And seeing him reminded me about everything at home – my family, my friends, everything that used to be so known and so comfortable. And his words made me wonder ... The summer had been wonderful, but where

81

was I really heading? I didn't see how I could make a career out of being a shop girl and surely Audrey wouldn't want me to stay on her floor forever. But then there was Simon ...'

Maggy trails off, her eyes misting over.

'I told Alan I needed to think about it, which he said he understood. He was the king of thinking things over, he always has been. He went back to Somerset to await my answer, and I went straight to Simon. I turned up in a bit of a state and I told him what Alan had asked me.'

'And what did he say?' Lou asks eagerly.

'He said I should say yes.'

'No!'

'Honestly, I was heartbroken. I didn't quite realise it until I saw him, but I think I hoped he would tell me not to, that he would give me an alternative offer. Because whatever my head told me, in my heart I knew I loved Simon. I couldn't stand the thought of my life without him. But he told me that he thought I should marry Alan and then he ushered me out of his flat in a hurry. And I never saw him again.'

'What happened? Where did he go?' exclaims Lou. By now her arms are wrapped around her knees, her eyes wide as she listens intently.

Maggy shivers, remembering it all. 'A couple of days later when I'd calmed down, I went back to his flat. But a neighbour told me he had moved out. We didn't have mobile phones back then and I tried his work and his friends, but no one knew what had happened to him. I had never met his family so I couldn't ask them. He had disappeared, and I had no idea where he had gone.'

'That must have been awful.'

'It was. Not long after that, I packed up my things and moved back to Somerset. It felt like that stage of my life was over. It was time to start being serious about my life. I accepted Alan's offer and shortly after that we got married and moved to this house.'

They both glance around them. The house might feel less lonely now that Lou is staying in the attic room, but it still feels too big for the two of them, meant for a different kind of life.

'Once I'd made the decision to come back, I threw myself into my life here. I worked for a while as a receptionist at Alan's family's firm, which he took over not long after we married. And then when the children arrived, that became my full-time job. I looked after them and Alan and became the woman my family always planned for me to be, perhaps the woman I was always meant to be. The yellow boots went up into the attic alongside all my other clothes from that summer in London. And the memories.'

And they stayed there for years. If Charlotte hadn't stumbled across the boots while rooting around up there, they might have stayed there forever.

'Did you ever try to find Simon again?' asks Lou.

'No. I thought about it occasionally, but it wouldn't have felt right, not once I was married.'

She never forgot about him completely, but over time that brief moment in her life came to seem further and further away, belonging to a different time and a different person entirely. Audrey stayed in London for years, but once Maggy had small children, trips to visit her became more difficult, so they mostly saw one another in Somerset. When Audrey talked about her life, usually while Maggy had a child balanced on her knee or a hand stirring something on the hob, she sometimes imagined what her life would have been like if she'd stayed. But the idea felt like trying to catch a snowflake; as soon as she thought she had it, it melted away. No, her life was in Somerset with her family, a family who needed her.

'But you're not married anymore!' says Lou. When Maggy looks across at her, there's an excited smile on her face.

She frowns. 'What do you mean?'

'You could try to find him now! Do you have Facebook?'

Lou pulls her phone from her pocket.

'I don't,' Maggy says. 'My children have tried to persuade me, but I've never got round to it.'

'I can help you set up a profile!' Lou shuffles closer to Maggy so she can see her phone, pulling up her business and personal accounts. 'That way, you can see if he's on there too and send him a message.'

'Oh, I'm not sure about that ... It's been such a long time. I don't know if I'd even recognise him. Or if he'd recognise me.'

'Go on!' Lou encourages. 'What have you got to lose? Do you really want to spend the rest of your life wondering what happened?'

Her heart races. 'I suppose there's no harm in looking ...'

Lou shows Maggy on her own phone what to do, and just a few moments later Maggy has her own profile.

'I can't believe it was that easy. My children have been pestering me to do it for years.'

'And now you just have to put his name in the search bar.'

Maggy isn't quite sure she's prepared for what she might find, or for the fact that she might not find him at all. But her new friend's enthusiasm is catching. And she realises Lou is right – she has nothing to lose in trying and maybe a lot to gain, even if just the answers to questions she has wondered about for years.

'Here goes, I suppose.'

It takes a while to find him, scrolling through tiny photos of other men with his same name. Maggy is starting to think that perhaps she won't find him at all; maybe, like her before today, he doesn't use social media. But then she stops, her eyes falling on a photo that makes her draw in a sharp breath.

'It's him!' she says suddenly. 'I can't believe it. It's him.'

Lou leans closer and together they look at the photograph. His hair might be grey, the curls shorter than when Maggy knew him, but the brown eyes are unmistakeably his. A jolt of electricity rocks through her as she finds herself looking at the eyes of the man she once knew.

In the photograph he is wearing a well-tailored grey suit jacket but with a loosely unbuttoned shirt, a colourful pocket square poking out of one pocket. He is smiling that same grin Maggy remembers but not looking quite at the camera, as though caught in the middle of laughter. Suddenly, everything seems to disappear and she is back in London that summer, holding his hand as they walked together down a night-time street, kissing him at the back of a cinema, his mouth tasting of popcorn, sitting on the edge of his bed watching him read and adoring him with every bone in her body.

'He's handsome,' says Lou, adding with a teasing smile, 'for an older guy.'

But Maggy is too on edge to pick up on the joke insult. She holds the phone as though it's suddenly hot to the touch.

'What should I do?'

'Send him a message!'

'But what if he doesn't remember me? Or he does but doesn't want to hear from me?'

'Maggy,' says Lou, looking her in the eyes. 'I mean this with great kindness. But you have raised two children and have helped raise three grandchildren. You can do this.'

Maggy lets out a small laugh.

'Sorry, you're right.' *Pull yourself together*, she adds to herself. A few moments later, she has typed the message and hit send before she has time to change her mind.

> Dear Simon,
> My name is Maggy Richardson (née Joyce). You might not remember me but we met in London in the summer of 1966. I recently joined Facebook and am trying to reconnect with some old friends. I know it's been a very long time, but if you'd like to get in touch I should be happy to hear from you. From your photograph you seem very well, and I hope that is the case.
> With best wishes,
> Maggy

'And now we wait?' she asks.

Lou wraps an arm around her shoulder and gives her a squeeze.

'Now we wait.'

DONNA

When Donna is stressed or anxious, she cooks. She has always loved recipes, and her kitchen shelves are stacked with cookbooks, arranged first by genre (sweet baking, savoury baking, food by region) and then alphabetically. Unlike most other things in life, if you follow a recipe exactly, you know how it's going to turn out. And if it doesn't come out of the oven looking perfect, you can start all over again and have another go.

The kitchen counter is covered in pies. There's a cherry pie with a neat lattice crust, an apple pie dusted in brown sugar and a pecan pie just out of the oven, steaming and filling the kitchen with its sweet caramel scent. Luna sits on the tiled floor, gazing up with wide eyes, tongue hanging out eagerly.

Once she has carefully wiped a dusting of flour from the counter, Donna pauses, playing the voicemail on her phone yet again.

'Hello, honey, it's me.' A pause. 'Mom.'

In the message, Shirley coughs and hesitates again.

'I know you're upset with me and you have every right to be. I understand the news came as a real shock. I should have told you years ago. But it doesn't change how much your dad and I love you. I'd love it if you could ring me back. Or come over whenever you like – I'm still stuck in bed, but I'd love to see you. We can talk about it all. OK, well, bye for now, Donna. Love you.'

Donna pictures Shirley in bed, her skin paler than usual and her hair limp, and her stomach knots. But then she thinks about how many times her mother – her adoptive mother – could have told her the truth but didn't. She chose to lie to her for her entire life. And Donna hates lies. Probably because she is incapable of telling them. It has got her into trouble many times throughout her life. When she was younger, it used to upset her when a friend would get cross after asking Donna's opinion on a certain outfit and then not liking her response, or if an acquaintance would say, 'Oh, we must meet up soon' and would then go pale when Donna took out her Filofax. But then Donna got older and she stopped caring as much what other people thought of her. She eventually gave up trying to learn all the social rules that often perplexed her and had decided to simply be herself instead. She might not have a wide circle of friends as a result, but she has always felt safe and secure in her hometown with her family. But now all of that has been turned upside down.

She puts her phone back in her pocket and scrubs furiously at a sticky patch on the work surface.

'Good morning,' says John, rubbing his eyes, then replacing

his round glasses as he steps into the kitchen. 'You've been busy.'

Donna looks up.

'Oh, hello,' she says, glancing to the window, where the fall sun shines down on the sycamore trees in the garden that is shared by both their house and the inn. She must have missed the sunrise.

John helps himself to a slice of apple pie and sits down at the table, pouring a coffee from the pot and topping up Donna's mug. Brooke, who is visiting from the city, steps inside next, still in her pyjamas.

'Busy night, Mom?' she says with a smile, kissing her mother on the cheek. Donna is still focused on scrubbing.

'Hmph,' she replies.

Brooke pulls out a chair, pouring herself an orange juice.

'Apple, cherry or pecan?' asks John.

Brooke stretches, rolling her shoulders. 'Mmm, pecan, my favourite.'

Donna had made her family's favourite flavours – apple for John, pecan for Brooke and cherry for her parents. She made that one without thinking. Later it will go across to the inn for the guests, just like the others she made earlier in the week. There's only so much pie that three people and a dog can eat.

As John and Brooke eat their unorthodox breakfast, Donna continues to clean up after herself. Then she stops suddenly, placing the rolling pin she'd been about to put away down on the counter with a bang.

'I just don't understand how they could be so careless!' she says crossly. 'To lose a whole file like that. I know it was a long time ago, but these are people's lives!'

'I know, honey,' John says with the gentleness of someone who has had this conversation before.

'If they even had her date of birth or last known address, it would give me somewhere to start. But nothing! A name and some photographs ...' She trails off.

The two photos from the adoption agency look down at her from the fridge, alongside the one Shirley gave her. Every day since the meeting, Donna has stared and stared at all three images, hoping that they might give her some answers. But despite knowing that the pictures once belonged to her birth mother, the woman in the yellow dress is still a mystery to her.

As she walks home from the bus stop after work, the sound of shouting reaches her before she turns onto her street. She pauses for a moment, her stomach dropping. Then she steadies herself, lifting her chin high as she braces herself for what is waiting for her. She knew it had to happen eventually.

She spots her mother and their neighbour, Mrs Walker, standing on the street outside her home.

'Irene,' she hears her mother saying in a pleading voice as she draws closer, 'I'm sure it's just a misunderstanding.'

As the young woman draws closer, Mrs Walker looks up, her face turning a violent red as she spots her.

'You!' she shouts, pointing at the young woman. 'You bitch!'

The young woman does her best not to flinch. It's only then that she spots the children watching the commotion from the street, still dressed in their school uniforms. She blinks hard and forces herself to look away from them.

'You're back,' says the young woman's mother. 'Now, tell Mrs Walker that there's been some mistake. I told her that she must have got it wrong. My daughter wouldn't have got herself caught up in a mess like this.'

The young woman says nothing, instead she smooths the fabric of her navy work dress. She wishes she was wearing a better outfit.

'I haven't made a mistake,' spits out Mrs Walker, the older woman's hair loose around her face and her eyes bloodshot. 'Sydney told me everything.'

At the mention of his name, the young woman's mind fills with images of him. He has always been a presence in her life, someone there in the background as she was growing up and who she was used to bumping into outside their neighbouring front doors or at church. But she only noticed him properly when he came in to the department store one day a year ago. He came right up to the counter where she was working and it had taken her a moment to realise who he was, being so out of context. He smiled and laughed about the coincidence of bumping into her there (something that she has since learned was not a coincidence at all) and then asked for her help choosing between several shirts, something she did, even though it wasn't strictly her department. As she helped him, they talked. She was surprised by how much they had in common – a love of music and a yearning to travel. She'd never had conversations like that before, conversations that took her mind far away from her Islington home.

The next day, he came in again and this time asked her to come out with him on her lunch break and mentioned a nearby restaurant. She hesitated, surprised by his offer. He was the husband of her neighbour and nearly twice her age. She knew she shouldn't say yes. But she had never been to a restaurant before. In the end, she couldn't resist.

'You're wasted working in that store,' he told her as he poured her a glass of wine, which she pretended to enjoy, wanting to seem sophisticated. 'Have you ever considered modelling? I can see you on the cover of a magazine. I have a few contacts I could put you in touch with.'

It was as though he had looked inside her heart and seen the secret dream that lived there.

'Yes please,' she replied, trying not to sound too excited.

After that, their meetings became more regular, always away from Islington where they might be spotted. He gave her gifts and compliments and talked about the future in a way that made her excited rather than daunted. She hadn't meant it to happen, she really hadn't. But somehow, it had.

'We're in love,' she says out loud, causing her mother and neighbour to turn to her, mouths open in shock. Mrs Walker looks as though she might slap her and the young woman readies herself for the sting. But as though all the energy has suddenly drained from her, the older woman's shoulders sag and she instead reaches for the hands of her daughters, who have been watching from the street.

'You are to have nothing to do with this family any more,' she says to them, 'do you hear me?' Then she drags them away, slamming their front door behind them.

The young woman is aware of the crowd that has gathered outside, their neighbours watching the drama unfold. She *doesn't want to give them the satisfaction of seeing anything else so heads inside, her mother following closely behind.*

Once the door is shut, her mother grabs her by the wrist.

'You can't be serious,' she hisses.

Her daughter takes a deep breath. Sydney had promised her that he would tell his wife and children soon. The fact that he has must mean he is serious about her and their plans together. Guilt and excitement collide inside her.

'But we are, Mother. He loves me and I love him.'

'What about Percy?'

She thinks of her first boyfriend, realising that he is exactly that – a boy. He is the kind of boy to bring her mother flowers instead of her and who is content to become a bus driver like his father and to stay living in the apartment where he grew up until getting married and maybe moving a few doors down with his wife. He would never think to take her out to a restaurant when his mother cooks such good pork chops. He is perfectly nice, but she wants more than that.

'Percy is sweet but boring. He doesn't have any ambition for his life. I could never marry him.'

'You can't marry Sydney either – you may have somehow forgotten, or are just too selfish to care, but he's already married.'

'He's getting divorced,' the young woman replies, her voice trembling slightly now. 'He wants us to be together. We didn't mean to hurt anyone, really we didn't. But he doesn't love her, Mother, they're not happy and haven't been for a long time. Can't we be happy instead? I deserve to be happy, and so does he.'

Her mother takes a step forward, her face close to her

daughter's. Her next words are delivered in a quiet but hard voice.

'It makes me glad your father isn't here any more. He'd be ashamed of you.'

Then she turns away, leaving her daughter in the hallway clutching her stomach as though she has just been kicked. For a second, she is overwhelmed by doubts. Maybe this was all a mistake. Maybe she never should have accepted that first invitation, however exciting the prospect of being out in a real restaurant with a man who seemed truly interested in her and her ambitions might have been. But it is too late to go back now. She has chosen her path and she has chosen him. She reminds herself that she loves him and that it will all be worth it in the end.

LOU

Lou and Maggy head to the shop together that morning.

'If you're not busy tomorrow,' Lou said the night before, 'I wonder if you'd like to come and spend some time at work with me? After hearing about your time in London, there are some clothes I'd love to show you.'

'I'd like that,' Maggy had replied. 'It will be fun to pretend to be a shop girl again.'

They start the morning with coffee at Beth's, who greets them both warmly.

'Have you thought any more about Latika's idea for a big relaunch on market day?' she asks as she prepares their drinks, the hiss and spit of the coffee machine rising above the background noise of customers chatting and a dog outside barking, its nose pressed up to the window, eyes fixed on the fresh pastries on the counter.

'I think I'm going to do it!'

'That's a wonderful idea,' says Maggy.

'If we can help at all, just let us know,' Beth adds. 'Maybe we could supply some cakes?'

'Thank you, that would be lovely.'

Lou and Maggy choose a pastry each, Lou picking a third at the last minute.

'Do you mind if we pop upstairs first?' she says as they leave the café, Lou balancing the coffees and the paper bag, the croissants inside still warm.

As they climb the stairs leading to the flat above the shop, they are met by the upbeat voice of Cyndi Lauper telling everyone how much fun girls want to have, followed by a decidedly rusty but equally enthusiastic male voice singing along. At the door Lou pauses, a finger to her lips as she and Maggy wait for a moment, both trying hard to suppress their laughter. As the song and the singer reach their triumphant end, Lou can't help herself – a giggle escapes.

She knocks lightly and pushes open the door. Pete spins round on the spot, nearly knocking over the portable speakers at his feet, a power drill held in his hand.

'I'm sorry to make you work so hard when you clearly just want to have fun,' Lou teases as he puts the drill down and pauses the music, 'but I come bearing coffee and baked goods.'

His cheeks flush, but he is smiling.

'I don't know, putting up light fittings is pretty fun.'

'I didn't have you down as a Cyndi Lauper fan.'

'Ah, but there's just nothing like an eighties anthem or singing your heart out to start the day. Perfect for a bit of shower singing too. Although I must admit I don't usually have an audience.'

It enters Lou's mind that it must mean he lives alone. She can't help but feel pleased. Then she shakes herself, surprised by the direction of her thoughts.

'Wow, it's looking great,' she says more seriously, taking in the transformation since her last visit. The space still looks far from finished, but she can see it beginning to take shape. Suddenly she can picture the freshly plastered walls painted a cheering yellow or perhaps a rich green, the old Chesterfield sofa she's had her eye on in a local antique shop reupholstered in a lush-coloured velvet and placed opposite the fireplace, thick printed curtains hanging in the windows.

'Sorry, this is my landlady, Maggy,' she adds. Then to Maggy, 'It was Pete who told me you were looking for a lodger actually. I think he knows your son-in-law?'

Pete and Maggy chat about their mutual connection.

'This space is wonderful,' Maggy says then, turning on the spot to take it all in. 'Gorgeous light. And what a lovely view.' All three of them step over towards the windows to glance down the cobbled hill, the colourful array of cafés and shops at ground level just opening their doors to customers. A mother pushes a pram bumpily over the stones as an older woman heads in the other direction, carrying a large bunch of flowers in autumn shades of orange and hot pink that Lou assumes must be from Zara's shop. Looking down at the pretty sight of the town waking up gives Lou a warm feeling. *I'm part of that too.*

'It is, isn't it?' she says aloud, turning back to the room that will soon be her living room.

Once again, Lou can't believe that the flat is going to be

hers. Excitement rushes through her, along with a little bit of regret that it means she won't be staying with Maggy for too much longer.

She hands over the coffee and pastry to Pete, who thanks her warmly.

'Right, I should probably get back to work.'

'And so should we,' Lou says in reply. As they head back downstairs, Pete resumes his music and singing, this time 'Total Eclipse of the Heart'. Perhaps he is putting it on for show, but he sings even louder this time and Lou laughs, thinking as she does that she hasn't laughed in quite a long time.

Now, Lou and Maggy stand side by side behind the counter waiting for the first customers of the day.

'Why don't I show you a few of my special pieces while it's quiet?' Lou says to distract herself. As she points out her favourites – a purple wool cape, a mint-green coat with white faux-fur collar and sleeves, a mustard-yellow pencil skirt – she tells Maggy how and where she found them and the life she imagines each piece having lived.

'Can't you just hear the fizz of the Champagne being poured and the sound of the band playing when you see this one?' she says of a black 1950s evening dress with a full skirt and white organza draped over the shoulders to form capped sleeves, a bow in the centre.

'Oh yes!' replies Maggy, reaching for a short sleeveless shift dress in red-and-white gingham. 'And I can feel the sun and see the picnic that went with this one.'

'Exactly!'

Lou watches as Maggy reaches out and strokes a hand gently along one rail of clothes, her fingertips brushing over cotton and lace, silk and denim.

'I think I'd like to update my wardrobe,' she says suddenly, turning to look at Lou. 'It's about time I tried something different. And finding my yellow boots again and talking with you about that time in my life has reminded me that I once had *fun* with clothes. It's also made me realise that I've probably … Well, I've probably let myself go.'

Both Lou and Maggy look in the mirror at Maggy's grey rollneck jumper, so long it comes down to just above her knees, and her plain black trousers and practical black trainers. Lou's mind runs its way around the shop, thinking of things Maggy might like.

'I don't think it's a case of letting yourself go, Maggy. You should wear whatever makes you feel good and that's not for anyone else to decide. But do your clothes make you happy?'

'Happy?' Maggy's face contorts as though it's a question she's never thought about before. 'They make me feel invisible. Which I suppose makes me feel safe. But happy? No. I don't think I've worn anything that's made me happy since I was about nineteen years old.'

Oh Maggy, Lou thinks, flooded suddenly with affection for the woman she has known for such a short amount of time but who has quickly become her friend. When she looks at her now, the black and grey outfit seems to sum up everything she's come to learn about her new friend: her recent divorce, her loneliness, the way she does so much for her family while

102

rarely taking moments for herself. But when Lou looks at her, she sees so much more than that. She sees the woman who took her in when she was at rock bottom, a woman who is kind and interesting and once wore bright yellow boots as she strode down the streets of London.

'Well,' Lou says, a smile breaking across her face, 'I think it's time to change that.'

Maggy stands in front of the mirror, taking in her reflection. She turns back and forth, dressed in a pair of navy high-waisted trousers with large white buttons up one side, a tangerine-orange jumper tucked in to the waistband and the collar of a white shirt just peeking out at the neckline. Lou added a chunky citrine necklace from the 1960s, which she fastened carefully at the base of Maggy's neck. Her grey hair is loose on her shoulders, hanging in slightly ruffled waves.

'I have a waist!' Maggy says suddenly. 'I thought I lost that in 1975.'

'It's been there all along. You were just covering it up.'

Maggy turns to the mirror again, taking herself in from all angles.

'I don't look like me,' she says hesitantly. 'I look … good.'

A warm rush of pride fills Lou's chest. This is why she wanted to open her shop, after all. It wasn't enough to keep building her vintage collection only to have it sitting in the wardrobe or in boxes. These things were made to be worn, and since opening the business, she has realised that her passion doesn't just end at *finding* the pieces – it's about finding new homes for them too.

'That *is* you!' she says, wanting to reach out to Maggy and hug her. 'You look beautiful.'

Lou notices Maggy's eyes shining before she turns hurriedly back to the changing room.

'Right, I'll try the next one.'

Some outfits are discarded as being uncomfortable or just not quite 'Maggy'. But others are met with 'oohs' and 'ahhs' by Lou and even Maggy herself. While she's showing Lou one of the outfits, a customer comes in to browse and tells Maggy she looks amazing, making her redden but smile.

'Maybe it *is* me,' she says once they are alone again, the customer having left with a couple of scarves and an embroidered shirt that was a particular favourite of Lou's. She was almost sad to see it go, but the woman had looked so happy when she spotted it on the rail. 'It reminds me of one my sister and I wore when we were young,' she said. 'We had matching.' Lou wondered from the wistful smile on the customer's face whether she and the sister were still close.

Maggy steps a little closer towards the mirror and swishes the fabric of the emerald-green dress she is wearing. 'It's me, just a different kind of me.'

In the end, Maggy buys several outfits and a plaid coat in shades of deep blue to replace the black winter coat she's had for years.

'Well, you've certainly buoyed today's sales,' Lou says as she folds each item carefully between sheets of tissue paper. Even with the generous discount she gave Maggy, it still constituted a substantial sale for Lou. 'I'm honestly not sure how long I'll be able to stay open if things stay like this.'

'But it's such a beautiful shop,' Maggy says earnestly. 'We just need to get the word out.'

Lou smiles at the use of 'we'. She thinks of Beth and the others and vows to take them up on their offers of help for the relaunch, as well as making more of an effort to support their businesses too. She makes a mental note to start buying her household essentials from Flic and Latika's refill shop, to pop in more regularly to the independent bookshop and to buy flowers for Maggy from Zara's shop – another little way of thanking her for everything she's doing for her.

'Now, tell me,' says Maggy once they are both back behind the counter again. 'There's one dress I'd love to know more about. What's this one's story?'

She points up to the yellow dress hanging above them, the fabric gleaming gold and the embroidered flowers shining cheerfully in the autumn sunlight. Lou remembers running her hands over the threads when she was a child, stroking as gently as if she'd been caressing a sleeping lion.

'Mum's yellow dress,' she says quietly.

When she started planning the shop, Lou knew her mother's yellow dress would have to hang in pride of place. The dress was one of the things that first sparked her love of vintage clothing after all, a spark that eventually caught and became a burning flame.

'It was her favourite dress. I don't actually know that much about it though. It was one of the only things in her wardrobe that I wasn't allowed to touch.'

She used to sneak into her mother's wardrobe when she was little and seek it out, drawn by the colour and the beautiful flowers that she sometimes imagined were real. She remembers her mother finding her there one day and snapping at her. Her mother never snapped and it startled her.

'You must be careful,' she said, 'that's very precious, it's not for playing with.' When Lou had cried in surprise, her mother had softened, handing her some scarves and a handbag to play dress-up with instead. But Lou remembers her mother moving the dress to the back of the wardrobe, zipping it carefully inside a dust cover.

'I hope she wouldn't mind me having it hanging here now,' Lou continues to Maggy, looking up at the dress, 'but it's the thing that most makes me think of her.'

In her mind, Lou sees her mum twirling in the kitchen in the yellow dress, dancing with her dad to a song on the radio while Lou perches on the kitchen counter as a child, licking a spoon from the bowl of the cake they had been making together. She sees her in the same dress at her university graduation ten years ago, her dad smiling and teasing her about how she must be the only mother there wearing a dress that's older than their child. Then she pictures the flash of yellow beneath the black coat that her mum wore three years later to Lou's father's funeral, Lou holding her mum's hand so tightly she lost feeling in her fingertips.

'It makes me feel like she's here with me,' she adds.

She lifts a hand to absentmindedly stroke the hem of the yellow dress. But as she does, one of her bracelets snags on the fabric and the dress slips from the hanger, falling to the floor.

'Oh no! I'm such an idiot!'

Both women bend quickly to the ground, where the dress fans out, creating a puddle of yellow.

'It's OK,' says Maggy, reaching the dress first and gently lifting it, inspecting closely. 'There are a few snagged threads, but nothing that can't be fixed.'

As she holds it closer to check the damage, something seems to catch her eye.

'E. M.,' she says aloud. 'Are those your mother's initials?'

'What do you mean?'

Lou leans closer to see where Maggy is pointing. On the underside of the lining is a small label that Lou has never noticed before. In scrolling embroidery stitched in bright red thread are two letters.

'E. M.,' she repeats, a frown appearing on her face. 'My mother's name was Dorothy Jackson, although everyone called her Dotty. Jackson was her married name. I never knew her maiden name. Her parents died before I was born, but I don't think they were close. She never really talked about them.'

'Perhaps the initials belong to the person who made it?'

Shaking her head, Lou traces the initials with her fingertip. 'I always assumed Mum made the dress herself. She made most of her clothes and worked as a seamstress doing alterations for individuals and theatre. This dress seems so *her* that I just can't imagine anyone else having made it. But I really don't know. And I don't suppose I ever will.'

Maggy carefully places the dress back on its hanger and passes it to her.

'Well, it's certainly a beautiful dress. And a lovely thing to have hanging in your lovely shop. Now, how about you show me how to use that steamer? I might as well be useful.'

Lou knows that Maggy is trying to distract her and as she hangs the dress back carefully on the wall, she tries her best to push the questions to the back of her mind. But even as she sets Maggy to work and serves a group of enthusiastic customers who tell her they will be back, she can't stop thinking about the initials 'E. M.' and how much she wishes her mum was there to answer her questions.

DONNA

'The photos!' Brooke says suddenly, making Donna jump. Her daughter is visiting for the weekend with her family, Tom and Chloe currently out at the park while Brooke and her parents catch up at home. Donna wishes she had more news to tell her daughter, but things have been much the same since she last saw her. She is still not talking to Shirley. And she still has no idea how to start the search for her birth mother. It's put her in a mood all week and she has been unable to focus on anything, her usual chores lying abandoned. But now her daughter's eyes are lighting up as she sits up straighter, pulling her phone from her jeans pocket. 'I don't know why I didn't think of it until now.'

'What do you mean?'

Brooke stands up and heads to the fridge, taking a photograph of the two images of Eleanor on her phone.

'I know it seems like you don't have any information, Mom,

but you do have these pictures. We can do a reverse image search and see if they match any that are online. It might not lead to anything, but it's a start.'

Donna glances at her husband, who shares her confused expression.

'How do you do that?' she asks.

All three of them gather round as Brooke shows her mother what to do. They start with the clearer headshot. There are plenty of 'matches', but as they scroll down they are met with dozens and dozens of similar-style photographs, but none that are Eleanor Morris.

'She's not here,' Donna says after a while. A sinking sense of disappointment takes over her as she looks down at the original image of Eleanor, staring towards the camera.

'Maybe it's for the best?' suggests John in a soft voice. 'You know I'll always support you, but perhaps it's best to let it rest? You haven't been yourself all week and I hate to see you like this. Perhaps it's best to try to let it go? Say you did find out more about her – you might not like what you find.'

'Maybe Dad's right,' Brooke says, giving her mother's arm a squeeze. 'I hate the thought of you being disappointed. Maybe it's better to just leave things as they are.'

Donna looks out the window at the view that is as familiar to her as the faces of her husband and daughter. The tree she climbed and hid in as a child when all the children in her class were invited to birthday parties apart from her, the tree that provided shelter from the sun when she sat and read, throwing herself into adventure stories that transported her far away without the anxiety and turmoil of ever having to actually leave.

The lawn where she learnt to walk and, later, her daughter did too. The inn porch which she repainted when she took over the business from her parents. She wanted to make her mark, but didn't want things to change, so painted over the peeling wood in a fresh coat of the exact same pale grey. Then her eyes drift to the photograph of herself as a baby, wrapped tightly in a blanket and with a fresh pink hat on her head. Someone put her in that blanket and chose that hat and the white dress that she can just see poking out from beneath the covers. Someone she knows nothing about.

'I haven't forgotten that she gave me away, if that's what you're worried about,' she says briskly. 'I know she didn't want me. But I don't know how old she was or where she was from or who my father was and if he knew about me. I don't know what her voice sounded like or if she liked cooking or reading or eating pie.'

'Everyone likes pie,' says Brooke.

'But what was her favourite flavour? And why did she give me up?'

The last words come out louder than Donna expected and leave her feeling breathless.

Brooke leans her head against her shoulder.

'Oh, Mom,' Brooke says. John steps closer too, taking her hand, their matching wedding bands tapping lightly together.

'I know it might be hard,' Donna continues after a moment's pause, 'but I can deal with the answers to all those questions. What I can't live with is not knowing. Especially when I thought I knew everything about my life and this town and my family.'

She closes her eyes and when she opens them, Brooke and John are looking at one another.

'Shall we try that last photo then?' says John. Brooke picks up her phone. Together they search for the photograph of the dancing woman in the yellow dress.

'Look!' says Brooke suddenly. 'I can't believe it. It's the same photo, Mom.'

Donna leans closer. The image on the computer is black-and-white, but there's no mistaking it. The figure is the same, as is the dress with its detailed covering of flowers.

'Well, click on it then!' she says, her heart thumping. The image is linked to a website.

'It looks like a thrift shop in England,' says Brooke. 'There are some cool things on here. And look, there's the photo of Eleanor!'

It is on the 'About' page, next to a modern photograph of a woman who looks around Brooke's age. She is wearing a red-and-white dress and red lipstick, her black hair styled in 1940s rolls. Donna quickly scans the text.

Hello, my name's Lou and I'm the owner of a new vintage clothing emporium in Somerset. I have always been passionate about vintage clothing, inspired by my mother. This year I decided to turn that love into a business. I look forward to greeting you in my shop, where I strive to match customers with unique pre-loved pieces that will hopefully become heirlooms in your own family for years to come.

Donna's mind buzzes, but she can't find any words. All she can do is stare at the face of the young woman on the website.

John is the first to break the silence.

'My God. She has your face shape exactly, Donna.'

'You know what this means, don't you?' says Brooke.

'What?' Donna manages, her mouth dry.

'You should go to England!'

Her daughter's voice is brighter than Donna has heard it since Shirley's stroke. It makes her look up from the screen. Brooke's eyes are sparkling with excitement.

'But I've never been to Europe.'

'Another reason why you should go! I know I might not have sounded that supportive before, but I can see now what this means to you. If you really want answers, phoning or emailing isn't enough. You should go there and meet her. Don't you think so, Dad?'

Turning to her husband, Donna waits for his response, not sure what she hopes him to say.

'I think you should do whatever you need to do,' he says. 'And if that means going to England, then I think you should go. I could come with you?'

The emotional part of Donna's brain sighs with relief; the thought of travelling with him is much more manageable than the prospect of doing the journey on her own. But then the rational side kicks in.

'No, we can't afford two tickets. Or to both be away from the inn.'

They have a brilliant team of staff, including a manager who went to school with Brooke and has worked there since she finished college. At this stage in their lives, Donna and John do far less of the day-to-day running of the place: Donna managing the finances from her quiet office and John meeting and greeting particularly important guests or big groups. But she still doesn't like the thought of leaving the place completely, even for a short period of time. The inn is her home as well as her business. And her husband knows that.

'OK,' he says seriously. 'If this is something you want to do, I'll take care of things here. You don't have to worry.'

'So, you're going?' Brooke says excitedly.

Donna looks again at the photograph of Eleanor twirling in a yellow dress and at the smiling face of the shop owner, a face that somehow seems unknown and familiar all at once. She thinks about all the reasons she shouldn't go – the cost, the upheaval, the stress of travelling so far on her own and the fear of what she might find, or not find, when she gets there. But for once all the rational arguments are silenced by the feeling in her chest.

'You can do this, Mom,' Brooke says, 'I know you can.'

When Donna eventually speaks, the words that come out are words she never would have imagined herself saying a week ago when everything in her life seemed known and stable. She won't be able to rest until she has at least tried to find out where she really comes from.

'I'm going to England.'

'Aren't you even going to say goodbye?'

The young woman is dressed in her travelling suit, a new suitcase resting at her feet. She adjusts her hat and tries to meet the eye of her mother, who is sitting on the stairs looking into the distance but saying nothing. She hasn't spoken to her since the altercation on the street. Since then, the young woman has been aware of the eyes following her whenever she leaves the house for work and the muttering that starts once she is out of earshot. But all of that will soon be a thing of the past.

'I'll miss you, Ma,' she says softly, her voice almost breaking. Because despite her excitement at everything that awaits her there's still part of her that quakes at the thought of leaving everything she knows behind. Her mother says nothing. The young woman's eyes flick for a second further up the stairs and then a knock comes on the door and her attention returns to the journey. It's time for her new life to begin. It's time to go.

'Darling,' Sydney says as she opens the door. He is dressed in a pale suit, a trilby hat pulled down low. 'You look beautiful as ever. Are you ready?'

She nods, looking down at her case and her freshly shined shoes.

'I'll take good care of her,' he says to her mother. 'You don't have to worry.'

She stands up and turns her back on them, disappearing back down towards the scullery. The young woman can hear the sound of the tap running and dishes clattering violently.

'Shall we go?' he asks her, and blinking back tears, she nods. She takes a deep breath, trying to settle her face into the calm, frozen smile of the models in her favourite magazines.

Outside, a taxi waits in the street. He carries both their suitcases and loads them inside. The young woman glances to the next-door building, trying not to picture Sydney's wife and children inside watching him leave. She forces herself to walk with her head held high.

As she steps inside the taxi, she turns her eyes up to the window of the room where she grew up. With one hand lifted, she mouths a silent 'goodbye'. When the car pulls off, she turns round in her seat, keeping her eyes fixed on the window.

It's only once the taxi has rounded the corner and disappeared that the young woman's mother runs out into the street calling her name.

MAGGY

Maggy tries out her new look the next day on her grand-children.

'Wow, Granny! You look amazing!' says Fleur as she opens the front door. Her cousins, Luke and Otis, come rushing up behind her, their faces flushed as if they have just been playing football or, more likely, fighting. They come to an abrupt stop.

'You look different, Granny,' says Luke.

'Good different?' she asks with a laugh.

Luke shrugs, then dashes round her and outside, Otis following behind.

Charlotte appears in the doorway, looking flustered. Her eyes widen as she sees her mother.

'Mum!' she says. 'Look at you!'

Maybe the outfit was a mistake, Maggy thinks, fiddling with the sleeves of her plaid coat and the hem of the orange jumper beneath. *I'm seventy-one, perhaps I'm too old for orange.* It had made her smile when she pulled on the new jumper from Lou's shop this morning, though.

'Don't you like it?' she asks her daughter, spreading her arms slightly to better show off the outfit.

'Sorry, Mum,' says Charlotte, 'you just took me by surprise. You look great. I've just never seen you in anything so ...'

Before she can finish, Fleur steps forward and wraps her arms around Maggy's waist, burrowing her face into the orange wool of her jumper.

'You look like sunshine, Granny,' she says, keeping her arms tight around Maggy but tilting her head back to look up into her face. Maggy smiles back and kisses the top of her granddaughter's head.

'Thanks so much for looking after them all today,' Charlotte says. 'Nick said to say thank you too when he dropped them off this morning – he and Sam had to run. You be good for your grandmother!' she calls out into the street, where all three children are now running up and down the pavement, Fleur chasing after her older cousins. They ignore her and Charlotte gives her mother a tired smile.

'We'll be absolutely fine,' says Maggy. 'I've got a nice day planned for us all. Plenty of fresh air to tire them out.'

With her three grandchildren jostling (Luke and Otis) and singing (Fleur) in the back of the car, she drives them out of the town and down the country lanes edged with brambly hedges and autumn trees. As the countryside rolls by, Maggy thinks back to the fun day she spent yesterday helping Lou in the shop. It gave her a thrill to work a till again after so many years and she even managed to persuade a few people to make purchases.

'You're a natural at this!' Lou had said to her, making her smile with pride.

It had felt energising to be surrounded by the glorious clothes, to chat to the customers and simply to do something a bit different, something where she felt truly part of the town where she has lived for years. And if she's honest with herself, as much as she loves her children and grandchildren, it had also felt good to do something that wasn't to do with her family but was entirely for herself. Looking out at the view around her, it suddenly strikes Maggy how different she feels to just over a week ago when her divorce papers landed on her mat.

'I feel happy!' she says aloud.

'So do I!' cries Fleur, lifting her arms in the air.

'I will be when there's cake. You promised there'd be cake, didn't you?' says Otis.

'Of course,' replies Maggy.

The car slows as they reach the edge of the village of Mells. It's one of Maggy's favourites in the area, with its pretty cottages, some with thatched roofs, others with latticed windows and ivy clinging to the stone walls. There's a village shop which also serves as a well-frequented post office and café, and a stall outside one house which sells jam via an honesty box. It always gives Maggy hope when she sees it there. A lot may have changed in the world throughout her life, but she is thankful that honesty boxes still exist.

She parks and the children hop out, leading the way towards

the walled garden that she has been bringing them to since they were tiny. It's been a while since she last visited though. For some time, it felt too painful because so many of her memories of visits here included Alan too. But today she feels ready to step back inside.

The garden is reached through a green wooden door set into a high stone wall draped with ivy. The boys dart straight off, chasing each other along the twisting paths that wind their way through the plants and fruit trees. They might be nearly teenagers, but Maggy feels thankful that at least for now they still enjoy running about just as much as they like computer games. It strikes her that this might be the last year when they are happy to come here on a day out and to be seen with their grandmother and younger cousin.

As the boys rush about, Fleur heads to the small green shed where cut flowers from the garden are sold in jam jars tied with ribbon. Today the jars contain messy posies of sunflowers and dahlias, delphiniums and lisianthus.

'Hello, ladies,' comes a warm, deep voice.

'Hello, Robert!' says Fleur, smiling up at the tall white-haired gardener who is dressed as usual in dark green overalls, a blue shirt rolled up to his elbows and a pair of battered green wellies on his feet. He has a pair of secateurs in one tough, tanned hand and in the other he delicately holds a bunch of dahlias.

Robert has worked here for as long as Maggy has been visiting. Over the years, she and Alan got to know him and his wife, Jane, who ran the garden's café. It was a tragedy for the whole village when she passed away five years ago. But somehow, through it all, Robert managed to hold on to his smile.

'Maggy, I haven't seen you in ages! You look lovely. No Alan today?'

It has been a long time, she thinks to herself, wondering where to start.

'Granny and Grandad have got a DIVORCE,' chips in Fleur, shouting the last word.

A couple of weeks ago, hearing her granddaughter shout that in the middle of a garden, heads turning in their direction at the sound, would probably have made Maggy cry. But now she can't help but laugh.

'Oh no, I'm sorry to hear that, what a shame,' says Robert.

'No it's not!' says Fleur. 'It means we get TWO sets of presents at Christmas!'

Then, without saying anything else, she rushes off after her cousins, leaving Maggy and Robert alone.

'Ahh, to be a six-year-old,' Maggy sighs.

Robert smiles back, but then tilts his head slightly. 'How are you doing?'

She breathes out heavily, feeling the late autumn sun against her cheeks and taking in the sound of the birds in the trees and her grandchildren's laughter.

'I'm actually doing OK,' she replies. 'And how are you?'

'Ahh, I'm good. How could I not be, working here? The best job in the world.'

Maggy wonders if he will ever retire – he must be a couple of years older than her. But the thought seems somehow ludicrous. Robert is as much a part of this garden as the walls that surround it and the plants that flourish here.

They catch up about their grandchildren, their children and

the garden. Then a pinging noise in Maggy's pocket distracts her.

'Sorry, Robert . . .'

Pulling her phone out, she spots the Facebook notification and her heart leaps. Since Lou set up the page for her, she's been checking it regularly, but until now there's been nothing.

'Will you excuse me?'

Robert waves and returns to the flowers as Maggy heads for a bench in the corner of the garden. Once she has checked that the grandchildren are happily racing around the garden, she sits down and checks the phone. There's a new message. And she sees immediately from the tiny icon of his face that it's from Simon. She steadies herself and then opens it.

Dear Maggy,
How wonderful to hear from you. Of course I remember you!

A sigh of relief escapes her. *He remembers me.*

She continues reading.

I'm delighted you found me – I only caved recently and got 'on' social media. How times have changed since we were young. That time in London feels so long ago but, in many ways, just like yesterday. Tell me, are you still living in Somerset? I have been living in New York for the past few years but come to the UK regularly for work. I am actually going to be visiting in just over a week and wondered – would you like to meet?

122

Her heart jumps. It's as though the garden and everything in it have momentarily disappeared.

> There are many things to say, and if you'd let me, I'd
> love to have the chance to say them, and to see you
> again.
>   Simon

The leaves in the tree above her rustle and her grandchildren laugh as they kick through piles of autumn leaves, but Maggy isn't there, she is standing alone outside the flat where Simon used to live, the question that has haunted her for years repeating itself in her head. *Where did he go?*

Before she can change her mind, she starts typing her reply.

> Dear Simon,
> Yes, I would love to meet ...

LOU

It's the busiest Saturday since the shop opened. Lou wonders if it's the weather – it's a perfect autumn day, the air crisp and the sky a fresh and brilliant blue – or if the marketing she's been working on is finally paying off. Either way, since opening her door that morning there has been a steady stream of customers. Several times people have had to wait to use the changing room, but they haven't seemed to mind; there's a buzzing, happy atmosphere in the shop as people browse.

Seeing the shop so busy makes her even more excited about her plans for the upcoming relaunch at the independent market. The day will be a chance to drum up new business, but it will be an opportunity to celebrate everything she has achieved so far too – and for the first time in a long time she thinks she might quite like to celebrate.

Lou offers guidance to the customers when needed, but mostly holds back, wanting to strike a balance between making everyone feel welcome and letting them explore, knowing herself the joy of rummaging. But while they browse she listens, loving hearing their exclamations and snippets of stories.

'What a gorgeous shade of pink. Doesn't it just make your mouth water?'

'My mum had a jacket just like this when I was growing up. I wonder if she still has it ...'

'What do you think of this dress? I love the sequins, but do you think it's maybe a bit too much?'

Lou couldn't help jumping in then.

'There's no such thing as too much,' she said passionately. 'If it makes you happy, that's all that matters. Although maybe I'm not the best person to ask about "too much".'

She gestured at her own outfit then – today a cropped cream jumper covered in cherries, paired with bright red-and-white striped trousers, a cream fascinator adorned with fruit tucked into her hair.

'But you look fabulous,' the woman had replied. 'I think I'll get it, you've inspired me.'

She's still on a high from the customer's comment, as well as from the regular ringing of the till. So when the woman in her sixties in the indigo jeans and plain blue sweatshirt steps inside the shop, she greets her with a warm smile.

'Hello! Do have a look around and let me know if I can help you.'

But instead of moving towards the rails, the woman stands dead still, staring at Lou and then up at the wall behind her. She is holding on tightly to what looks like a piece of paper and her expression is so intense that it unnerves Lou. Just as she is trying to think of something to say, another customer steps towards her, holding a dress on a hanger.

'Is it OK if I try this on?'

Before Lou can answer, the older woman in the blue jumper interrupts.

'Yes, you can help me.' She speaks with an American accent and her voice is too loud for the environment, coming out sounding something like an order.

Ruffled, Lou tries to remind herself that difficult customers are part of working in retail. She pulls out her best smile and glances first at the other customer, directing her towards the changing room.

'Of course you can try it on, please help yourself and shout if you need help with the buttons or anything.'

The customer nods, glancing at Lou and then at the American woman briefly before turning away.

Clinging on to her customer service smile, Lou turns her attention to the American.

'Is there anything particular you're looking for?' she asks brightly.

The woman continues to stare. There's something about her blue eyes that unsettles Lou. But perhaps it's just because they are fixed unblinkingly on her.

'We have some lovely knitwear,' suggests Lou in an attempt to break the awkward silence. 'Or perhaps you're after directions? I grew up here so know the town well and should be able to—'

But the woman cuts her off. 'No!' she barks. 'I'm not interested in clothes. Or directions.'

'OK…'

Lou is just wondering whether this is some kind of strange robbery and the woman is about to pull a knife from her jeans pocket, although she doesn't look much like a robber. *But then maybe that's me stereotyping,* she says to herself. *There's no reason why a sixty-year-old woman in a blue sweatshirt couldn't be a robber.*

But instead of a knife, the American shows Lou something even more surprising.

'I'm here to see you,' she says as she hands over what Lou thought was a piece of paper but is actually a photograph.

'How did you get this photo?' Lou asks quickly, looking down at an image she knows well.

Lou found it when she was packing up some of her mother's things, which are currently sitting in a local storage unit waiting for the day when Lou has the energy to sort through it all.

Most of the belongings were boxed up by the removal company as Lou was too overwhelmed to tackle the task. But she sorted through her mum's bedside table herself. She wanted to hold the book her mother had been reading, see where the bookmark was and wonder what the last sentence she read might have been.

As well as the book, there was a bottle of perfume – a perfume that Lou has taken to wearing herself – a pair of reading glasses, an assortment of pills, some rose-scented hand cream and at the back of the drawer two photographs. One was the photo that Lou now has tucked into her wallet – a picture of her, her mother and her father when she was a child. But the second image was one Lou had never seen before. It was a black-and-white photo of her mother as a young woman, the image blurred as she twirled in the dress Lou recognised even in black and white. Her mother's face might have been unclear in it, but she loved the sense of energy and joy in the image. When she opened the shop, she decided to frame it and hang it next to the yellow dress, both reminders of her mother.

The photo the stranger has handed her is exactly the same, except in colour, the yellow of the dress shining brightly.

The woman doesn't answer Lou's question. Instead she points up at the matching photograph above the till. 'Is that your mother?'

Lou softens slightly. Perhaps this woman is an old friend of her mother's and doesn't know she has passed away.

'Yes, it is. Although she passed away recently. She was ill for quite some time.'

The American opens her mouth, then closes it again. An expression of great pain passes across her face. By now Lou is aware of the other customers in the shop watching them.

'Did you know Dotty?' she asks, trying to keep her voice gentle. 'Perhaps you can pop by another time when it's quieter and we can talk?'

But the woman seems oblivious to the people around them, including the customer just behind her who is holding a jacket and clearly waiting to pay.

'Dotty?' she says. 'But that's Eleanor. Eleanor Morris.'

Rubbing her forehead, Lou feels her skin prickling beneath her jumper.

'I don't know an Eleanor Morris. That's my mother, Dorothy Jackson.'

'No, it isn't,' insists the woman, 'that's Eleanor Morris. They told me.'

'Who told you?' Lou's head spins. 'Look, I don't mean to be rude, but I'm not quite sure what you want and there are customers waiting. You haven't even told me who you are.'

At that the American woman opens her mouth again, but then closes it abruptly. Then she snatches the photograph back from Lou, turns round and dashes out of the shop, letting the door shut loudly behind her.

Lou stands dead still, flustered and confused, a feeling of anxiety pressing down on her.

Taking a deep breath, she forces a calm expression onto her face.

'I'm sorry about that,' she says to the woman waiting to pay, 'let me take that for you.' But as she serves the customers, wrapping each piece carefully and telling them to come back soon, all she can think about is the strange woman who somehow had a copy of her mum's photo. Who is she and why was she here? And who on earth is Eleanor Morris?

DONNA

'I never should have come here!' Donna says into the phone.

She is video calling with John and Brooke from her room in the pub in town where she is staying. Her room is pleasant enough, although if it were at *her* inn, she would have insisted on giving the surfaces an extra scrub. And the selection of teas by the kettle could be improved – she makes sure to provide a vast array of herbal and fruit teas, as well as decaffeinated and caffeinated coffee too. She has to admit the bed is comfortable though – it wasn't just jet lag that was responsible for the thirteen hours she slept last night after arriving. And the view out over the town square is undeniably pretty.

Although she spent a long time looking up images of the town before arriving, nothing could quite prepare her for how quaint it all is in real life. The higgledy-piggledy old buildings, the stone fountain in the square and the red postboxes were all things she'd imagined when she pictured England in the past but didn't think would *actually* be as charming in person. The few holidays she's been on with her family over the years were pretty much always disappointing, which is another reason why she chose to stay in Cold Spring instead. Why leave when she had everything she needed there?

She certainly isn't in Cold Spring any more though, and even the squishy bed and the postcard-perfect view can't make up for how awful she feels after her visit to the vintage shop.

'Take deep breaths, Mom,' says Brooke, her face freezing, thanks to the pub's slightly dodgy Wi-Fi.

'Damn!' Donna shouts, before the connection resumes and both Brooke and John reappear in sync.

'It's OK, we're here,' says John reassuringly. Donna fights hard to stop herself from pointing out that *no, they're not*. Why did she think she was up to doing this trip on her own? But she knows he is just trying to help, so tries her best to remain calm. 'So, tell us exactly what happened?' he asks.

She tells the story right from the beginning when she landed at the airport, feeling totally disorientated until she thankfully found the taxi driver she'd booked in advance to meet her, through to arriving in the town when it was already dark, sleeping through breakfast the next morning and then spending the day walking up and down the streets, building up the courage to face visiting the vintage shop and the reason she was there.

'You have to go back and ask her more questions!' Brooke says once Donna finishes, ending her story feeling breathless and with the shop owner's shocked expression lingering in her mind.

'I don't know if I can. This whole thing was a terrible idea.' She smooths the blanket on the bed beneath her, straightening it so the lines on the checks match up to the edge of the bed. Despite how comfortable the mattress might be, more than anything she wishes she was back at home in her own bed, with her husband beside her and the weight of Luna's warm body on her feet.

'But she might be able to help you find out about Eleanor,' presses Brooke.

'I think Brooke's right, honey,' says John. 'You've gone all that way. It would be a shame to quit now.'

But that's exactly what Donna wants to do. She wants to give up and get back on the plane. More than that, though, she wants to go back to the time before her mother's stroke and before she knew the name Eleanor Morris.

Out the window the sun is beginning to set, casting a golden wash over the warm yellow stone of the buildings. She watches people moving about in the street, some in groups talking to one another and others on their own. When she was younger, she used to watch people and wonder if they ever felt as disorientated and overwhelmed as she often did. Then she got older and worked hard to build a life that suited her, a life where she knew what was going to happen next and didn't feel different or out of place. But now, thousands of miles away from home and totally out of her comfort zone, those thoughts come rushing back in.

'I don't know. I don't know,' she says, her head spinning.

'Mom, you just need to take a moment to calm down and things will seem better.'

'Is there something you can do that will make you feel more settled?' John suggests. 'Something that might make you feel like you're at home?'

Donna looks quickly around the room. She could read her book, but she feels too distracted. The minibar isn't an option either – she has never been a drinker. Why would she ever *choose* to lose control? Then an idea comes into her head.

'I've got to go,' she says into the phone. 'I love you both.'

She hangs up before they have time to finish saying good-bye, then walks out of her room with purpose and down to the pub's restaurant. A young waitress with pink hair leads her to a table in the corner. It's a nice table, Donna has to admit. It's tucked away from the noise of the bar and sits alongside a wall of bookshelves, the glow of the fireplace behind warming her back.

'Can I ask, is this where you hold breakfast for your guests?'

The girl looks a little confused but nods.

'So that means you have breakfast foods in your kitchen?'

'Er, yes.'

Donna leans back in her chair with a smile. 'Then I'll have half a grapefruit, a bowl of Cheerios and a black coffee.'

'Um, but it's dinner time?'

'Do you have those things in the kitchen?'

'Er, probably yes.'

'So that's what I'd like. Please.'

She pushes the menu that had been placed on the table to the corner. The waitress glances towards the kitchen, frowning. But then she nods her head, a small smile on her face.

'All right, I'll ask the chef. Breakfast is my favourite too, actually.'

As the pub fills with conversation and the smell of chips, warming pies and homemade gravy, Donna sits in the corner eating Cheerios and grapefruit, sipping her black coffee while she reads a book pulled from the shelves.

When she returns to her room, carrying a pile of books borrowed with permission from the pub landlord, she sends a message to both John and Brooke.

'I think I might stay here for a bit longer after all.'

The next morning Donna wakes late and groggy after a restless night. After breakfast and a slow start, she heads out into the morning air, the streets already busy with shoppers. Before she can stop herself, her feet have taken her up the hill until she is standing outside the vintage shop, unable to bring herself to step back inside. As she lingers outside, the shop door opens and its owner comes rushing out.

'It's you again!' the woman says, but unlike when Donna left yesterday, the woman's face is softer now. She glances briefly into the shop, then turns back to Donna. Today she is wearing another outfit that makes Donna's head hurt with its mix of colours and prints. She blinks rapidly. 'I'm sorry about yesterday,' the woman continues. 'It was a busy day in the shop and you totally took me by surprise. What did you say your name was?'

'I didn't. It's Donna.'

'Donna. Nice to meet you, my name's Lou.'

'I know,' replies Donna.

Lou frowns momentarily. She turns back to the shop, where Donna can see a few customers browsing, and then returns her attention to Donna.

'I'm working now, but perhaps we can meet later and properly talk? Here's my address. Well, it's where I'm staying at the moment.'

Donna takes the piece of paper with the handwritten address with a nod.

'So, you'll come over?' Lou asks eagerly.

'If I have time,' Donna replies. She tucks the paper with the address into her handbag alongside the photos that are stored safely in the inside pocket, trying hard to stop her hands from shaking.

She isn't sure what she was expecting New York City to be like, but it surprises her in every way. To start with, she'd pictured herself in Manhattan, perhaps a few paces away from the Empire State Building, not in a tiny tenement apartment in Brooklyn where the sounds of families cramped into the flats above and below can be heard at all times of day and night, smells of foods she cannot recognise creeping in through the floorboards.

Then there's the heat, unlike anything she ever experienced in London. Even with the windows in the apartment left wide open, the air is still and heavy, feeling as thick as hot soup. The pavements steam and the entrance to their building becomes crowded during the day and often into the evening, mothers sitting on the steps fanning themselves as their children play in the street below.

The noises are different here too. She might have grown up in a city, but everything here feels amplified. Trucks trundling down the streets, the brush and sweep of garbage collectors out with their pails and brooms, the thud and bounce of basketballs in the courts at the back of their building, where children and teenagers congregate after school and on weekends. Door-to-door salesmen visiting the street on Saturdays with their carts, shouting up at the apartments their offers for fish, fruit and veg, kitchen pans or freshly baked pies and women shouting back at them until a price is agreed and the women descend to complete the transaction. Families conversing in more languages than she has ever heard before and the piercing twang of a mother shouting at her children from a window to, 'Hurry up and get back home, macaroni's on!'

'This flat is just temporary,' Sydney assures her most days, planting a kiss on her forehead. 'Just until I get myself set up with a job and till we find you work as a model. We just have to be patient, it's all ahead of us.'

Despite the feeling of having arrived in a totally different world, Sydney's sense of optimism is contagious and she tries to make the best of things, cleaning the apartment until it shines and hanging the few clothes they could fit in their suitcases into the rickety wardrobe. And they might be on what she can't help but think of as the 'wrong' side of the city, but she has to agree with Sydney that the view across the river is pretty spectacular when they take an early evening walk down to Prospect Park and stand arm-in-arm gazing across at the jagged skyline.

He buys her a gold ring from a local pawn shop which she wears on her left hand.

'It's simpler that way, don't you think?' he tells her and she nods, trying just to enjoy the glint of it winking there on her finger.

She tries to tell herself that this is a new start. That the small, hot apartment is just temporary and that she will find her place in the city and in this new life. She just needs to give it time. This is what she wanted, a life full of adventure and with the man she loves and can now sleep beside every night.

But sometimes she stirs in the very early hours, the only time when the city seems almost quiet, and she looks around the semi-darkness expecting to see her old room back in London. And in the fog between sleep and wakefulness she feels the unshakeable sense of having forgotten something, something important that she never should have left behind.

MAGGY

'So, tell me again who this woman is?' Maggy asks as she prepares for their visitor that evening, arranging mugs and biscuits, as well as a wine bottle and glasses on the coffee table too, just in case.

'That's the thing,' Lou replies, pacing in the kitchen, 'I don't know. She just came into the shop with a photo of my mum – the one I have up in the shop of her wearing her yellow dress.'

'I know the one,' Maggy says. It's blurry, but it's a nice photo – the woman in it looks so happy and carefree.

She listens intently as Lou tells the rest of the story.

'Hmm. It all sounds very mysterious.'

'You don't mind that I invited her over, do you?'

'Not at all, I'm glad to help. And offer refreshments,' she adds, gesturing to the table with a smile.

'Oh, but you're doing so much more than that, Maggy,' Lou replies hastily. 'I'm actually really nervous about seeing her and hearing what she has to say. I partly invited her here to have you around for moral support.'

'Well, that I can do.'

Maggy watches as Lou fiddles with her necklace distractedly.

'Maybe she's an old friend of Mum's. But that doesn't explain the fact she thought Mum's name was Eleanor Morris.'

Something flashes suddenly into Maggy's mind.

'Eleanor Morris? That's funny ...' She trails off, frowning.

'What is it?' asks Lou.

'Don't you remember?' Maggy continues. 'E. M. The initials we found stitched into your mother's yellow dress.'

Lou's face lights up and then darkens again, a frown appearing between her eyebrows.

'I can't believe I hadn't even thought of that. There's been so much else going on that I haven't thought much about the dress. But you're right. I wonder what it means ...'

The doorbell rings and both Maggy and Lou turn in the direction of the sound. 'Shall we?' asks Maggy, and Lou pauses, then nods.

At the door, Maggy steps back to let Lou answer, smiling encouragingly at her as she does.

The woman standing outside is a little younger than Maggy, she guesses, and dressed in a blue sweatshirt that matches the blue of her jeans exactly. Her dark grey hair is short and neat and she has an uncertain expression on her face, her handbag held tightly under one arm, the other tensed at her side. Lou greets her and introduces Maggy, then opens the door wider for Donna to step inside. She does so hesitantly, looking around her.

'I like your house,' Donna says. 'It's exactly how I pictured an English house.'

'Thank you,' Maggy says, trying to get a smile back from Donna, but not succeeding. 'I've lived here for years. It could do with a bit of a tidy.'

'Yes,' nods Donna, taking Maggy by surprise.

'Yes, well. It's nice to meet you, but I can leave you two to it now ...'

'Oh, do stay,' Lou says rapidly, her eyes pleading.

Maggy must admit she is interested by Donna's story; her appearance in Somerset, and now in her home, is certainly a change from her normal routines and day-to-day life. She doesn't want to interfere but is also just as intrigued as Lou to find out this stranger's story.

'OK then! Why don't we go and sit down in the living room and we can get to know one another?'

Maggy busies herself in the kitchen while Lou and Donna sit down on the sofas on the other side of the open-plan living area. As she fills the kettle, she feels thankful for the reassurance of mundane tasks during difficult or unusual situations. She takes orders and prepares a coffee for Donna and tea for her and Lou. As she carries them over, Donna looks up suddenly.

'I don't think you turned the tap off fully,' she says, her blue eyes meeting Maggy's.

'Excuse me?'

'The tap,' Donna repeats, looking over at the sink with a strained expression on her face. 'It keeps dripping.'

Maggy catches Lou glancing at her as she places down the drinks, then walks back to the sink.

'Oh, you're right, thank you.' She tightens the tap and as she joins the others in the living area, it seems as though Donna has relaxed slightly, her body less tense.

Once they are all settled, an awkward silence descends. Lou is the first to speak.

'So, I have to know, Donna, where did you get that photograph you showed me?'

The American woman takes a deep breath. And then she tells them, talking in an even, precise tone, her eyes on her coffee mug as she explains how she was adopted sixty years ago by the couple she has always believed to be her parents, Shirley and Ken, and that she only recently found out the truth.

'Eleanor Morris was my birth mother,' she says finally. 'They gave me this photograph of her at the adoption agency, it's how I found you. Well, my daughter did actually. She showed me how to do a reverse image search and we found the matching photo, the black-and-white one, on your website. And then I decided to come and meet you. I couldn't have told you all of this over the phone, I don't think I would have been able to get the words out.'

Lou's mouth is open and she shakes her head slowly from side to side. When it's clear that she isn't going to say anything – that she isn't *able* to say anything – Maggy chips in.

'And they didn't have any other information about your mother at the adoption agency?'

'No,' Donna replies, shaking her head. 'All I have are these photos.'

She shows them a picture of a small baby and a black-and-white headshot of a young woman. Lou peers at it closely.

'I just don't understand,' she says finally, her voice choked with emotion. 'Mum never went to America, not as far as I know. And this photo … It *could* be her, but …' She swallows hard then, blinking back tears. 'I just can't imagine Mum giving away a baby, even when she was really young, and never telling me or Dad.'

Maggy glances at Donna, who is sitting very still, her face unreadable. Could this woman be Lou's *sister*? It seems impossible – they seem so different, with their age gap, their different accents and how Donna's plain, straightforward outfit couldn't be further from Lou's colourful and creative sense of style. But as Maggy looks closer, she sees a flicker of something – a similarity around the mouth and jawline, perhaps?

'I know what we should do,' says Lou suddenly, a new sense of energy in her voice that makes both Maggy and Donna sit up a little straighter. 'I've been putting it off for ages, but I think it's time I went and sorted through my mum's things. They've just been sitting in a storage unit since she died. There must be something in there that can help us figure all of this out. If Mum did have a baby when she was very young, before she met Dad, maybe we'll be able to find something about what happened among her things. Donna, do you want to come too? I warn you, it might take us a while – I don't think the removal company packed things in much of an order. It's probably a total mess.'

For the first time since arriving on Maggy's doorstep, a smile spreads across Donna's face.

'I happen to be very good at organising. If there's anything in there that might help us, I'll be able to find it. Shall we go there now?'

She stands up in readiness, but Maggy glances outside – it is dark, the sky flecked with a smattering of stars.

'Oh, I didn't mean now,' Lou says, seeming startled. 'It's been a long day. But perhaps we could meet tomorrow morning before I have to head to the shop? Seeing as you're only here for a short time, it does make sense to start as soon as we can.'

They agree to meet at the storage unit at 7.30 and then Lou and Maggy wave Donna off. Once the door has closed behind her, Maggy lingers at the window. The evening has been a whirlwind and she can't quite make sense of everything that has happened. She worries about Lou and what might be going through her mind, but among it all she can't deny a sense of excitement too. There's a new energy in the house that arrived with Lou and her boxes and has grown ever since. After all the years of family life and then the past year's unexpected loneliness, Maggy's home has become the setting for a new story.

LOU

In the attic bedroom, Lou sits on the edge of her bed and unfolds a letter she has read countless times. The fold line is soft from being opened and refolded so often and the handwriting on the page is as familiar to her as her own. She scans the text again, trying to find some clue that might explain Donna's sudden appearance in her life. But there is nothing new, only the words that she knows so well she could probably recite them from memory.

She refolds the letter and tucks it into the back of the book she is reading, alongside a photograph of her parents that she takes out now, looking closely at her mother's face. Like the letter, she has looked at this photo many times too, but this time as she studies it, she searches for traces of the American woman who turned up in her shop unannounced and who has just left Maggy's house, leaving Lou's thoughts in disarray. Running a finger over the image of her mother, her eyes locked with Lou's father's and a smile taking up her entire face, she thinks she sees a hint of something that was there in Donna's face and she feels as though the room is suddenly spinning.

Maybe it would be easier for Lou to send Donna away and to go back to living her life, as it was before she knew the name Eleanor Morris. But there are a few things she can't ignore, like the photo Donna has that's a twin of the one in Lou's shop, the letters 'E. M.' stitched into her mother's favourite dress and the eyes that gaze back at her now from the photograph in her hand that look so similar to Donna's.

'Oh Mum,' Lou whispers. 'What secrets were you hiding? You know you could have told me anything. I wouldn't have judged you.'

On the floor below her, Lou can hear Maggy pottering about, preparing for bed. Then comes the sound of creaking floorboards and footsteps on the stairs and a gentle knock on her door.

'Come in, Maggy,' Lou says, wiping her face with her sleeve.

Maggy pops her head round the door and then pushes it slightly wider, pausing in the doorway.

'I just wanted to come and check that you're doing OK.'

She is wearing an elegant pair of navy pyjamas, a grey jumper thrown over the top, an expression of concern on her face.

Lou sighs, pushing herself back further onto the bed and lifting her knees up, wrapping her arms around them.

'I don't know what to think. It's a lot to get my head around. And I just hate the thought that Mum might have kept something so huge from me.'

Maggy nods. 'It's hard to think that there are parts we might not know about the people we love. But people keep secrets for a lot of reasons. Sometimes because it's too painful to speak the truth.'

Could that explain things? If her mum really *was* Donna's birth mother, then she must have been so young when she had her. Maybe her parents forced her to give the baby up; that would explain why she never spoke about her family. Lou's mind races with questions.

'I just wish she was here so I could ask her about it all.'

'I know,' replies Maggy.

Lou sniffs, rubbing her eyes again.

'Look, it's late and there's nothing you can do now,' Maggy says. 'Tomorrow maybe you'll find some answers. It's probably best to just go to bed, you must be tired – it's been a shock.'

'I don't think I'll be able to sleep.'

'Why don't you have a bath? A hot bath helps most things. I saw you admiring the tub when you first came to visit, but you haven't used it yet, have you?'

Lou shakes her head. She has been using her en-suite shower room instead, but suddenly the thought of a bath seems like exactly what she needs.

'That's a good idea, thank you, Maggy.'

Lou follows her down to the large bathroom on the floor below. Maggy gets out a box of bath products and hangs a clean towel on the radiator.

'Right, I'm off to bed. You take it easy. We'll tackle everything together in the morning, OK?'

'Thank you, Maggy,' Lou says. 'For everything.'

*

A few minutes later, alone in the bathroom, Lou swirls the steaming water and slowly undresses, her toes sinking into the soft bath rug that lies over the floorboards. Then she climbs into the tub. As she sinks into the hot water, the smell of bluebells rising from soft piles of bubbles on the surface, it hits her that until she moved in with Maggy it had been a long time since anyone looked after her and not the other way around. As she thinks it, she feels a stab of guilt – she knows how much her mum hated becoming so reliant on her towards the end. But then Lou closes her eyes and lets herself sink lower into the bubbles. The thoughts of her mother and Donna and even the name Eleanor Morris grow blurry as the hot water soothes her body and sends pleasant tingles up her spine. She lets herself breathe slowly. Just for a moment, everything else fades away.

DONNA

'I told you it was a mess,' says Lou as she, Donna and Maggy peer inside the storage unit at the piles and piles of boxes. They are stacked from the floor to the ceiling, the boxes right at the top somewhat precariously balanced. None of them have labels.

Donna begins to sweat as she takes it all in. She was at the storage unit by 7 a.m., ready and waiting for Lou to arrive. She had been too early for breakfast in the pub, but the young waitress, who has become her ally, left her grapefruit, Cheerios and coffee outside her bedroom door.

'I hope you don't mind me joining,' says Maggy, 'but I thought an extra pair of hands might be helpful. And I've brought coffee!' She gestures at a green Thermos under her arm and three tin mugs in pleasingly matching tones of green. Donna decides she likes Maggy.

While Maggy distributes the coffee, Donna and Lou decide what to do next.

'I don't really know where to start,' says Lou despondently, chewing on her bottom lip. She is dressed for the occasion in a pink boiler suit with a striped Breton top underneath, her hair tied back in a matching striped scarf, and a pair of heeled boots on her feet that Donna thinks are somewhat inappropriate for a morning of hefting boxes around. She holds herself back from saying anything.

She still can't work out what she makes of Lou, or how their stories are connected. She insists her mother was called Dorothy, not Eleanor, but last night, as Donna stayed up late running through everything, it hit her that her birth mother could have changed her name, maybe after she had given Donna up for adoption, as a way of starting a new life? Then there's the age difference – Lou is much younger than Donna and while their mothers *could* be the same, it had been a surprise to see Lou in person that first time and to realise she looked even younger than the photograph on her website. Donna feels overwhelmed and disorientated, two feelings that she has spent many years trying very hard to avoid.

'We should begin at the top and work our way down,' she says, trying to focus on the practicalities of their search. 'It would help to have some space to lay everything out so we can unpack each box and check for clues before repacking.'

She looks around her. They are already somewhat cramped, standing in the corridor facing the storage unit, two rows of identical metal doors stretching away from them on either side.

'I'll be back in a moment,' she says, before turning and walking off with purpose.

A few minutes later, she returns with a small folded ladder under one arm and a pair of keys in her other hand.

'The manager has let us borrow this,' she explains, gesturing to the ladder, 'and he says the unit opposite this one is currently empty, so we can use it for a few hours.'

'That's brilliant, Donna, thank you,' says Lou.

Donna shrugs. 'I run an inn, I'm used to solving problems.'

'Why don't I climb up and pass the boxes down,' suggests Lou, 'and you two can set them up in the empty unit. Then we can go through them together.'

'Good idea, Lou,' says Maggy, Donna nodding in response.

Donna has to hand it to Lou – she is surprisingly nimble on the ladder in her heels. The heavier boxes don't seem to faze her either; there are many that she passes down that Donna and Maggy then have to manoeuvre into the other room together.

'Ahh, to be young again,' says Maggy with a wink.

'I would hate to be young again,' says Donna as they place the box down and catch their breath for a moment. 'You care far too much about what other people think about you when you're young. When you get older, people stop noticing you as much, which means you can do whatever the heck you like.'

'I hadn't thought of it like that,' Maggy replies. 'Maybe you're right.' She gazes away, her expression thoughtful.

Once there is a small pile of boxes laid out in the empty unit but still enough space to work, they all gather in there.

'Look what I found in a bag in the corner,' says Lou, lifting up three cushions.

'Thank goodness. I don't think my knees – or my bottom

– could have managed sitting on a concrete floor,' says Maggy.

'Me neither,' agrees Donna.

The three women settle themselves around the boxes.

Lou reaches for the first box, pulling it in front of her and resting her hand on the top. She pauses like that for a while.

'Are you OK?' Maggy asks, reaching out to gently rub Lou's arm.

Lou sniffs and nods. 'Yeah, I'm OK. It's just I haven't looked at any of this stuff since Mum died.'

'We're here with you,' Maggy says gently, 'you're not alone.'

Looking at the two women in front of her, Donna can't quite believe she is here. When she messaged John and Brooke last night to update them, they were so supportive.

'I'm proud of you, Mom,' Brooke wrote. 'I know you were nervous about this trip, but I really hope you're going to find the answers you're after.'

Donna barely slept again last night, lying awake thinking about Lou and how they might be related. She seems so different from Donna – she must be twenty years younger and has a look that couldn't be further from Donna's plain, simple and comfortable clothes. But there is something about her that feels almost familiar; every now and then when she smiles, Donna gets hints of her own daughter.

'Right, I suppose we better make a start then,' says Lou, peeling the tape off the top of the first box. Donna leans forward eagerly. Maybe the answers to her questions about who she is and where she comes from can be found among these things. And then perhaps she will know how to move on with her life.

*

Together, the three of them work their way through the boxes. Lou takes out item after item, sometimes stopping to look more closely or tell a particular story about her mother, other times handing things over to Maggy to sort into a pile for the charity shop or to Donna to bag up for the recycling centre.

Lou pauses briefly as she holds up a silk scarf patterned in roses, lifting the fabric to her face and breathing deeply.

'It still smells like her,' she says quietly, her eyes glistening.

'It sounds like you were close,' Donna says.

Lou nods, a faint smile on her face. As she speaks, she winds the silk scarf around her neck, tying it at an angle. 'We were very close. I feel so thankful for that. Are you close to your mum, Donna?' An uncomfortable expression appears on Lou's face. 'Your adoptive mother, that is,' she adds.

Donna lets out a sigh. Shirley contacted her again this morning, wanting to talk. But she doesn't feel ready yet.

'We were, yes. We always have been, actually. But we haven't spoken since she told me about Eleanor.'

'I can understand that,' says Maggy, her voice softer than earlier. 'If I'd found out something like that at this stage in my life … It must be hard to have everything you thought you knew about who you are thrown up in the air.'

'Yes, exactly,' replies Donna. 'And I just can't get over the fact that she kept something so huge from me. Perhaps when I was a kid it made sense not to tell me. But I'm very much a grown woman. I'm a grandmother, for crying out loud. I had a right to know the truth.'

It's Lou's turn to sigh then.

'But we don't seem to be any closer to finding answers. Look

154

at all this stuff...' Donna follows Lou's gaze around the storage unit – clothes, books and trinkets strewn everywhere. 'And so far, there's nothing at all that mentions an Eleanor. What if we don't find anything?'

The panic in Lou's voice is catching and Donna feels her own heart rate rise. Lou's right. They've been through a dozen or so boxes already, Donna checking everything meticulously in case the others have missed anything, and while she feels she knows the woman Lou calls Dotty better now – colourful like Lou, a keen seamstress, a fondness for detective novels – there has been nothing that connects her to the name Eleanor Morris.

Seeming to sense the anxiety rising in the room, Maggy steps in. 'It looks like we've got another hour until you need to get to the shop, Lou. Why don't we keep going for now and then we can always come back another time to tackle the rest?'

Donna glances at Lou, who returns her uneasy expression. For the first time since arriving, Donna feels a sense of solidarity with the younger woman. They might not know how or why they are connected, but a photo of a yellow dress has brought them together. Donna can read the sadness on Lou's face and understands at least a part of it: Lou is realising that her mother kept secrets from her, just like Donna's did.

'How about some more coffee to perk us up?' Maggy offers.

'OK, let's keep going then,' Donna says.

Maggy refills their tin mugs and they take a moment to sit and drink before diving in to the next box.

'Ahh, Mum and Dad's wedding photos!' Lou exclaims in a happier voice, pulling out an ivory photo album embossed with gold. She flicks through, showing Donna and Maggy the black-and-white photos of a young woman in a knee-length satin dress with three-quarter-length sleeves and a bow at the waist and a man in a grey suit with a carnation buttonhole. Both of them are smiling broadly.

'These are wonderful,' says Maggy, leaning closer to get a better look.

'I always thought I might wear Mum's wedding dress one day,' Lou says, brushing her hand over one of the pages.

'You still might,' replies Maggy.

'She made the dress herself,' adds Lou. 'You can't see from the photo, but it was cornflower blue. And her shoes were yellow.'

'I can see now where all this comes from,' Donna says, making a gesture that takes in Lou and her outfit.

Despite the tears gathering in Lou's eyes, she smiles. 'You're right, Donna,' she says, brushing her eyes, 'I definitely got my love of clothes from Mum.'

'I wonder what I got from Eleanor.'

They grow quiet again. The shadow of a young woman in a yellow dress flickers through the room.

Lou places the album carefully in the pile labelled 'Lou's flat' and then reaches further inside the cardboard box, pulling out three old biscuit tins. The smallest one rattles when Lou shakes it and is filled to the brim with buttons in an assortment of colours. The second contains photos of Lou as a child, which they all look at, laughing at some of the particularly funny expressions and outfits. The lid on the third tin is tightly wedged shut and takes a good amount of jostling to pry open. When it finally does come loose, the force of Lou's pulling means she loses grip of the tin and drops it, the metal hitting the concrete floor with a loud clatter and a bundle of papers scattering everywhere. All three of them bend to pick them up. As Donna reaches down, she realises that they are in fact envelopes.

'Oh my God,' says Lou suddenly.

'Look!' adds Maggy.

Donna brings her own envelope closer. There is no stamp and no address, simply one word handwritten in spiky letters. *Eleanor.* As Donna looks at Lou and Maggy, she sees that they are both holding envelopes bearing the same name in the same handwriting. Her heart races as she runs her hand through the pool of envelopes on the floor. As she does, the name flashes again and again before her eyes. *Eleanor, Eleanor, Eleanor.*

'That's Mum's handwriting,' Lou says. As she says it, Donna's eyes fall on something else among the pile – an official-looking document. She picks it up and realises it's a birth certificate.

'I think you should look at this,' she says, handing it to Lou, whose mouth opens in surprise.

'Mum's birth certificate. I've never seen it before. Her name is listed as Dorothy Morris.'

Unable to stop herself, Donna slices her finger along the top of the envelope she is holding and pulls out a letter. With her heart pounding in her ears, she begins to read.

Dear Eleanor ...

'Stop,' Lou interrupts, jolting Donna and making her look up. 'Can you read it out loud? We should hear this together.'

Donna nods. Lou is right. This isn't just her birth mother's story, it is Lou's too.

'The letter is dated 24th December 1955,' she says. 'The year before I was born.'

'Mum would have been twelve.' Lou lifts a hand up to her mother's silk scarf around her neck, rubbing a corner of the smooth fabric between her thumb and forefinger, her eyes glistening.

'Shall I carry on?' Donna asks, her clear voice reverberating around the metal-walled storage unit where a lifetime's collection of things lies strewn across the cold grey floor. Lou nods. Donna clears her voice and then begins.

Dear Eleanor ...

In a small house in Islington, a girl stands by the window of her bedroom, watching the postman on his morning round. As he draws closer to the house, her heart skips and dances. Maybe this will be the day. Maybe the letter she has been waiting for will finally arrive.

The postman glances down at the pile of letters and parcels in his hands and then up again. He takes a step closer, then another. And then he continues on to the house next door and the girl's stomach sinks.

She drops down onto the bed below the window, the bed that used to be occupied but is now empty. She still regrets not having come down into the street to see her off properly. But she was crying too hard and didn't want the neighbours to see, especially not Jackie and Christine from next door, who had stopped talking to her ever since The Incident in the street. In some twisted way, it had been a relief when she arrived home from school that day to hear the argument erupting in the street. It meant she didn't have to carry her secret any more. Because the truth was, she knew, ever since she stirred one night to find the bed beside her empty and to hear voices she thought she recognised in the street below. She had tiptoed to the window and seen the two figures on the street corner. What she saw didn't make sense to her, but she still knew that it was something she couldn't tell anyone.

Now, she pushes herself off the edge of the bed and steps over to the wardrobe. It still feels strange to see it so empty, her own clothes only taking up less than half the space. Tucked at the back is the dress she is looking for. Carefully, the girl slips it from the hanger and holds it up to the light, the yellow fabric shining and the embroidered flowers seeming even more realistic close up. She runs a finger over the threads. As she holds it, the words come flashing back into her mind. 'You keep it safe for me until I see you next.' Then a tight hug and a goodbye that ended too quickly. She watched from her bedroom window as the taxi drove down the road and then round the corner and out of sight, taking her favourite person in the world with it.

Resting the dress gently on the spare bed, the girl steps out into the hall and calls down the stairs to her mother.

'Has there been any post?' she asks. She has to make sure.

Her mother's voice rises up the stairs, cold and bitter.

'You really think she's going to write to us? She's gone. She forgot about us the second she stepped inside that taxi.'

The girl doesn't believe it though. She can't let herself believe it. She would never forget about her. The letter will arrive soon and when it does, the girl will find some way of leaving too, whatever it takes. Then they will be together again, the way it's meant to be.

LOU

As Donna reads the letter, Lou closes her eyes, trying to hear her mother's voice in her head. Her heart thuds inside her chest as she listens, and everything Lou thought she knew about her mother rearranges itself in her mind.

Dear Eleanor,

Tomorrow is Christmas Day. But it doesn't feel like Christmas without you. There's only one thing I want for Christmas this year and it's for you to come back. Or to be able to come and join you there. I know you said I was too young to come with you, but I think I'd manage. I'd like to see the Empire State Building.

Do you remember when we used to go to Trafalgar Square to visit the Christmas tree together? And how you used to sing when we got there as though no one else was around? I wish we could go together now.

What is Christmas like in New York? Is there snow? We haven't had snow here yet, but it is very cold. Ma is calling now so I should stop writing. She doesn't know about these letters. I think she misses you too but doesn't know how to show it, so she is just angry instead. The house feels too quiet without you here. I hope you have a Happy Christmas, Eleanor. I miss you.

Love, your sister Dotty.

Tears sting Lou's eyes, the figures of Donna and Maggy and the object-strewn storage unit swimming before her.

'Mum had a sister,' she says, her throat tight. She tries to picture her mother as a child and now she adds a second figure beside her. Eleanor. She struggles to hold the image in her mind. With one hand she rubs her face, her head suddenly aching. 'Why did she never mention she had a sister?'

She and her mum used to talk about everything. Maybe it was partly because Lou was an only child, but they had always been particularly close, Lou often thinking of her as a friend just as much as a mum. Lou could never keep a secret from her, even things she knew her mum wouldn't approve of, like when she accepted a promotion at the recruitment firm even though she knew her mum wanted her to leave and follow her dream of opening the shop instead. She always thought her mother was honest with her. And in her mum's final year while they lived in the same house and Lou cared for her, they had plenty of heart-to-hearts, trying to fit in all the conversations that they would never have a chance for in the future. Why didn't she tell her then? The fact that her mother could keep something so huge from her stings.

'Maybe it was because of me,' replies Donna. 'My mother gave me away, didn't she? Maybe my birth caused a family controversy and your mother cut ties with her when she found out.'

Lou shakes her head, wiping the tears from her eyes. 'I just can't imagine Mum doing something like that. She was always so kind to everyone …'

Her voice catches then and Maggy reaches out and rubs her arm.

'It's OK.'

Sniffing, Lou looks again at the envelope in her hand, the name on the front written in her mother's handwriting and addressed to a woman Lou never knew existed. 'And besides,' she adds, 'from this letter, it sounds like Eleanor must have moved to America and they lost touch somehow. Maybe she never knew about you? But why wouldn't her sister tell her?'

Another silence descends.

'You know what this means, don't you?' Maggy says, her voice suddenly bright as she looks from Lou to Donna and back again. 'You two are cousins!'

Lou glances at Donna. When she was growing up, she sometimes pictured what it would be like to have a brother or sister or a big family with aunts and uncles and cousins her age. In her imaginings, she never once conjured a fastidiously neat American woman twice her age. Donna meets her eye, a somewhat wary smile on her face. And as she looks at Lou, she finally sees it: Donna has her mother's eyes.

Lou takes a deep breath. However much finding out such a huge secret might hurt, her mum must have had her reasons for keeping her past life secret. Whatever those reasons were, Lou feels certain that if she were here right now she would want Donna to feel welcome. Despite what Lou has learned, she still believes that's just the person her mother was. So Lou steps forward and reaches for Donna, pulling her into a hug.

'Oh Donna, I'm sorry I wasn't more welcoming when you showed up at the shop. I didn't know what to think. I *still* don't know what to think. But you're family. I can't believe it. At the start of the week, I didn't have a family.'

Clearly startled, Donna pauses stiffly before softening slightly and hugging Lou back.

'There's no need to get so emotional,' Donna says brusquely. But she squeezes Lou a little tighter. 'You should read your letter too,' Donna says, nodding to the envelope in Lou's hand that she has been too dazed to actually open.

'It's from much later,' she says as she slides out the folded paper. 'It's dated 13th July 1965.'

She scans the lines of ink.

'Well, go on then,' says Donna impatiently.

'Sorry. Here goes.' As Lou reads, her mother's voice sounds in her ear. It feels as though she is there with them in the room, the air scented with her familiar perfume.

Dear Eleanor, it's been a while since I last wrote. I promise
I haven't forgotten about you, but I've been rather busy. I
am settling in well to my new home and my role as au pair
to little William and Amy. William is six and loves animals,

*sticks and learning the names of new countries. Amy is four
and a sweet little thing with the funniest laugh. I wish that
you could meet them. Their mother, Marion, has found out
that I can sew (she admits herself that she is useless at things
like that) and has started paying me extra to fix some of
the children's things and has even asked me to make a dress
for her – we are going next week to pick the fabric. But the
most important thing that I have to tell you is that I've met
a man.*

Lou pauses here, breathing in quickly.

'*His name is Jeremy and he works here too.* That's my dad!'
she adds breathlessly. 'The family were quite wealthy, I think,
but the house was old and needed a lot of upkeep. He did odd
jobs for them – bits of gardening, repairs, that sort of thing. I
remember Mum telling me how she saw him for the first time
out the nursery window when she was with the children she
looked after, back before she became a seamstress. She told
me they had a beautiful rose garden. Mum says she looked down
and spotted him there, surrounded by roses. She said he saw
her looking and smiled. Later, he found her and gave her a
rose he'd secretly cut from the garden for her.'

'How romantic,' says Maggy.

'What else does the letter say, though?' urges Donna.

'Yes, sorry, I'll carry on.

*He is just lovely and always manages to make me laugh.
He's so sweet with the children too – it's wonderful to see.
This weekend, we're going on our first date. It's my day off*

and he's taking me to a pub in the village. I am going to wear your yellow dress. It fits me now, although I am sure it doesn't suit me as well as it suited you. It makes me feel as though you are with me, though. If I wear it, you will be giving me courage and you will be meeting him too, this man that I can already feel myself falling for. I will write again after our date and tell you how it went.

As I write this, I realise how ridiculous this all seems, given this letter will just go in the tin with all the others. But I suppose there is part of me that still hopes I might see you again one day. And when I do, I can give you all these letters and you will know that I thought of you, and that you were there with me for all the most important moments in my life. I hope you are well and happy.

Yours, Dotty.

Lou barely manages to finish the final words. She looks down at the dozens and dozens of envelopes lying at her feet, trying to picture her mother at various ages writing them to a sister that for whatever reason she had lost. Is there a letter in the pile that she wrote when she found out she was pregnant with Lou? Or after she was born? In each image her mind conjures, she sees the yellow dress there with her mother.

'So, the yellow dress was Eleanor's, originally, not Mum's,' she says, the realisation dawning on her.

'That explains the initials we found in the label, then,' adds Maggy.

'And it seems like Eleanor never came back from America,'

166

Donna says. 'They never saw each other again. I wonder what happened.'

Lou's eyes sting again as she thinks about her mother writing letters to a sister who would never read them.

'I wish Mum had told me about these,' she says, picking up a handful of envelopes from the floor. All that paper, all those words written in ink, and all shut away inside a biscuit tin with a stiff lid. 'I don't think Dad even knew. How lonely she must have been, keeping that to herself.'

'I wonder if we can find out more about Eleanor if we go through them all,' says Donna, reaching for a few more of the envelopes herself and stacking them neatly. 'We already know that she went to New York, but maybe there's more in here that can help me find where she might be now. If she's still alive, that is.'

Lou brightens. It might have shaken her to learn that her mother kept such a huge secret from her, but these letters have given her an opportunity too – a chance to hear her mother's voice again and to learn more about her, both things that she thought had gone forever when she died.

'That's a good idea.' She may never be able to talk to her mother again, but maybe these letters will at least let her hear more of her story. She glances at her watch, then wipes hurriedly at her eyes. 'Oh no, I really need to get to work.' She pauses, for the first time since opening her shop, wishing that she didn't have to go in today. 'Can I see you later, though, Donna? Maybe we can sort through the rest of the letters and decide what to do next?'

Donna nods and Maggy chips in.

'We can tidy up here, can't we, Donna? And I have been meaning to ask, where are you staying?'

Donna names a pub in town.

'I'm here for a few more days. It was such a long journey, it seemed sensible to stay awhile.'

'Why don't you come and stay with us for the rest of your trip?' offers Maggy. 'There's plenty of room for another guest and that way you and Lou will have time to get to know one another properly before you have to leave?'

Donna tilts her head slightly. 'Well, the pub is terribly noisy. It does have a comfortable bed though.'

'I promise I have one of those, too.'

'And are you sure you don't mind, Lou?' she asks.

Lou shakes her head. 'It's a good idea. We can go through the rest of these together.'

There's so much that Lou suddenly wants to find out about Donna. *She's family*, she says to herself, still not quite used to the idea but filled nonetheless with a sense of excitement. Donna may not have known her own birth mother, or Dotty, but she is still a link to Lou, and to Lou's family, that she had been missing.

'Well, all right then. Thank you.'

Lou gathers her bag and jacket and takes one last look around the storage unit, taking in the piles of her mother's things. This task seemed so daunting for so long, but now that the boxes have been opened, it strikes her that the things are just things after all. Some are precious and will find a home in her flat when she moves in, like her mum's nicest clothes, the photos and a few of her favourite books. She's put aside some things to use for the shop's upcoming relaunch too – some fabric she intends to make into bunting and an old tea set that she thinks will be the perfect, quirky thing to use to serve Prosecco to her customers. But there's so much too that didn't hold the significance she had expected and feared: papers and crockery and the less well-loved things from her mum's wardrobe that will now be given away or sent off to be recycled. Lou had worried that every single item of her mother's would spark some memory, but what she hadn't been prepared for was how opening these boxes would show her how much she *didn't* know about her mother.

As she glances at Donna, who is neatly stacking up all the envelopes and placing them back in the tin, Lou wonders how much more they both might discover in those words about the women who gave birth to them.

DONNA

'Wow, I don't think my kitchen has ever smelt so delicious.'

Donna tries to ignore the note of surprise in Maggy's voice. She did tell her that she was a good cook, after all, when she offered to make dinner for them all this evening as a thank you to Maggy for letting her stay. She had been unsure whether to accept the offer of accommodation – she doesn't usually like staying at other people's houses – but the thought of getting to spend time with her new relative and the possibility of them discovering more about Eleanor together had been too good to turn down. When she messaged John to update him, he had agreed. 'Wow, your trip hasn't been for nothing then,' he wrote. 'You've met your cousin!'

It still feels strange to think of Lou that way. As she glances at her now, looking more casual than usual in her socked feet and with her hair loose on her shoulders, the pins taken out when she arrived home from work, Donna feels a surprising rush of warmth. Since the visit to the storage unit and the discovery of the letters, Lou has let her guard down. Finding out that her mother had a sister had clearly been a shock, but now she seems calmer and is clearly making an effort to get to know Donna, asking her questions about Cold Spring and her family.

Donna wipes a hand on the front of the borrowed apron that is tied around her waist and then gives the frying pan a gentle shake, the oil sizzling and the smell of butter and lemon wafting into the air. She carefully checks the scallops, noting with satisfaction the perfect golden-brown colour on both sides and turning down the heat.

'Plates, please!'

Lou, who has been acting as Donna's sous-chef since returning home from work, quickly fetches three plates from the dresser and lines them up next to Donna, who turns off the hob and lifts the pan, carefully scooping a serving of scallops onto each plate and drizzling over a spoonful of the lemon, butter and caper sauce, sprinkling a garnish of freshly chopped chives over the top. Lou carries the plates to the table, where a loaf of crusty bread and a bowl of salad tossed in a lemon, orange and mustard dressing awaits them. Maggy lights the candles, Lou brings over the wine and Donna unties her apron and joins them, taking satisfaction in the smell of the food and Lou and Maggy's expressions as they admire the meal before them. She was pleased she managed to find scallops, although it had required visiting four of the supermarkets in the town. The task had proven a welcome distraction, though, giving her time to think.

'This looks wonderful,' says Lou appreciatively. 'Such a treat to come back to after a day at work.'

'How were sales today?' asks Maggy, pouring wine for them all.

'Not too bad. And I had someone stop in and ask about selling me her vintage collection, so I'm going to go and see it soon. I'll be needing new stock before long and it sounds like she has some great things. How was your day?'

'I showed Donna around the town,' Maggy replies, turning to Donna. 'I just hope I didn't bore you too much!'

Maggy had pointed out certain buildings to Donna, telling her snippets of history – both the town's and her own personal history, like showing Donna where her children went to school and her favourite cafés and shops.

'Not at all,' Donna replies now. 'It was nice to see you love your town as much as I do mine.'

Donna watches as Maggy tilts her head now, her eyebrows knitting together.

'I suppose I do,' she replies. 'It's funny, recently I've been thinking a lot about my life and how it might have been different. I sometimes wonder if I've missed out by not living it bigger and bolder. It's something I'd maybe like to change. But I *do* love it here.'

A pang of homesickness hits Donna in her chest. Suddenly, she is not in Maggy's kitchen but back in Cold Spring. Her mind floods with images of her home. The bandstand looking out over the Hudson where she likes to stop on her morning walks with Luna, the sycamore trees in the garden of the inn, the sunflowers that grow in pots along Main Street in the summer, the nearby marshland where she likes to go birdwatching with John. Among the images, she sees her family – John greeting guests at the inn, Brooke riding her bike along the sidewalk as a child and her parents sitting on their porch swing drinking coffee together and smiling.

'It's your home,' Donna says in reply. She sniffs and then straightens slightly, trying to push away her emotions. 'Oh, I meant to tell you, Lou, I organised Dotty's letters to Eleanor this afternoon. I ordered them by date and thought we could read them together this evening.'

It had been so hard not to race through them all herself. She nearly did, but as she started to read the first line of the first letter in the incredibly neat stack she'd arranged, she stopped herself. Dotty was Lou's mother. These letters might have been addressed to Eleanor, but they belonged to Dotty, and now to Lou. With great restraint, Donna folded up the letter again and put it back with the others.

'Oh wow, that's so kind of you,' replies Lou. 'I can't wait to read them. I've been thinking about them all day, too.'

'I just hope there's something in there that can help us find Eleanor,' replies Donna, rubbing her forehead in an attempt to loosen the pressure that has built behind her eyes. 'In a way, it's worse now I know a tiny bit more about her – I would find it very hard to let it go and carry on with my old life if we don't find anything about where she went and why. Does that make sense?'

Across the table, Maggy nods and takes another sip of wine.

'I can understand that. It's not at all the same, but I'm meeting with an old friend soon, someone who left my life very suddenly and without explanation. I did quite a good job over the years of boxing away my thoughts of him, but now that they're back in my mind again, I don't think I could stand it if he called to cancel our meeting. It would be like coming to the end of a puzzle, only to find there was a piece missing.'

'That's why I always count the pieces before starting one,' Donna replies.

The two women opposite her smile back at her with such warmth that it makes Donna's cheeks turn pink.

'We should eat now,' she says briskly. 'This meal deserves to be eaten warm.'

'It looks delicious, Donna,' says Lou.

Maggy raises her fork in one hand and her glass in the other. 'A toast to new friends. And family.'

As Donna joins the two women in their toast, she tries to remember the last time she made a new friend. If she's honest with herself, she's not sure if she really has any proper friends at all, unless she can count her family and the people she works with at the inn. She's had friendships over the years, but they have always fizzled out eventually. She never means them to, but too often she has found herself in a position of accidentally offending someone and feeling too perplexed or perhaps simply too stubborn to try to fix things. Like the time she laughed her way through her friend's daughter's school play, not realising it wasn't supposed to be a comedy. Or the time another friend got upset about her not attending her anniversary party because it was on the last Sunday of the month and on the last Sunday of the month Donna cleans her office from top to bottom, and besides, she didn't really like her friend's husband anyway.

For the most part, she has been content to surround herself with her family and her work, but as the three of them eat and drink and Maggy and Lou ask her questions about life in Cold Spring, she wonders if perhaps she has missed out. Despite being thousands of miles from home and despite all the questions and uncertainties that still linger in the air, the room is filled with a sense of warmth, as well as conversation and the smell of lemons and hot butter.

Donna takes a sip of her wine and realises she feels relaxed, something she hadn't imagined she could feel when she boarded the plane alone in New York, riddled with anxiety. Maybe after this trip and all its surprises, she might clean her office on a Friday occasionally instead of a Sunday. And go into the city to visit her daughter and granddaughter more often. And perhaps go on a cruise with her husband. Because if she can come to England by herself and find a cousin she never knew she had and make a new friend too, maybe it's possible to live a different kind of life after all.

LOU

Lou wakes the next morning with a sense of optimism. As she props herself up in bed, leaning back on the mound of cushions, she thinks back over last night's delicious meal, followed by the sugar-dusted apple pie baked by Donna with the neatest crust Lou had ever seen, plus the generous glasses of wine poured by Maggy and the general sense of warmth in the room. Donna might be completely different to Lou, but now that she knows they are related there's a definite sense of connection, a feeling of having roots again after months of feeling as though she'd been wrenched from the ground.

Lou had enjoyed hearing Donna talk about her home town, thinking how pretty it sounded. Maggy seemed to come alive in her role as host, the wine doing its bit to make her tell her own stories, making Lou laugh with funny things her grandchildren had said and sharing memories of family life over the years.

When they eventually retreated to the sofas, Donna presented

Lou with the carefully organised stack of envelopes and they read her mother's letters together eagerly, sitting close to one another so they could both read at the same time.

It was sad, of course, that the letters never reached their intended recipient and that her mother never shared her story with Lou. But Lou tried her best to see the positives in the situation. When her mum passed away, she thought it meant never getting to hear her mother's voice again, and yet there she was reading words she wrote at eighteen, twenty-five, fifty. It felt like being gifted a glimpse of versions of her mother that she remembered, as well as others she had never met before.

Through the letters, she learnt what she had for breakfast on her wedding day (a slice of toast with marmalade and half a glass of champagne), the list of potential names her mother considered before settling on Louise and how upset she had been when Lou discovered the truth about Father Christmas. There were sad letters, like the one she wrote after Lou's father died, a letter which made Lou well up, reliving that time all over again. But there were happy ones too, like the letters that described her work as a seamstress and all the exciting projects she worked on with the local theatre, something that Lou always knew brought her so much joy. Among them were many that simply described the everyday details of her life.

'I think Mum lived a happy life, overall,' Lou thought out loud to Donna and Maggy. 'It was obviously a great source of sadness that she lost touch with Eleanor and I wish she'd talked about it with me and Dad. But reading these … it makes me glad too. There were sad moments in her life, of course, but I think she was happy for the most part.'

'Isn't that all we can hope for?' said Maggy.

The only real clue they gleaned about what happened to Eleanor was the mention of a man's name: Sydney. Lou and Donna agreed that, from Dotty's mentions of his name here and there in her letters, Eleanor must have gone to New York with a man, a man whom their mother, and perhaps Dotty herself, didn't approve of.

'That would make sense,' Donna had said, nodding seriously. 'And it explains me.'

'I'm sorry there's not more in here that could help us find her,' Lou had replied, turning to her cousin and giving her a consolatory smile.

'That's OK. At least I feel like I know who my aunt was now. I think I would have liked her.'

Lou had smiled, a bittersweet feeling filling her body. 'I'm sure she would have liked you too.'

Stretching, Lou kicks off the covers and steps out of the bed, smiling to herself as she thinks about the fact that under this same roof are a cousin she never knew she had and a friend she couldn't have imagined making just a few weeks ago.

'Good morning,' she says as she enters the kitchen, where Maggy and Donna are already sitting at the table drinking coffee.

'Good morning,' replies Maggy brightly. 'You look lovely! I don't think I've ever seen you without make-up before.'

Lou suddenly realises that she forgot to put any on. She is still in her pyjamas too, her feet bare and her hair for once loose and unbrushed around her face.

'Oh, I suppose you haven't,' she says, not mentioning that very few people ever have. Even when she was looking after her mum, she forced herself to put make-up on each day. It was part of trying to feel normal when everything was falling apart. When she and Richard first got together, it took her months to let him see her without make-up; it felt more intimate somehow than being naked – her make-up a mask she very rarely let slip. But right now, and with these women, she doesn't feel the need for it. She feels relaxed enough to be herself. 'Is the kettle still hot?'

They share breakfast and their plans for the day. Lou is heading to the shop as usual and Maggy and Donna plan to visit the library to ask advice from the archivist there about how they might find out more about Eleanor.

'Good luck,' says Lou as she drinks the last of her cup of tea and clears up, 'and keep me updated if you find anything.'

Once she is ready, make-up applied and her favourite embroidered waistcoat thrown over a 1970s denim dress, a chunky-knit yellow scarf twisted around her neck, she sets off, humming to herself. Her mind turns to her to-do list, and in particular the things she has to sort for the upcoming independent market and the relaunch of the shop. Everything that's happened over the past couple of days may have distracted her from her plans, but as Lou walks through the park, her boots scuffing through the piles of dry leaves, she runs through the things she has left to do. There are the cakes, which Beth and Danie have offered to supply, and Lou has booked a swing band for a couple of hours for the event. Maggy has promised to help her whip up some strings of bunting one evening using a combination of Lou's collection of vintage fabric and some old curtains Maggy has in the attic. Maybe she will run some more online ads too in a bid to attract more visitors and potential customers. Donna's flight may be in a few days, but perhaps Lou could persuade her to stay for a little longer and join the celebration.

It feels to Lou as though the market really could be a new start for the shop. It's given her something to work towards and a renewed sense of enthusiasm for the business. She's determined that the day will showcase exactly why she loves vintage clothing so much. Above all, she wants it to be a happy occasion, a moment of colour and celebration after what has been the hardest year of her life.

She turns onto the street that leads down towards the shop with a vision in her mind of relaunch day, bunting fluttering in front of an autumn window display she's been coming up with and music spilling out onto the street. Her head is so filled with the image that it takes her a while to notice the police car pulled up at the top of the hill and the small crowd gathered nearby. As she draws closer, she spots a man talking animatedly with a police officer and as he turns she recognises Pete. His face is stricken as he mouths something Lou can't hear to the officer and then points in her direction.

The first shard of broken glass sparkles at her from the pavement, making her think for one bizarre moment of one of her mother's favourite bracelets. But then she spots more and more of it, her shoes crunching through the jagged pieces. She starts to run.

As she reaches the shop, Pete starts talking rapidly to her, his voice strained.

'I just arrived to start work upstairs and saw what had happened. I called the police first and was just about to call you. Maybe I should have done that first. Shit, I should have called you first, shouldn't I? I'm sorry. But I panicked.'

But Lou barely registers what he is saying. She is too busy staring at the gaping hole smashed into her shop door and the shards of glass scattered on the street. The door is ajar, the trail of glass continuing inside. Through the windows, she takes in the sight of her shop.

The table where she keeps her bags and accessories has been swept clear and a few of the rails are in disarray, one nearly empty and another with clothes half-clinging to hangers, others lying piled on the floor. As she takes it all in, her mind fills with memories of the months she spent preparing for the shop's opening. In the thick of her grief, she came here and lost herself for hours in fittings and fixtures and steaming her stock, hanging it all neatly in anticipation of her customers. Now, she barely recognises the place.

'Hello, love,' says the police officer, her voice gentle. 'This gentleman tells us this is your place?'

Lou ignores the officer too, pushing past her and through the small crowd of curious onlookers and stepping into her shop.

A scattering of leaves has blown in through the open door and she treads through them and the splinters of broken glass as she makes her way into the centre of the room. It's then that she spots the missing till from the counter and the empty hanger on the wall behind. The yellow dress is gone.

She sinks down to the ground. After a few moments, she is aware of Pete at her side, resting a warm hand on her shoulder.

'What can I do?' he says gently.

Lou begins to shake.

'Maggy,' she finally manages to say. 'I need Maggy.'

MAGGY

Maggy finds Lou sitting in the middle of the shop floor, her arms wrapped around her knees. She picks her way through the broken glass, a lump forming in her throat as she looks around the shop, taking in the damage. It had been such a shock to see the shattered glass on the street and the police car parked outside when she and Donna arrived on the road, Maggy's hair dripping down her neck from where she had just finished washing it. She didn't have time to dry it, instead she rubbed it quickly with a towel, threw her clothes on and told Donna that they had to go. Lou needed them.

Outside, Maggy can hear Donna's voice as she interrogates Pete and the police officer, asking a series of questions about what has happened and what is going to happen next. Maggy doesn't try to listen to the answers, though. Her focus is on the young woman huddled on the floor. Besides, from what she's learnt so far of Donna, she feels confident that she will be making a careful note of every answer. Possibly in a notebook kept on hand in case of moments exactly like this.

She approaches Lou slowly and crouches down, her knees clicking as she does.

'Lou?' she says softly.

Lifting her head from her knees, the young woman sniffs loudly. Maggy's heart breaks a little as she takes in the lines of eyeliner that have dripped down Lou's cheeks and onto her scarf, staining the yellow with streaks of black. Her nose and cheeks are red and her eyes shine an even brighter shade of green.

'You're here,' is all she manages to say.

'Of course I am. Sorry about the hair,' she tries to force a smile, gesturing at the wet tangle on her shoulders. But as Lou tries to smile back, tears sliding down her cheeks at the same time, Maggy feels her heart give another crack and her expression grows serious. 'You poor thing. Your beautiful shop.'

Lou lets out a sob then, her shoulders shaking.

'They took the till,' she manages to say through her tears. 'And look!' As Lou points behind her, Maggy looks up to take in the bare wall, the hanger that used to carry a yellow dress covered in flowers now hanging bare.

She lifts a hand up to her mouth.

'Oh Lou.' Maggy adjusts herself so she can wrap her arms around her, pulling Lou into a tight hug. Lou's body shakes as she cries into Maggy's coat.

At that moment, Donna bustles inside. She is holding a tiny spiral-bound notebook in one hand.

'The police think it was probably opportunists trying their

184

luck,' she says. 'Maybe people from out of town – I take it you don't have a particularly high crime rate here.'

Maggy tries to remember the last time she saw a police car in the town before today. Not that Maggy would wish a break-in on any of the local shops, but a fierce protectiveness whispers, *Why Lou?* Hasn't the poor girl had enough to deal with?

Donna stops still as she spots them. Over Lou's shoulder, Maggy meets her eye, her lips spreading in a thin smile, but a concerned frown still around her eyes.

'Oh,' is all Donna says. She shifts uncomfortably on the spot, clearly unsure what to do next.

'Thank you for speaking with them,' Maggy replies. 'Thank goodness one of us is thinking straight.' She wipes her own eyes quickly, not wanting Lou to see the emotion on her face. She has to stay strong for her.

Lou peels herself away slightly, her sobs turning to sniffs.

'Thank you, Donna,' she manages weakly.

Donna seems to relax slightly. She consults her notebook.

'They are going to give you a crime number so you can report it to your insurance provider. Officer Haynes did say it was strange that the security alarm wasn't triggered – none of the neighbours heard it.'

Lou's face turns pale. She bites her lip and another silent tear drips down her face.

'Oh my God,' she says in a shaking voice. 'The alarm. I forgot to set it last night. I can't believe I'm such an idiot!'

She wipes a hand across her face, her make-up totally destroyed now.

'That means I probably won't be able to claim on the

insurance. Without that, how am I going to manage the repairs? And it means it's all my fault. The break-in, losing Mum's dress ...'

She turns to Donna now. 'I'm so sorry, Donna. The dress was your mum's too, of course. I can't believe it's gone.'

Donna glances up at the back wall, taking in the empty space where the yellow dress used to hang. Her face suddenly hardens, her cheeks turning an angry red.

Maggy braces herself, involuntarily squeezing Lou's shoulder. She understands Donna must be upset to have lost such an important part of her birth mother's history, but getting angry isn't going to help anything. Can't Donna see how upset Lou is?

'Lou, I want to make myself quite clear,' Donna says firmly. 'This is absolutely *not* your fault. You cannot think for one second that it is. The only person who is responsible for all this is that disgraceful criminal who violated several laws, not to mention common human decency, when they decided to smash that door and take whatever they liked. I will absolutely not have you think that you are in any way to blame. You are not. And I may not have met either of them, but I know for a fact that your mother and Eleanor would agree with me. As would the very nice Officer Haynes and the rest of the Somerset police force. So you must stop that thought this second, OK? This is not your fault.'

'You're not angry about the dress?' sniffs Lou.

'I'm absolutely furious!' Donna replies in an almost shout, making both Lou and Maggy jump. 'But not at you,' she adds, softer this time.

A weak smile appears on Lou's face, but then her expression clouds again.

'I can't believe it's gone. And what am I going to do about the shop? I can't afford to fix the door and buy a whole load of new stock, and a till and …' She trails off dejectedly.

'It's going to be OK,' Maggy says, trying to make her voice sound more confident than she feels.

But Lou's eyes are filling again as she slowly reaches into her handbag and pulls out her book and out of the back she takes out a letter, which she hands to Maggy.

'But you don't understand. This place isn't just a shop. It was a promise. And now I've let her down.'

Maggy takes the letter from Lou's outstretched hand and with one hand resting on Lou's shoulder for support, Donna close beside them, she begins to read aloud the inked words that match the handwriting on the letters they found in the biscuit tin.

Dear Lou,

My darling girl. I have left this letter with my solicitor alongside the rest of my instructions, so if you are reading this it means that I have gone. I hope that you are managing OK, or as OK as can be expected. You are braver than you think you are, my darling, and I know you will be all right once you have picked yourself up and brushed yourself down. You were so good at doing that when you were young.

It's hard to put into words how thankful I am for everything you have done for me over this last difficult year.

The way you left the life you were building for yourself in Brighton to come back to 'boring old Somerset' (as you called it when you were a teenager) to look after me … It's more than I could have asked for and I have cherished this time together, even if bits of it were frankly awful thanks to this ghastly illness. Your dad would be so proud of you and would thank you too for taking care of me, I know it.

Now it is time for you to follow your own path. I have left you the house, of course. I have some savings too, not much, but something. And Louise, my girl, I want you to use the money for you. Why not finally quit that recruitment job you hate and open the shop you have always talked about? I can picture it so clearly from how often you've described it. You might prefer to go back to Brighton or to somewhere new entirely, but I have also had my solicitor make some enquiries about a few buildings in town just in case. I can't say that it doesn't cheer me to think of you brightening my own town – the town where I've been very happy over the years – but that has to be your decision. Whatever you decide, I want you to live your life and to live it colourfully. Because you have filled my life with every colour of the rainbow, my darling girl.

I know you will make me proud. You always have.

I love you.

Mum xxx

The words swim before Maggy's eyes as she folds the letter and hands it back to Lou, who holds it tightly to her chest and takes another heaving sob. Even Donna is sniffing now, looking down at the floor and wiping her eyes subtly with her sleeve.

'You see,' says Lou, her words coming out choked. 'If the shop has to shut, it won't just mean I've failed as a business owner. It will mean I've failed Mum too. I've let her down.'

Maggy looks at the young woman, her face blotchy and red and lined with make-up, and something inside her breaks. She squeezes Lou's shoulder and turns to make sure Lou can see her face as she speaks.

'Lou, listen to me. Speaking as a mother, I can tell you that there is nothing you could ever do that would let her down. I may never have had the pleasure of meeting her, but I can tell you with absolute certainty that she would be incredibly proud of you and of this shop.'

'Maggy's right,' Donna chips in. 'You've done a brilliant job here. And besides, as a parent, you're not just proud of your children when things go well for them. You're even prouder when they go wrong and they work their way through it. Which you will.'

'I don't know …' Lou trails off.

'Have you had a proper look around?' Donna asks, glancing around the shop.

'Not really,' admits Lou. 'I came in and just got totally over-whelmed.'

Donna nods. 'Well, we need to take an inventory of exactly what is missing. I can make a note in here.' She lifts up the trusty notebook.

'That's probably a good idea,' says Maggy gently. 'Come on, love.' She shifts to help Lou off the floor, but her knees tighten and she winces. The two of them end up pulling each other up. Maggy brushes her knees and Lou does the same, looking around and blinking.

After the initial shock of seeing the shop in such disarray, Maggy tries to take in the positives.

'Look, there's a lot of stock they haven't even touched,' she says, pointing out a couple of the rails where the clothes still hang neatly. 'And at least they went for the door rather than the windows. That surely has to be less expensive to fix.'

'I guess.'

'Come on,' says Donna, taking out her pen and holding the notebook in her palm, 'let's go around and you can tell me exactly what you think has gone. We can give the information to the police in a minute. I told Officer Haynes you probably needed a moment.'

Maggy glances outside to where the police car, the officer and Pete still linger on the pavement. She is surprised not to see Beth and Danie there but remembers that the café opens late today. Would the break-in have happened if they'd been there? Maggy tries to shake off the thought. The crowd has dispersed slightly now, a few early morning shoppers glancing in curiously every now and then as they pass the window.

Together, the three women make their way around the shop, Maggy with her arm around Lou, and Donna doing an excellent job of making clear notes and asking questions. The shop has definitely taken a hit: all of the bags and accessories are gone, as well as a couple of leather jackets, some of Lou's evening dresses, and of course, the till.

When they reach the counter, Lou runs a hand lightly over the surface. 'I found the till on eBay,' she says, staring ahead with a glazed expression. 'I know it sounds a small thing, but buying it felt like the moment my plans all became real. I wasn't just playing shop – I was really going to have my own business. I was so excited. And now ...'

'It's not over,' Maggy says reassuringly. 'We can fix this.'

Lou doesn't say anything in reply.

Maggy wishes she could do more to cheer her up. She thinks back to when she first visited the shop, drawn in by the brightness of the yellow dress behind the counter. Lou had seemed so enthusiastic, something that Maggy has seen since every time she talks about her business or her love of vintage. She had no idea when she first met Lou how much she was hiding and quite how much the business meant to her. Maggy thinks that quite possibly it has been the one thing keeping her going.

As they stand by the counter, Donna moves behind it, crouching down for a moment. There's a sound of shuffling, then an, 'Oh!' She reappears a moment later. In her arms is a crumpled pile of yellow fabric.

'Look what I found!' she shouts. 'It must have got knocked down and slipped under the counter.' Donna hands over the bundle and Lou reaches out eagerly, her mouth opening wide. Lou lifts it up and the fabric becomes a dress covered in flowers, a little dusty, but still as bright as a lemon.

'The dress!' she says, her face lighting up. 'It's here!'

She holds the fabric up to her cheek.

'There's quite a lot of dust on that,' Donna points out, but Lou doesn't seem to notice. She hugs the dress tightly.

'See,' says Maggy, 'it's not all bad. It's going to be OK. And we'll help however we can, won't we, Donna?'

Maggy smiles encouragingly at her new friend.

'Well, of course,' Donna says simply, as though the suggestion is ridiculously obvious. 'That's what you do for family.'

LOU

When Lou wakes up the next morning, she glances at her phone to check the time and how long she has until she needs to get ready for work. And then she remembers. It all comes back in a rush: seeing the police car on the street, spotting Pete, the broken glass and realising the break-in was at *her* shop. The police officer had been kind, as had Pete, who fixed a board to the shop's door to cover up the broken window-pane. And Maggy and Donna might be determined to help her rebuild her business, but as Lou taped a hastily written sign in the window reading, 'Closed until further notice' and then locked up, she couldn't help but feel like she was saying good-bye.

'Knock, knock,' comes a quiet voice outside the door. It creaks open and Maggy pops her head round the gap, Donna at her side. Maggy is carrying a steaming mug and a plate piled high with toast.

'We thought you deserved breakfast in bed this morning after the day you had yesterday.'

'You didn't have to do that.' Lou sits up a little straighter in bed, tucking her hair behind her ears and pulling her pyjama sleeves down over her hands.

'That's OK,' Maggy says, perching on the end of the bed and passing Lou the mug and plate.

'Thank you, that's really kind of you.' She doesn't feel particularly hungry, but doesn't want to seem ungrateful, so takes a small nibble of the corner of one of the slices.

'So, what do you want to do today?' Maggy asks. 'Donna and I can come and help you tidy up at the shop?'

'I'm good at tidying – we'll have the place sorted in no time,' adds Donna.

But Lou shakes her head.

'Thanks for the offer, I really appreciate it. But I don't think I'm ready to go back yet. I think I need to take a few days. Have a bit of a break from it all.'

The two other women frown at each other, but then Maggy nods.

'Of course. If that's what you need.'

Lou doesn't want to see the shop. She doesn't want to think about it either. Her phone buzzes and she picks it up. There is a stream of messages from Beth and the others, telling her how sorry they are and asking what they can do to help. Pete has messaged too, asking how she's doing. Lou turns the phone over and places it back on the bedside table.

When she eventually gets out of bed, instead of reaching

for one of her colourful outfits, she pulls out a pair of black leggings and a faded blue shirt from the back of a drawer, the outfit she usually reserves for cleaning. She pulls her hair back in a simple ponytail, leaving her face bare.

'How about a walk?' Maggy suggests.

'I might just watch some TV, if that's OK? I'm feeling pretty tired.'

Lou doesn't leave the house for several days. Maggy and Donna cook for her, Donna making a series of different flavoured pies that Lou tries her best to eat. They are delicious, but she doesn't have much of an appetite. They don't talk much more about Eleanor. Maggy and Donna head off to the library together a few times and Lou assumes they are doing more research. But Lou doesn't ask. Donna's flight back to America is drawing closer and Lou knows she should join them both and help, but she can't find the energy. Every time she thinks about the unsolved mystery of what happened to her aunt, an overwhelming sense of failure washes over her, despite Maggy's and Donna's words of encouragement. She couldn't keep her business going, how is she possibly going to find a woman she didn't know existed until a few days ago? Her emotions manifest in a sense of extreme lethargy; her limbs feel heavy and every time she thinks about getting off the sofa, she spots another home renovation or cooking show and decides she might as well watch one more.

On the second day, the doorbell rings. Maggy answers it and comes back into the living room, where Lou is curled on the sofa, having just woken from a nap, carrying an enormous bunch of orange and yellow flowers.

'They're from Zara at the flower shop, aren't they lovely?'

Lou sends her a message to thank her. She knows she should call, or pop in and see in person the new friends who have been so supportive since the break-in. But she can't stand the thought of seeing the sympathy on their faces. It feels like when she lost her mum all over again. Because she knows that's why the break-in has hit her so hard. Since her mum passed away, she has put all her energy and focus into preparing, opening and running the shop. It's been a bright spot of colour and hope in the darkness. Now that she isn't heading in there every day, it's as though everything she thought she was managing to hold up has crashed down on top of her, crushing her. Her mum's illness, leaving her life and friends behind to come and care for her, her break-up with Richard, her mum's death ... Now that it's all knocked her over again, she isn't quite sure if she'll be able to get back up again.

LOU

A few days after the break-in, Lou, Maggy and Donna are having dinner together – a comforting macaroni cheese with a crusty breadcrumb and bacon topping. Lou is feeling slightly brighter today – she at least managed a shower and helping out with dinner – and the macaroni cheese smells so delicious that she feels her stomach rumbling eagerly.

'This looks amazing, thank you, Donna,' she says, trying to make her voice sound bright.

'It's one of my family's favourites,' Donna replies.

Donna is just passing Lou a bowl when a phone rings. All three of them look up.

'I think that's mine,' says Donna, placing down the serving spoon. 'Do you mind if I take it? It might be my husband or daughter.'

'Of course not, go ahead,' says Maggy.

Donna steps out of the room to take the call. As she answers, Lou turns to Maggy.

'I might check in on the shop tomorrow,' she says, twisting a piece of hair around one finger. 'Maybe make a start at sweeping up.'

Maggy's face brightens. 'That's brilliant. I'm sure once you start it won't be as bad as you think.'

Lou isn't sure if Maggy is right, but she doesn't have any other source of income. She quit her job to start the business and while moping on the sofa for a few days felt absolutely necessary after what happened, she knows it's time to pull herself together.

'I hope so,' she replies. 'I'm sorry I've been so hopeless these past few days. It just hit me really hard after everything. But I know I haven't been much fun to be around. I really appreciate you and Donna looking after me.'

In the corridor, she can hear Donna's murmured voice, although Lou can't make out what she is saying.

'You don't need to apologise. I completely understand,' Maggy replies, pouring them both a glass of wine and filling Donna's glass too. 'You've had so much to deal with that it's quite understandable that this has shaken you. But I do think it's fixable. You have a beautiful shop and it has so much potential. I don't want to overstep at all, but I've been thinking about a few ideas actually ...'

The sound of Donna's raised voice interrupts them. 'What? Really?'

Maggy raises an eyebrow at Lou. They both pause to listen.

'Can you email it to me? Yes. OK. Thank you. Goodbye.' There's a pause and then Donna says aloud, 'I can't believe it.'

She returns to the kitchen with flushed cheeks, her phone

still held in one hand. Her eyes are wide and shining brightly.

'What is it?' asks Maggy. 'Is everything OK?'

Donna opens her mouth and then closes it again. She looks at Lou, fixing her with an intense gaze.

'They found her,' she says. 'They found Eleanor.'

Lou can't speak. She just looks at Donna, the two of them not breaking each other's gaze. It's Maggy who asks Donna to explain.

'What happened? Who was that on the phone?'

Donna looks down at the phone in her hand as though disorientated, before putting it in her pocket and placing her hands on her hips.

'That was the adoption agency. When I first went to see them, they told me that they were in the process of organising their old files after an office move. They thought they didn't have any more information about Eleanor for me – that it had been misplaced somehow over the years. But they were just sorting through a particular filing cabinet and they found something.'

'Oh my goodness!' says Maggy excitedly, reaching for Lou's arm and squeezing it. She smiles and Lou tries to smile back, but her mind is racing, trying to process.

'They have her address!' Donna says breathlessly, lifting her hands slightly in the air as though they are being pulled by strings. 'Apparently she supplied them with her new one every time she moved, just in case I ever wanted to get in touch.' She sniffs slightly then, turning away, her eyes gaining a faraway look. When she turns back, her lips are set in a determined line. 'She only lives a few hours away from Cold Spring. I'm going to call the airline to bring my flight forward. I need to go and see her as soon as possible.'

For the first time in days, Lou feels truly awake, her body wired and alert.

'Oh Donna,' she says, standing up and reaching her arms out for her cousin, 'I'm so pleased for you. You found her!'

They hug tightly.

'Mum would be so pleased. And I can't believe you're going to finally meet your birth mother, it's just wonderful.' But at the same time a sadness wells up inside her. 'All this time,' Lou adds, shaking her head in disbelief. 'All this time, she was right there nearby and you never knew.'

Not for the first time that week, tears spring quickly to Lou's eyes.

'It all seems so unfair,' she says sadly. 'I mean, it's brilliant that you know where she is now, but it seems so ... pointless, I guess, that it's taken us this long. That she was right there, but you never even knew she existed. And from Mum's letters and how she treasured the yellow dress, it's clear Mum loved her sister. It's just so sad that they lost touch. And it's not fair that Mum has missed out on all of this, on meeting you, Donna, and now potentially seeing her sister again ...'

'You're right,' Donna says, nodding firmly. 'Life is not fair. That's just the way it is, and it's taken me a long time to realise it. I've always wanted my life to fit neatly into a box, because it's easier that way. To know what's coming next and how everything joins together. But the trouble is it just doesn't work. Surprises happen. People get sick and sometimes you find out something that totally changes what you thought you knew about someone, and what you knew about yourself. In the past, I might have tried to fight against it, or ignore it, or to somehow control the uncontrollable. But I'm starting to think that doesn't always make sense either.'

She pauses, taking a breath.

'Yes, life is not fair. But it's still your choice how you react to knowing that. That's something I've learnt on this trip. I could have just stayed in my comfortable life and not tried to find answers about my past. But I chose to come here and I'm glad that I did. It might not have turned out exactly how I hoped it might, but that's OK. It's not fair that I have spent my life not knowing my birth mother and that your mother never got to meet her sister again. But now I know where she is and so I'm going to go and talk to her. And you should come with me.'

Donna folds her arms across her chest as though signalling that she is finished.

'Come with you to America?' says Lou, frowning. 'I can't do that.'

'Yes, you can,' replies Donna.

Lou's mind races, filling with all the reasons why Donna's suggestion doesn't make sense. But among them all is a rising sense of trepidatious excitement.

'But what about the shop?'

'I can take care of it!' says Maggy encouragingly, her face lighting up. 'It's the perfect time for you to go away, given the shop is closed anyway. I can handle everything with the police and with that nice builder … Pete, is it? You don't have to worry about anything. Getting away for a bit might be good for you. And I'm sure you would love to meet your aunt too, wouldn't you?'

Lou tries to picture meeting her mother's sister for the first time. She must be an old woman by now, nothing like the photographs of her when she was young. Lou tries to imagine how she might have aged and whether she will look like her mother.

'We could take Mum's letters with us,' she suggests.

'So that means you're going?' asks Maggy, placing her hands together.

Lou glances at Donna, who is watching her carefully. And she finds herself nodding.

'OK. I'll come with you.'

Maggy cheers and pours them all more wine while Donna goes immediately into action mode, researching flights on her phone.

'I should probably call John too and let him know the change of plans.'

She heads to her room to make the call and continue her research, and Lou and Maggy are left alone at the kitchen table.

'I probably shouldn't be spending money right now,' Lou says sheepishly. 'Not with the repairs to sort in the shop. I do have some of Mum's money left though.' She twirls a strand of hair around one finger, a mix of excitement and nerves lacing her insides.

'And I am certain this is exactly what she would want you to spend it on,' Maggy replies with a warm smile.

Maybe Maggy is right and this trip has come at the perfect time. Just the thought of seeing the boarded-up door and the broken glass and empty hangers in her shop makes Lou feel sick, especially when she can't stop thinking about the fact she forgot to set the alarm that night. She hasn't had the energy yet to think in detail about what will happen next for her business or how viable its future really is. But now she doesn't have to, at least not yet, anyway. For now, she doesn't want to focus on the future, instead she wants to finally uncover the secrets of the past.

'I've never been to America before,' she says hesitantly.

'And now you're going!'

'As long as you really don't mind keeping an eye on things here? I don't want to impose on you, Maggy, you've already done so much for me.' She glances at her, overwhelmed suddenly with affection for the woman who gave her a room and has become her friend. But Maggy shrugs off the thanks. Lou takes her in for a moment, the orange of the jumper paired with dark jeans and a coral lipstick that is brighter than any shade Lou has seen her wear before.

'It's OK,' Maggy says. 'You go and have your adventure. I've got things covered here, really.'

Looking at her friend, Lou realises that Maggy isn't the same woman she met just a couple of weeks ago, who seemed cautious and uncertain, hiding herself behind layers of black and grey. She really *has* got this.

'OK. I guess I'm going to America!' Lou lifts her hands in the air, her face brightening for the first time in days.

'Excellent! I think that's a reason for another glass, don't you?' Maggy tops Lou up and they clink glasses, sharing a warm smile.

Now she just has to decide what to pack.

DONNA

Everything is sorted. The flights are booked and Donna has printed her ticket and folded it neatly into the transparent ziplock bag that also contains her passport, a small bottle of hand sanitiser, a packet of tissues, a sleeping pill and a pair of foam earplugs. John will be there to collect her and Lou from the airport when they land. Donna wanted to head straight from there to Eleanor's house, but John managed to convince her that late evening, and after an eight hour flight, might not be the best time to confront her birth mother for the first time. Instead, they will head back to the Sycamore Inn – Donna has made sure the manager has put aside one of the nicest rooms for Lou – and Donna will drive herself and Lou the next morning.

Now, she packs the last of her belongings carefully in her suitcase in her room at Maggy's. She folds the final T-shirt, smoothing it neatly, and then zips up the case, entering the pin number to lock the padlock. She pauses next to the bed (which she stripped earlier this morning, placing the bedding inside one of the pillowcases) and looks around to see if she has forgotten anything. But the room is back to the way it was when she arrived. Which means she can't blame having forgotten something on the sense of unease she feels. She unzips the transparent bag again and checks the flight details for the tenth time that morning.

'The taxi will be here soon,' says Lou, poking her head round the door.

Donna spots the suitcase at her side – it is bright yellow. *Of course it is*, she thinks with a smile. She and her cousin might be very different people, but Donna has come to feel a deep sense of affection for the younger woman. Lou's outfits still make her eyes hurt – and today's is no exception. But they share a sense of understanding. Lou might show it in different ways, like the way her make-up is particularly meticulous again today and how she keeps touching her hair, but Donna can tell that she feels just as nervous about this trip as she does.

'I'm excited, are you?' Lou says, her voice full of energy. Because that's another thing they have in common – despite the nerves coursing through Donna right now, there is also a fizzing, popping-candy type of feeling too.

'I am,' she replies, slipping her travel wallet inside her handbag. 'I can't believe we're really going to see her.'

'She might not be home, though,' Lou replies, biting her bottom lip. 'I guess we have to brace ourselves for the fact she might not be there. Are you sure you didn't want to send a letter first?'

But Donna shakes her head. 'No, it's better to go in person. It's too much to fit in a letter, and besides, I couldn't bear to wait for the reply, could you?'

She doesn't mention the fear that she might not receive one.

'I suppose you're right,' Lou replies. 'Can I help you with your bag?'

Maggy is waiting for them in the hallway downstairs. She seems almost as excited as they do.

'I can't wait to hear how it all goes. I hope you find what you're looking for.'

'Thanks, Maggy,' Lou replies, giving her a big hug. 'And I hope your meeting tomorrow is everything *you* hope for too.'

She smiles and raises an eyebrow and Maggy's cheeks pinken.

'Ah yes, my meeting with Simon. I'd almost forgotten.'

Donna knows that isn't true though. Maggy has a hair appointment booked for later that day; Donna heard her booking it. They talked about Simon last night, too, Maggy sharing memories with them both about her time in London in the sixties. Donna had listened with fascination, trying to square up the stories of miniskirts and art student parties with the grandmother of around her age that she has been staying with. But then it struck her that, of course, people change. *Maybe it's just me who hasn't,* she thought.

'I hope it goes well,' continues Lou. 'And that you get some answers.'

'You too, and you, Donna. I'll be thinking of you.'

To her surprise, Maggy reaches out for Donna, pulling her into a hug. And perhaps even more surprisingly, Donna finds herself hugging her back warmly.

'Thank you for having me,' she says once they have parted. 'If you're ever visiting the States, you make sure to come to Cold Spring, OK? I mean it. There's always a room for you at the Sycamore Inn.'

'Thank you, Donna. You know, I haven't taken a holiday in quite a while. Maybe I should change that someday soon. Anyway, I think I hear a car out there ...'

Maggy opens the front door just as the taxi driver parked on the street steps out and walks round to open the boot.

'This is it then,' says Lou. 'I'll be back in a few days. Are you sure you don't mind being on hand for any emergencies at the shop? I've told Pete and the police officer that I'll deal with it all when I get back ...' Lou frowns, a shadow passing across her eyes.

'Stop worrying,' says Maggy. 'And go on, I don't want you to be late for your flight.'

Donna doesn't say that there is no *way* they would be late. She booked the taxi two and a half hours earlier than strictly necessary.

Lou picks up her suitcase and bumps it down the steps to where the driver is waiting to help them and then comes back for Donna's. She gives Maggy a final wave and then heads to the waiting car, Donna following behind, taking one last look up at the town house and at Maggy, who stands in the door-way.

Once the taxi has set off, it hits Donna that although there is still a long journey ahead of them, they are on their way. She is going home, and then after that ...

'Are you OK, Donna?'

She sniffs and pulls out a pair of sunglasses from her handbag.

'Allergies,' she replies, putting the glasses on and squeezing her eyes tightly shut. Her eyes are still closed as she feels Lou's hand wrap around her own.

MAGGY

The house feels quiet after Lou and Donna leave, but for once it doesn't bother Maggy. She has too much to do to notice.

First, she calls the number of Lou's builder that Lou left along with some other key contacts. They speak for a few minutes and then say goodbye, agreeing to talk again in a couple of days.

'Nice man,' Maggy says aloud to herself. When her phone rings, she wonders if it's perhaps Pete again with another question for her, but it's her daughter Charlotte.

'Hi, Mum.'

'Hello, darling,' replies Maggy, putting down the list she had been consulting, the list she wrote this morning while Lou was packing. 'How are you?'

'I'm OK, but annoyingly I've had a meeting come up for this afternoon. I know it's not one of your days, but do you think you could collect Fleur from nursery and have her till the evening?'

Maggy catches her reflection in the mirror as she listens to her daughter. It still surprises her not to see a woman dressed all in black and grey looking back at her. She hasn't totally thrown away her old wardrobe, but since treating herself at Lou's shop, she has been making sure to wear at least one thing that's colourful each day. It makes her smile to see the red silk scarf tied around her neck today. She didn't quite have the confidence to go for a matching lipstick, like Lou would have done, but she did try a slightly brighter shade than usual. She isn't sure if it's just her imagination, but she can't help but think that her skin looks less pale than usual and she wonders whether black ever actually really suited her.

She turns away from the mirror and back to the list in her hand.

'I'm sorry, darling, you know I would normally love to have Fleur, but I'm afraid I'm busy today.'

'Oh.'

There's a moment's silence that Maggy so nearly fills; it would be so easy to change her mind and to say that of course she can help out. It's what she would normally do.

'I'm actually going to be quite busy this whole week,' she forces herself to say instead, determined not to lose her nerve. 'Something has come up, I'm afraid. So it might be better to make alternative plans for Fleur's childcare this week.'

'But—'

Before Charlotte can continue, Maggy chips in. 'Perhaps you could ask Alan and Tracy to help out? I'm sure your father would love to see his granddaughter – it's been a while now, hasn't it? I'm sorry to do this, but I knew you would understand, darling, after all, you know exactly what it's like to have things come up at the last minute.'

Once Maggy has finished, she braces herself for Charlotte's reply, not quite believing she managed to get through her whole speech without giving in. Despite feeling bad about letting her daughter down, there's a strange rush to having stood up for herself for once and also for the truth of what she just said. She *does* have things to do.

Charlotte clears her throat. There's another moment's silence and then she eventually replies.

'Of course, Mum. I'll work it out.'

'Oh, that's brilliant. Now, I've got to run, sweetheart, but let's catch up soon, OK?'

A few minutes later and Maggy is throwing on her coat and stepping outside with purpose. She cuts through the park on her way to town, taking in the autumnal scenes around her. Children kick their way through piles of crunchy leaves, parents nursing steaming drinks in paper cups purchased from the small café in the park following in their wake. Maggy smiles to see them, remembering the countless times she has done the same thing over the years with both her children and her grandchildren. In the bandstand, a choir made up of all ages and wrapped up in scarves and gloves are practising a cover of a show tune, attracting a small group of onlookers on the grass below.

Over the past couple of weeks, Maggy has been forced to confront so much about her life, questioning her choices and what the point of it all has been. The divorce left her feeling as though her home had been taken away from her as well as her marriage. But as she walks through the park that she has walked through thousands of times throughout her life, it strikes her that her home isn't just a house, or even the people who once shared it with her. Her home is this town. Which is why she feels so determined to help Lou. Because this town is Lou's home too.

Beth looks up with a smile when Maggy pushes open the door of her café. Other than a few customers sitting quietly at the back, Maggy is the only customer so steps straight up to the counter.

'Hello, you might not remember me, but I'm a friend of Lou's. She's been staying with me.'

'Of course, hello, Maggy,' Beth replies warmly. Her face falls then, glancing to her right, as though imagining herself in the shop next door, picturing the broken glass and debris. 'It's so awful what happened. We're all just gutted for her. It's so un-fair. How's she doing? I've tried to get in touch, but she hasn't seemed to want to talk.'

'She's doing OK,' Maggy replies and then quickly explains about the last-minute trip to America.

'Oh wow!' replies Beth. 'That's amazing.'

'It is ... at least I hope it will be. But what I'm worried about is how she's going to feel when she gets back and has to face everything again. I really want to help. And that's actually why I'm here ...'

Maggy explains her plan to Beth, who listens intently. When Maggy finishes, Beth nods firmly.

'Well, you can count me in, Maggy. And I'll speak to the others about it too. I know there are lots of people who would want to help.'

'That's so kind, thank you,' says Maggy, sighing in relief.

'Of course. It's hard starting a new business – I remember it well. We have to help each other out. Besides, I like Lou a lot.'

Maggy smiles. 'So do I.'

'And she certainly helps to keep us afloat with the amount of coffees she buys from us,' adds Beth. 'It's nice to have a neighbour who's such a loyal customer. The last owners used to come in to collect parcels left here while they were out, clutching their Costa cups.'

'The cheek!' replies Maggy. She says goodbye and leaves the café with a hot chocolate, a pastry and a renewed sense of determination.

Maggy continues down the hill through the town, popping in to a few shops she hasn't visited in a while. She stops at the flower shop, where a bicycle hangs in the window, the basket over-flowing with orange roses, dark green foliage woven through the wheel spokes. Inside, she asks for Zara and, after compli-menting her on the window display and choosing a bunch of dahlias to take back to the house, fills her in on her plan.

'Of course I'll help,' Zara says as she wraps Maggy's flowers in brown paper, tying them with shiny orange ribbon. 'I was so sad to hear about the break-in. It kind of shakes your faith in the world, doesn't it? But then I look around and I see so much good stuff too. I think most people genuinely do want to help one another.'

Maggy takes the flowers, tucking them under the arm of her plaid coat. 'I think so too. And the reaction I've had so far to my idea makes me think you're right, Zara.' At that moment, she spots the time on the clock that hangs at the back of the shop. 'Oh, I've got an appointment to get to. But we'll be in touch again soon?'

She waves goodbye, buoyed up by the reaction from Beth and Zara. She understands why Lou might feel alone at times; after everything she's been through, it's not surprising. But Maggy is determined to make her see that she isn't. The whole town is behind her, and so is she.

The smell of hair products and the background whirr of dryers greets Maggy as she steps into the salon. She looks around at all the tall mirrors surrounded by lights, women in various stages of transformation sitting in black chairs facing them, the stylists behind them chatting away as they work their magic. Maggy can't remember the last time she treated herself to a proper haircut; she always used to cut Alan's hair for him and eventually worked out it was easier and cheaper to trim her own too.

A chirpy young woman with a glorious halo of red curls greets her, taking her coat and bag.

'I'll pop these in some water for you to keep them fresh while you're here,' she says, reaching for the flowers.

'Thank you, that's kind.'

'Now, can I get you a tea or a coffee? We have regular tea, all sorts of herbal ones and a nice coffee machine.'

Maggy is taken aback; the service is nothing like this when

she does her own hair. She opts for a herbal tea and is handed a black robe before being led to the washing station at the back of the salon.

'Would you like the massage chair turned on? And a head massage with your wash?'

Maggy nearly waves a hand dismissively, habit making her want to tell the young woman not to go to any bother. But instead she changes her mind and nods her head.

'Yes, actually, that would be lovely. Thank you.'

For ten minutes, Maggy sits perfectly still as the massage chair ripples up and down her back and warm water washes over her head, gentle fingers rubbing shampoo into her hair and sending shivers down her spine. For a second, she almost feels guilty, thinking about Charlotte and Fleur. But then the young woman begins to massage Maggy's scalp and she closes her eyes. She breathes in the smell of the shampoo and lets herself fully relax into the chair, her limbs growing heavy and her skin tingling.

'Right, you're all done,' a voice says what could be minutes or hours later, lifting Maggy up out of her dreamlike state. 'If you'd just like to lean forward, I'll wrap your hair and then you can go upstairs.'

Maggy sits up and opens her eyes, blinking rapidly.

'Oh my God, are you OK?' the young woman says anxiously. 'Did I hurt you? Was the water too hot?'

But Maggy shakes her head, wiping quickly at her eyes.

'No, nothing's wrong. It's just …'

She pauses, not quite sure how to explain to this young

woman that she hasn't been touched like that in a long time. That it's the first time, maybe for years, that she has felt like someone was looking after her and not the other way around. That she is starting to realise that perhaps she misses the thought of her marriage, rather than her actual husband, and that she doesn't know quite what to do with that realisation or what it means about the way she has lived her life.

'It was lovely, thank you,' she says.

The woman smiles in relief.

'Right, let's get you upstairs. Sal will be doing your hair today. She's great.'

Maggy is led to a chair on the upper floor of the salon, where a floor-to-ceiling window looks out over the street below. Waiting for her by the mirror is a tall woman with a perfectly trimmed pixie cut. She introduces herself and compliments Maggy on her red silk scarf.

'That colour really suits you.'

Maggy thanks her, feeling herself sit up a little straighter in the chair.

Then Sal places her hands on the back of the chair, looking at Maggy in the mirror.

'So, what are we doing today?'

Maggy explains what she wants and Sal listens intently, nodding and unwrapping the towel around Maggy's head and then picking up strands of her hair, not breaking her gaze in the mirror.

'OK, no problem,' she says with a confidence that reassures Maggy. 'Is it for any particular occasion or was it just time for a trim?' she asks as she starts combing Maggy's hair.

Maggy's eyes dart towards the window, but then she looks back in the mirror. 'A little of both,' she admits. 'It has been a long time since my last haircut. A *very* long time actually. But I'm also seeing an old friend tomorrow for the first time in years. Is that a silly reason to get a haircut?'

Sal continues to gently brush out Maggy's damp hair, spraying it with some sweet-smelling product and then reaching for the scissors in her belt.

'You are talking to the wrong person. There's never a silly reason to get a haircut in my opinion. I've been doing this job for twenty-five years and I've seen the difference a good haircut can make. People come in as one person and leave as someone different. That's the magic of hair. It's also one less thing to worry about if you're feeling nervous about say a date or a job interview. If you *know* your hair is looking great, you can focus on killing it at what you're doing without having to keep fussing with that bit of fringe that keeps falling in front of your face or whatever. There's a freedom that comes with a great haircut.' She pauses then, the scissors held aloft. She lets out a laugh, smiling at Maggy. 'Sorry I'm going on, I just love my job.'

Maggy smiles back. 'No, it's nice to hear someone talk so passionately about what they do.'

Maggy's thoughts turn to the questions that have been filling her mind recently: *What is my passion? And what am I going to do with the rest of my life?* For once, she realises that she might be getting closer to an answer.

'So, tell me,' continues Sal, returning to Maggy's hair, 'how long has it been since you saw this friend? Did you say it had been a few years?'

'Try more than fifty!'

'Wow! Now I have to hear that story. Which is another perk of my job. If you don't mind telling it, that is?'

She may have spent most of her life keeping the story of Simon secret from those closest to her, but now that Maggy has revisited the memories with Lou and then Donna, she finds that she doesn't mind talking about it again. In fact, she wants to, reminding herself of the woman she used to be.

'And you never found out why he left like that?' Sal asks once Maggy finishes speaking. By now, Maggy's hair is nearly finished too, Sal moving around behind her making the final adjustments.

'No,' Maggy replies. Then, as she looks more closely at her reflection, she adds, 'Wow, this is perfect, thank you.'

She turns her head, taking in the shiny grey waves that now bounce at her jawline. Sal holds up a mirror to show her the back, Maggy thanking her and Sal smiling appreciatively.

As Sal helps to remove the protective cape, she says, 'Well, I hope tomorrow goes well.'

'Thank you, so do I.'

Maggy steps out into the street with a bounce in her step. Her phone buzzes. She has two notifications, one a WhatsApp message and another from Facebook. She opens the WhatsApp first; it's Lou saying they are about to board their flight. Maggy types a quick reply, wishing her a safe journey. Then she opens the Facebook message. It still gives her a jolt to see Simon's face in his profile picture, so different and yet also somehow so similar to the young man she knew.

'Looking forward to seeing you tomorrow x,' he writes.

She had offered to travel to London to meet him, but he said he would come to her, something which secretly relieved Maggy as it means she could choose the location, picking a place that always made her feel calm. 'You too,' she replies, hesitating for a moment and then adding a kiss too.

LOU

The plane cabin is dimly lit and quiet, apart from the background hum of the engines and the symphony of snores coming from various passengers. In the seat next to Lou, Donna sleeps soundly, her head resting on her wraparound neck pillow, an eye mask pulled over her face and orange earplugs in her ears. Lou glances at her, wishing she'd thought to pack a pillow too. She can't sleep. Although, as she glances around the plane, she wonders how much of that is to do with the wafer-thin cushion provided by the airline or whether her racing mind is to blame instead.

Lou catches the eye of a passing air steward.

'Can I have a gin and tonic please?' she whispers.

The attendant nods and returns a few moments later with a plastic cup half-filled with ice and two miniature bottles. Lou twists the cap of the tonic slowly, watching Donna beside her in case of any signs of movement. But she doesn't stir. She has been asleep since take-off when Lou watched her take a sleeping pill and then settle herself.

Lou reaches for the touchscreen in front of her, considering watching another film, but instead clicking on the information panel. The cartoon icon of the plane is currently halfway across the Atlantic and as she watches it she feels a sudden pang of homesickness, knowing as she does that it's not just her shop or the town or Maggy that she's missing. It's what her grief has felt like – an intense and all-consuming homesickness. Over recent weeks, it has started to fade somewhat, other brighter feelings finally able to find their way to the surface. But she wonders if it will ever go away completely.

Reaching under her seat for her rucksack, she opens it and after a bit of digging pulls out the biscuit tin filled with her mother's letters. She didn't trust putting it in the hold. Switching on the tiny reading light above her, she pulls out a small stack of the letters. Thanks to Donna, they are now grouped in smaller piles secured by rubber bands, a Post-it note on the top of each stack detailing the time period that the letters cover. Lou finds the most recent pile and pulls the one she is looking for out from the very back – the last letter her mother wrote but never sent to Eleanor.

In the strange no-man's-land between two continents, two time zones and between wakefulness and sleep, Lou reads the letter again.

3 May 2018

Dear Eleanor,

It is late and Lou is asleep upstairs. I have waited until now to write this as I have still never told her about these letters. I thought about it over the years, but it felt too complicated to explain, or maybe I thought she might think I was mad. I can't quite believe myself that I have been writing for so long. But there is a comfort to putting my thoughts down on paper. I suppose it's why some people write diaries. These letters are my diary, my life on paper.

I am tired, Eleanor. I don't like to admit it, but I am. There's nothing that feels easy any more and on the rare occasions when I let myself catch a glimpse of myself in the bathroom mirror, I don't know who it is that is staring back at me. Certainly not me.

In my mind, I am still young. I am about thirty-five, married to a man I love and with the most gorgeous girl as my daughter. Perhaps I might have liked more children, but she is enough. She has always been enough for me and Jeremy. In my picture of myself, I am wearing your yellow dress, never looking quite as beautiful as you did, but feeling when I wear it like I have my whole family with me.

When my time comes, I hope that I can close my eyes and see myself like that. Wearing a dress the colour of sunshine with my beloved husband and daughter at my side. You will be there too.

I'm tired now, I think it is time to sleep. I will write again when I can.

Your sister,
Dotty

PS I was just putting my pen away when it suddenly

struck me that sometime soon, sooner probably than she
realises (I like to think that I have grown accomplished at
hiding my pain from her, it's what you do as a mother), Lou
will be left to sort through my things and will eventually find
these letters. So, this last part is for you, dear Lou.

By now you will know about my sister, Eleanor. You will
know that she was once my favourite person in the world,
the person I looked up to and admired more than anyone.
I know it might seem strange that I never mentioned her to
you or your father, but over the years, it became too painful
to talk about her. It was easier to pretend that I had never
had a sister than to dredge up the memories.

She left for New York when I was twelve years old and I
never saw her again. I still don't know why. I like to think
that something happened which meant she wasn't able to
get in touch, not that she merely forgot about me. Even after
all these years, I can't let myself think that she might have
forgotten.

I of course considered the fact that she might have died.
Perhaps she grew ill on the crossing to America or there
was some accident with a taxicab on some street in New
York and she became yet another unknown woman who
disappeared from this world before she had a chance to
make her mark. But I don't like to imagine that either.
In my mind, she became the model she wanted to be, her
picture finding its way into magazines (although not any of
the ones I flicked through on countless newsstands, searching
for her familiar face). Perhaps she and Sydney really did

get married like she'd hoped, or maybe – and this was my favourite version of her story – she ditched him quickly after arriving in America and met a dashing young man of her own age – Italian perhaps – who loved her as she deserved to be loved and gave her a brood of cheerful children.

I tried to find out what really happened to her over the years but never made any progress. Perhaps you might have better luck, though. You have a skill for finding clothes that tell a story, after all. Maybe you can find her story.

If you do by some chance manage to find her, can you do something for me? Will you hug her as tightly as you would hug me? And tell her that I never forgot her.

MAGGY

The next day, Maggy glances at her watch for perhaps the hundredth time that afternoon. Except this time, it's not still far too early. It's time to leave. Pulling herself up from the armchair in her bedroom where she had been staring at her book without really reading anything, she steps in front of the full-length mirror propped against the wall for a final check.

Carefully, she smooths the fabric of her dark green wrap dress, one of the outfits bought at Lou's shop, and adjusts the chunky citrine necklace nestled between her collarbones. In the mirror, her eyes fall on the sensible brown shoes she had planned to wear and, next to them, the bright yellow Mary Quant boots that she hasn't had the heart to return to the attic just yet. On a whim, she reaches for the yellow boots and pulls them on.

They shine brightly back at her in the mirror and she smiles. She looks so unlike the woman she has been for years, the woman she's avoided catching sight of in reflective surfaces because the person staring back didn't look like the woman she felt like inside. Without the cloak of her black baggy clothes, she feels truly visible for the first time in years and there's something terrifying about it, but exhilarating too.

For an instant, she falters, torn between excitement and nerves. She sends a quick message to her WhatsApp group with her old girlfriends, telling them she's about to leave. A few messages ping back instantly, wishing her luck. And then she grabs her handbag and heads downstairs, pulling on her blue coat and stepping out the front door into the brisk but bright afternoon.

The ten-minute drive to the nearby village feels like a particularly long ten minutes today. She chose the walled garden as their meeting place as it felt like a good neutral location. It's a place she often brings visitors to the area, liking to show off this little slice of countryside. But did she also choose it for the romance of the place? The smell of the late autumn flowers in the air, the golden leaves on the trees dancing in the breeze? She pushes the thought from her mind. *He might not recognise me. He might have changed as much as I have. He might be nothing like the young man I once loved.* She tries to prepare herself for disappointment as all the while her heart beats hard and fast.

As soon as she steps through the gate and within the garden walls, she calms a little. This is a place she has visited countless times over the years, after all, and she is greeted by the familiar sights and sounds of the garden in autumn.

The first person she spots is the gardener Robert, leant over

226

one of the beds with a large watering can in his hand. As she sees him, she feels her shoulders relaxing slightly, the sight of his familiar figure as comforting as the view of the garden itself.

He looks up and catches her eye and his eyebrows rise in surprise.

'Wow. You look wonderful, Maggy. Those boots!'

Her cheeks grow warm.

'Thank you, Robert. You don't think they're a bit ... much?'

She looks down at her feet now, suddenly worried. *Who am I kidding with my new haircut and new clothes? I'm still just the same me.*

But Robert's smile reassures her.

'I might not know much about clothes, but I do know a lot about plants and those boots are pure daffodil. Brilliant. You look lovely, Maggy.'

She tucks a strand of hair behind her ear and suddenly scans the garden.

'Thank you. I'm actually meeting an old friend ...'

The nerves return in a flash, making her almost want to turn round and walk straight back out through the garden gate.

'Ah, I think he might be out the back on the terrace,' replies Robert.

Maggy glances to the archway at the rear of the garden that leads out onto the walled walkway overlooking the meadow.

'Can I get you anything from the café?' Robert asks.

'Perhaps a pot of tea, please,' Maggy says quietly, her eyes not moving from the far side of the garden.

'I'll get one of the girls to bring it over.'

'Thank you, Robert.'

There's a pause, Maggy suddenly not able to move. But then Robert's voice reaches her again, its tone kind and encouraging.

'Go on, Maggy, you can't waste an outfit like that on a scruffy old gardener like me.'

They share a final smile, and with Robert's encouragement still in her ears, she makes her way through the garden that is so familiar towards the man who was once just as well known and dear to her, but long ago disappeared from her life.

When she reaches the archway, she ducks beneath the hanging branch of a climbing rose, a few peach-coloured blooms still clinging on and filling the air with their scent. And then she is out on the terrace, facing a figure with his back to her and the stretching view of the meadow beyond, the large oak tree dripping orange leaves onto the long grass. He is tall and has filled out a little, but is still slim, dressed in dark jeans, a tweed jacket and with a navy woolen scarf tucked in at the collar. Unruly curls brush the nape of his neck, but they are grey now and shorter than when they were both young.

At the sound of her footsteps, he turns round. His face is lined, his eyebrows flecked with grey, and unfamiliar tortoiseshell glasses resting on his nose, but his dark brown eyes are the same and as his mouth spreads into that smile she could never forget, Maggy feels the years dropping away.

'Hello, Yellow.'

His voice is deeper than she remembers and coloured now with an American accent, but his voice is still so familiar that it makes her skin tingle as she looks across at the man he has become, leaning against the garden wall and with a smile still on his lips. *It's really you*, she thinks, *after all this time*.

'Hello, Simon,' she replies. As she takes in the lines on his face and the grey of his hair, she feels suddenly conscious of how much she must have changed too. She's an old woman now, nothing like the girl she once was. But if he feels any shock or disappointment, he hides it well.

He opens his arms slightly and steps forward.

'May I?' he says, the first hint of hesitation appearing in his voice.

And then, more than fifty years since their last meeting, they are stepping into one another's arms and hugging tightly. He smells like expensive aftershave and old books and she takes a shameless breath of him, feeling her heart race all over again, just like it did when she was nineteen years old and falling in love against all her better judgement.

Once they part, they are suddenly a little awkward with one another, Maggy not quite knowing where to look.

'Um, shall we sit down?' he says, gesturing at the wooden picnic table beside them. 'I thought this could be a good spot?'

'Perfect,' replies Maggy, lowering herself somewhat slowly onto the bench, feeling her knees ache as she does so. 'I ordered us some tea.'

'Oh, marvellous. I must admit, I do miss British tea, there's really nothing quite like it.'

The waitress arrives and sets out the tea things. Once she's gone, Simon reaches for the pot to pour, and Maggy notices the flash of a wedding band on his left hand. She can't help it;

her heart sinks a little. *What was I expecting?* she tries to tell herself. *What was I hoping for?*

They sip their tea, Maggy burning her tongue slightly but grateful for something to do with her hands. They both place their cups down at the same time, a silence descending.

'So,' Maggy says eventually, 'here we are. I hope you like it, this is one of my favourite spots.'

She glances around, taking in the view of the meadow, the trailing ivy and roses on the wall and the sound of birdsong in the trees. But Simon isn't looking at the meadow or the garden, he is looking straight at Maggy, his eyebrows knitted together and his smile long gone.

'Maggy, I owe you an apology.'

His tone is so serious that it makes Maggy squirm slightly. In all their messages, this is the thing they've skirted around, keeping the conversation light and friendly. For her, the questions have been at the front of her mind, but she's wondered if perhaps he had forgotten how things ended between them. He certainly hasn't hinted at it until now.

'Oh, that was all so long ago,' she says, waving a hand in the air. 'It's OK.'

Simon shakes his head. 'No, it's not OK, Maggy. What I did to you was terrible. To just leave like that without saying goodbye. It's unforgiveable.'

He looks in pain as he speaks and despite the shock and hurt she felt all those years ago at being left so abruptly, she finds herself feeling sorry for the man who sits in front of her now, something she could never have imagined feeling back then.

'So why did you leave? And where did you go, Simon?'

Maggy asks a lifetime later as the breeze wraps around them both in a garden that she has come to love.

Simon rubs his chin.

'I should have reached out years and years ago, I know that. It might have been due a long time ago, but now we're here, I need to tell you how deeply sorry I am for how I treated you, and to try, well, not to excuse myself, as I don't believe I deserve that, but at least to explain.'

'Go on,' Maggy says, her heart thumping, 'I'm listening.'

The last of the summer swallows loop above them in the sky and autumn leaves rustle in the garden's trees behind them, but Maggy and Simon are focused only on one another as Simon finally tells his story.

'I should start by saying how happy those months we spent together that summer were for me. From the moment we met, you were just such fun, so quick to laugh, so joyfully light-hearted.'

Maggy wonders if anyone she knows now would ever think of her in such a way.

'And you were such a good listener,' continues Simon. 'I remember the long talks we'd have, although, to my shame, if I think back now, I realise it was mostly *me* doing the talking. But it was such a relief to have someone I felt I could talk with so freely. You just had that effect – you were so easy to be with, so easy to talk to. I didn't really have that in my life at that point. I had friends, yes, but I never felt I could truly be myself around them. With you, I felt like I could relax and be me. But even that was a lie. There was so much about myself that I hid from you. But somehow when I was with you I forgot about all of that. The way you looked at me ...'

He blushes now and Maggy feels her own cheeks growing warm. Thinking back to it all now, she realises how young she must have seemed, how much like a doting puppy following him around everywhere and looking at him with such open adoration in her eyes.

'It made me feel wonderful. *You* made me feel wonderful, Maggy.'

If only he knew how much the same had been true for her. But, of course, he must have done. It was so obvious, Maggy can see that now. She was about as subtle in her love as a male peacock flaunting his feathers. She wants to say something but senses that he has more to share and that the saying of it isn't easy for him. She lets him continue.

'But then when you told me about Alan's proposal, it was like being shaken awake from a dream. I realised I'd been taking advantage of you. What Alan was offering you ... I could never give you that.'

He hesitates and she takes her chance to speak.

'You know that stuff didn't matter to me back then – the house, the money ... I was quite ready to live life as a happy pauper.'

She laughs a little, trying to make light of her words. But his expression is serious.

'It wasn't about all that,' he says with a shake of his head, 'No, the problem was that I knew that however much I loved you, I could never love you like he loved you. I could never love you like you deserved to be loved.'

He fiddles with the wedding band on his hand, his hair falling slightly in front of one eye.

'It was cowardly to leave like I did without giving you a proper explanation. You deserved that at the very least. But back then I was still so confused, so ashamed. And the more time that passed, the more I convinced myself that I had no right to contact you. Why would you want to hear from me? The years went by and I never forgot you, but I never searched for you either. I couldn't bring myself to. And then when I received your message a few days ago … I showed my husband and he convinced me that I had to contact you. I had to see you again and I had to apologise to the only woman I ever loved.'

Husband. Understanding arrives for Maggy like the onset of dawn. After all these years, here it finally is, the real answer to the question that has never left her. There are tears in Simon's eyes and Maggy realises her own are damp too.

'Oh Simon,' she says, reaching for his hand.

For a while they stay like that, holding hands across the table and letting their tears fall quietly, old pain, old memories and old love flowing with each drop.

'Goodness me,' Maggy says eventually, reaching for a tissue in her handbag and passing one to him too, 'what are we like? We're far too old to be sitting in a garden weeping into our tea like this.'

As he accepts the tissue with a sniff, he finally smiles.

'You're right. What would our younger selves think?'

'Well, they'd be appalled at our wrinkles for starters.'

He lets out a laugh, still dabbing at his eyes.

'But I think they'd be proud too,' she says, her voice

softening. 'Proud of us for finally speaking the truth with one another.'

A feeling of relief washes over her. She may have come to this garden hoping for a different outcome, perhaps even a second chance at love, but, more than anything, what she wanted was the truth. Finally knowing it feels like shrugging off a heavy layer and turning to face the elements bare-skinned but free.

'Dear Maggy,' Simon says, his eyes welling a little again. 'I'm just sorry it took so long.'

Maggy swallows hard, trying to hold back another wave of tears. After all this time, it's a sort of comfort to hear that he *did* love her, just not quite the way she loved him.

'So, what happened after you left?' she asks finally. 'I came to your apartment, but your neighbour told me you'd moved?'

'Ah.' He readjusts his glasses and rubs his chin. 'I still feel awful about that, I was such a coward to just up and leave. But as much as I wanted to tell you the truth about myself, I knew that first I had to finally tell my parents. I took what little I owned and headed back to visit them, thinking that I might stay there for a while and figure out my next steps.'

'How did they react?'

His eyes glisten again now.

'Not well.'

He lets out a long sigh.

'I knew they might be upset, but I wasn't prepared for how angry they'd be. My father told me I wasn't welcome in their home – my home – any more. I didn't even have time to pick up the last of my things that I'd left behind when I moved to London. He threw me out.'

Maggy tries to imagine anything her children could possibly do that would make her turn her back on them like that. She can't think of a single thing. They might be adults now, but they are still her babies. They always will be and there's nothing they could ever do to stop her loving them. Even when they have their misunderstandings, she thinks, suddenly recalling her last somewhat strained conversation with Charlotte and experiencing a stab of regret.

'Oh Simon. I'm so sorry you had to go through that. I just don't understand how any parent could do that to their child.'

'I think it was quite common back then,' continues Simon. 'I've since made many friends who, unfortunately, had similar experiences. But the thing I've found is that family isn't always the people you were born to. You can create your own family, built up of people you choose and who choose and accept you exactly as you are.'

'I'm so glad you've found that. I'll admit, when you left, I was sad and confused and at times angry. But I always wanted the best for you. I hoped that you'd made it to Los Angeles and made it big as an actor. I kept wondering if I'd see your face on a film poster one day.'

Simon laughs now and the sound transports Maggy back through the years again.

'Well, I did make it to Los Angeles. After my parents threw me out, I took a live-in job at a local hotel for a while to scrape together enough money for the tickets and then I left. But I can't say I ever had any great success. I got the odd bit part here and there, but my career never really took off. I eventually switched to working as an assistant at an agency that represented actors and found I was much better at getting other people's careers off the ground than I was my own. It's what I've done ever since – I have my own agency now.'

'You seem happy,' says Maggy.

Simon smiles. 'I am.'

'I'm so glad to hear that. I suppose dreams can change over time – just because we had one dream once doesn't mean that's the only life we could find happiness in. And I've found that life is less straightforward than that. So much seems down to chance and choices that could have gone differently. But maybe that's OK.'

Maggy's life could have taken a different turn all those years ago. But despite how real her feelings for Simon felt back then, she's glad that their relationship never lasted beyond that summer, for both of them. What felt like an ending at the time became a new beginning for each of them.

Now she feels at a crossroads again, uncertain of the way ahead. Her marriage is over and her children are grown up. She realises that she has been trying to hold on to a life that doesn't exist any more. Instead of looking back, she needs to start looking forward and planning how she is going to spend the rest of her life.

'So, how's Alan?' Simon asks.

'Actually, we separated a few years ago.'

'Oh, I'm sorry to hear that.'

'Don't be. It has been hard, of course, really hard actually, but I think I'm getting ready to move on. We had a happy life and I really was blessed with our children. But I don't know … Perhaps it ran its course.'

She feels a sense of peace descending as she says the words aloud. Over the past week or so, she's taken more action in her own life than she has done in years – finding Lou, meeting Donna, helping out in the shop, changing up her wardrobe and tracking down Simon. None of this would have happened if she and Alan were still together and she finds herself thinking how sad it would have been if she'd missed out on these experiences.

The old friends drift into a long conversation about their lives. Maggy tells Simon proudly about her children and grandchildren and he shows her photos in his wallet of his godchildren. He tells her about his agency and about his husband Michael, an art dealer, and their home together in Manhattan.

'So, are you seeing anyone then?' Simon asks eventually, making Maggy laugh in surprise.

'I think I'm too old for that.'

'Never! You're still a spring chicken.'

She raises an eyebrow, his brown eyes sparkling at her as she smiles back at him.

'Simon, I don't think anyone would describe either of us as spring chickens any more.'

'You're probably right. But there's still plenty of time.'

LOU

The Sycamore Inn is everything Lou imagined it would be. The lawn in the garden is bright green and perfectly trimmed, the sycamore tree in its centre showering the grass with golden leaves that look as though they were placed there on purpose.

Her room is on the second floor and looks over the garden and out to the forest-covered hills in the distance beyond the river. The striped white-and-navy sheets are soft and crisp at the same time and the lines match up perfectly with the edges of the bed, which is positioned exactly in the centre of the room, with a series of photographs of autumnal trees hanging above. Everything has been thought of, from the robe and slippers in the wardrobe to the travel iron, the extra blankets and the vast array of tiny sachets of tea and coffee on the dressing table. The whole place is ordered and neat with an underlying warmth. *Just like Donna*, Lou thinks to herself.

She is alone in her room, settling herself, while Donna and

John catch up downstairs. Donna's husband collected them from the airport earlier, greeting Lou warmly, and the rest of the family – Donna's daughter, granddaughter and son-in-law – will be coming in a couple of days. Brooke and Tom took time off work to be able to meet Lou before she heads home again; when Donna told her this, Lou struggled to hide her emotion. After having felt so alone for so long, it feels a little overwhelming to have acquired a new family so suddenly.

Lou and Donna are planning on making the trip upstate to the address given to them by the adoption agent tomorrow and Lou can't decide whether she is more excited or nervous about what might happen when they arrive.

The jet lag is kicking in and her head swims, her limbs heavy. She leaves her suitcase unopened and flops down on the bed, kicking off her shoes. The afternoon sun streams in through the windowpane, warming her cheeks as she closes her eyes.

She is woken by a light tapping on her door. Lou stretches and looks around, disorientated. Her phone tells her she has been asleep for over an hour.

'I'm coming!' she replies, straightening her dress and pulling herself up from the bed, her socked feet stepping across the pristine, soft carpet.

Donna is standing in the hallway. As she sees Lou, she smiles.

'Ah, I was right, I thought you must have fallen asleep.'

'How can you tell?' replies Lou, opening the door wider so Donna can step inside.

'Your hair,' replies Donna, gesturing at her own head.

Lou catches sight of herself in the mirror and laughs – one side of her hair is still pinned neatly, but the other is a messy tangle of pins. She pulls out the remaining pins, shaking her head.

'That's better.'

'I must admit, I don't know why you go to so much effort,' says Donna. 'You'd look just fine in regular clothes and with your hair as it is.'

Lou perches on the edge of the bed and Donna sits in the armchair in the window opposite. Somewhat self-consciously, Lou arranges the skirt of her green fifties dress, worn with thick black tights and a chunky-knit cream cardigan embroidered with colourful flowers. She feels overdressed opposite her cousin, who is in her standard outfit of jeans and jumper, but this time with the embroidered name of the inn on the chest of her sweatshirt.

'I guess I just love to dress up,' Lou says, trying to put the way she feels about her relationship with clothes into words. 'I got my love of bright colours and patterns from my mum. And I love the style of vintage clothes – I feel like the shapes suit me better than the clothes that are in shops now. But it's more than that. When I get dressed each morning, it's like I'm choosing the kind of person I want to be and the way I want to feel, even if I don't always actually feel that way on the inside. And there's a kind of sense of order to doing my hair and make-up in a similar style every day. I suppose it makes me feel in control.'

'Hmm, I hadn't thought of it like that,' says Donna thoughtfully, frowning slightly. 'Maybe we're not so dissimilar after all.

Even if you might not think that from looking at us.'

She smiles then and Lou smiles back. Then her eyes drift behind Donna to the view outside, where she can see a family walking down the sidewalk towards Main Street, flags fluttering from the doors of shops, the sky above the town a sharp blue, the orange of the trees standing out like fireworks.

'Your town is beautiful,' she says.

'So is yours,' replies Donna.

Lou returns her attention inside, looking down for a moment in her lap, fiddling with a loose thread on her jumper.

'I suppose it is,' she says hesitantly, 'but if I'm honest, I'm not sure how much longer I'll stay there.'

She hasn't told anyone yet. But as Donna slept beside her on the plane, Lou spent the journey thinking it all through. By the time they had landed, it felt like she had made a decision.

'What?' says Donna now, her eyebrows rising in surprise. 'I thought you were going to be moving into your own flat soon? And I know the break-in was a setback but ... moving?'

Lou sighs, the jumper thread wrapped tightly around her finger. 'It's not just the break-in. The shop was struggling before then. But having to sort the repairs and everything on top of that ... It's just made me think that the whole thing might not be viable. Maybe it's better just to close now before I work my way through the last of my savings. If I sell the building, I could do anything. Travel, maybe.'

She tries to picture herself on a sunny beach somewhere, a cocktail in her hand. It doesn't feel exactly her – she's not that much of a beach person. But wandering around unknown cities, perhaps? She could come back to America, maybe. Spend some time in New York, perhaps come back to Cold Spring and visit Donna again.

'But what about Maggy?' asks Donna. 'And didn't you say you'd made friends with some other people who have their own businesses?'

Lou shifts uncomfortably as she pictures Maggy, bringing her tea in the room that quickly felt like hers, and Beth and Danie, chatting away with them over Lou's morning coffee.

'I love Maggy,' Lou admits, 'and the other business owners have been really kind and welcoming. But with Mum and Dad gone, I don't know if I really belong there any more.'

She isn't really sure that she belongs anywhere.

'But anyway,' she says, turning back to Donna and pushing thoughts of home away, 'we're here now. I'd love to see more of the town. Have you got work to do now or would you like to come with me on a walk?'

'I can give you a tour!' Donna says brightly, her expression turning from concerned to eager.

They don't talk any more about Lou's plans or about what will happen tomorrow when they reach Eleanor's. Instead, Lou tries to just focus on the here and now as she and Donna set off down the streets that Donna has walked up and down her whole life, Luna trotting at her heels. Lou pushes away thoughts of Somerset as she takes in the clapboard houses and the many antique stores and cafés that line Main Street, Donna pointing out particular points of interest as they go. For now, Lou is here in Cold Spring with her cousin. Everything else can wait.

MAGGY

Eventually, the two old friends have to say goodbye, Simon heading back to his brother's house in London where he is staying.

'I think I'll stay here for a while,' Maggy says as he stands to leave. The sun is starting to dip on the horizon, washing the meadow in an apricot glow. There's a chill in the air, but she wraps her coat tighter around her, enjoying the feeling of being wrapped up but with the chilly air on her cheeks.

'Please say we can stay in touch?' says Simon.

'Of course.'

They reach for one another a final time, holding each other tightly.

As they part, they both brush their eyes rapidly and laugh.

'And if you're ever in New York, please do come and visit.'

'Thank you, I'd like that.' For once, the thought of a trip to New York some day in the future doesn't feel like such a crazy idea. It's a place Alan would never have agreed to visit, Maggy thinks with a thrilling sense of freedom.

And then with a final wave, Simon turns away, ducking under the climbing rose and then disappearing from sight.

For a few moments, Maggy sits at the bench surrounded by the finished tea things and her memories of their conversation and their time together all those summers ago. Sparrows flit in and out of the vines growing along the garden wall, the grass in the meadow swaying in the afternoon breeze.

'Is everything OK?'

It's only as she hears Robert's voice and looks up to see him looking at her with concern that she realises her cheeks are damp with tears. She wipes her face, regarding the moisture there with surprise, and smiles.

'Yes,' she says, 'everything actually is OK.'

He puts his hands in his pockets and then removes them again.

'Would you like to join me?' she asks on a whim, pointing at the empty seat on the bench. 'If you have time for a break that is? It seems too gorgeous here to leave just yet.'

A broad smile breaks across his face.

'It would be my pleasure. Just give me one sec …'

He disappears, returning with a tray laden with two large slices of carrot cake. Then he settles himself opposite her and they begin to talk. She tells him about her time in London as a teenager and about Simon and Alan. He listens earnestly, nodding and chipping in with questions every now and then. To her relief, he doesn't express any judgement about her fling with Simon; he isn't the judgemental sort. And she does her best to explain the whirlwind of it all, how for a few months she got caught up in this other possible story before returning to the pages of her own, settling down and finding happiness in her marriage and her family life, even if it felt as though by doing so she was closing a door too. Eventually, she describes to him the recent divorce and how hard she has found it living alone.

'Oh, I can understand that,' he says. 'Ever since Jane died, I must admit even my little cottage has felt too big, unless the grandchildren are over, of course. I'll be honest with you, I've even found myself talking to the cat every now and then. Does that make me mad?'

'Not at all. It's understandable. You and Jane were married a long time. I miss seeing her here.' Maggy glances around, half expecting to see the woman who she encountered so many times on visits over the years bustling out through the archway with a pot of tea on a tray. But it's been a long time since that happened.

'I miss her too,' says Robert. 'I think I always will, in a way. But it's been a while now. Things change. Just like this garden.' He gestures around him. 'I felt so grateful for this place when Jane was ill and then after she passed away. However bad the night might have been, I knew that in the morning I would come here and the flowers would still be growing, the birds would still be singing. That's the thing about nature, it just keeps on going. Even if there's a tough winter and it looks like everything's died back, come spring, new shoots always force their way out of the earth. I've learned a lot from this garden.'

Maggy looks at him a little more closely. It's the most he's opened up since she's known him. They usually exchange news about the grandchildren – both his and hers being frequent visitors of the garden – and make comments on the weather or what's in bloom. It's one of those acquaintances that she wouldn't exactly go as far as to call a friendship but that she would miss deeply if it were to be removed from her life.

As she looks at him, she notices a few dark spots appearing on his shirt and overalls. She tilts her head to the sky just as the heavens open, raindrops falling heavily on her face.

'Oh!'

The air rings with the sound of rain falling into the empty teacups and onto the leaves of the plants and trees in the garden.

'Come on,' says Robert, reaching for her arm.

Arm in arm, they hurry back through the archway and into the main garden, which Maggy notices is completely empty, the usual volunteers nowhere to be seen.

'Where is everyone?' she asks as he ushers her into the greenhouse. Rain clatters against the glass roof, but it is at least dry in here.

'Oh, I sent them home,' Robert says, pulling out a chair at one of the tables for her to sit down and sitting opposite. 'We're technically closed now, so I told the other staff I'd do the final bits and lock up.'

'Oh, I'm sorry! You should have told me to leave too!'

'Don't be silly,' he replies. 'It's nice to talk, honestly.'

'It is,' agrees Maggy.

'Unless you want to leave, that is. Please don't let me bore you.'

'You're not boring me at all, Robert. And I don't want to leave,' she says, realising how true it is as she says it.

'Good,' he says, his tone relieved.

As the rain drenches the empty garden outside, they continue their conversation, drifting from their pasts to gardening to their grandchildren and round again.

The sound of Maggy's phone buzzing suddenly interrupts them.

'Oh, do you mind if I take a look? It might be one of the children …'

'Of course not, I know what it's like.'

But as she draws her phone out of her bag, she sees it's not from her children. It's a message from Pete, giving her an update about the progress he has made today.

'I should probably head back and let you go home too.'

'Of course,' replies Robert. He hesitates, rubbing his hands on his overalls. 'Well, this has been nice.'

He looks down at his muddy boots before glancing up again, his cheeks pink.

'Do you think we could perhaps do it again some time? It's been nice to talk.' He coughs now, clearing his voice, 'I can't remember when I last had such a nice conversation. And with such nice company.'

It's Maggy's turn for her cheeks to glow. This whole day has been so unexpected, but she knows she will be leaving the garden feeling lighter and happier than when she arrived. She looks at the gardener she has known for years, wearing his muddy overalls and anxious expression, his hands rough from gently tending the plants, and thinks back to what Simon said earlier. *'It's never too late.'* She remembers something that Robert said earlier too, about how spring buds manage to poke their way out of the soil no matter how long or cold the winter.

And then she smiles.

'How about a drink at the pub tomorrow night?'

DONNA

The address takes Donna and Lou to a town three hours north of Cold Spring, a town not dissimilar to Cold Spring itself, Donna thinks as she drives them both past the town's welcome sign and along the main street. They had set off that morning, both of them waking early. John had hugged Donna tightly as they said goodbye.

'Good luck,' he whispered to her, 'I hope you find what you're looking for. And I'll be here when you get back.'

Both Donna and Lou have been quiet on the journey, the radio filling in the long gaps in their conversation. Donna doesn't mind the quiet – it has given her time to think. Now, she glances briefly at Lou in the passenger seat, who is resting one hand on the windowsill, her head tilted to look outside at the town around them.

Donna pulls up at a red traffic light, watching as an elderly woman crosses the road, her arm linked with what looks like her son. Behind them follow a woman in her forties holding the hand of a child. A jogger runs by, a dog on a lead following beside.

'It's so . . . normal,' she says as she waits for the light to change. 'I don't know why, but I imagined her living on the other side of the world. Maybe in a beach hut somewhere exotic.'

Donna does know why. It's easier to accept that her birth mother was living in a totally different world from her, not *here* and so close by all along.

'I know what you mean,' replies Lou. 'It seems nice, but I don't know how you end up in a small town like this if you're not from here. And we know Eleanor was not from here.'

'Maybe she married someone who was,' Donna thinks aloud.

'Well, we'll hopefully find out soon,' Lou replies as Donna pulls away as the light turns green.

A glance at the satnav tells her they are just five minutes away. They pass through the centre of town, through a square with a bandstand not dissimilar to the one in Cold Spring, before crossing through to the other side of town, where the houses eventually become further apart, woodland interspersed in between. Following the instructions on the screen, Donna takes a turning through an open gate with a mailbox and down a bumpy track, pulling up outside a cottage clad in a similar-coloured wood to the surrounding trees, making it almost disappear into the forest. There is a separate garage with a car parked in front.

They both sit in silence, looking ahead at the house. It has a wraparound porch and Donna spots marks on the boards where it looks like a bench used to be. There is an empty bird feeder hanging from one of the posts. She tries to glimpse inside the house, but the curtains are drawn.

A tapping makes both Donna and Lou jump, turning away from the house to look out the passenger window, where an elderly woman is standing with her hands on her hips. She is wearing jeans and hiking boots, a set of keys in her hands. Donna takes in the woman's lined face and grey eyes, trying to spot something of herself. The woman's expression is suspicious, one eyebrow raised.

With a shaking hand, Donna presses the button to wind down the windows.

'Can I help you?' asks the woman sharply.

Donna can't speak.

'Hello,' Lou says, leaning slightly out the window. 'My name's Lou and this is Donna. We're looking for Eleanor.'

'You're from England like Eleanor?' the woman replies in an accent not dissimilar to Donna's.

Donna blinks rapidly, her shoulders sinking slightly. Lou looks at her for a second, but when Donna says nothing, she turns back to the woman outside.

'I am, yes. Although we've come from Cold Spring, today, where my friend lives. So, you're not Eleanor? We were given this as her home address.'

The woman shakes her head, the keys in her hand jangling as she does.

'No, I'm her friend. Have been for more than fifty years. The name's Connie. I'm just checking in on the place for her.'

'So she's not here?' asks Lou.

The elderly woman pauses, a frown on her face.

'No,' she replies after a moment's hesitation. 'How did you say you knew her?'

Finally, Donna finds her voice. She leans forward to get closer to the window.

'We're family.'

For the first time, Connie looks properly in Donna's direction. She frowns, then her mouth opens slightly.

'How old are you?' she asks, pointing at Donna. 'If you don't mind me asking.'

Donna tells her.

'Oh,' replies Connie, her face turning pale and her hands dropping away from her hips. 'Oh. I think I know who you are.' She stares at Donna and Donna stares back, her heart pounding.

Eventually, Connie collects herself and gestures towards the cottage.

'It might be better if we talk inside.'

DONNA

The cottage is sparsely furnished, the walls decorated with faded squares marking out where pictures must have once hung. It is light and airy, with white floorboards and large windows that look out into the woodland, making it feel as though the house is part of the forest itself. Connie leads them through to a room that is only identifiable as a sitting room by the large navy sofa in its centre, the rest of the room bare, apart from a few boxes stacked in one corner.

'Have a seat,' says Connie.

Donna hesitates and then sits down on the very edge of the sofa cushions. She has a strong sense of not wanting to touch anything, but at the same time wanting to spend a long time looking around every single room in this house.

'I'm fine here,' Lou says, perching on the edge of a large box labelled 'books'. 'You take the sofa, please.'

Connie shrugs and then sits down next to Donna, letting out a little grunt as her knees creak.

'So,' says Connie, making the one small word sound like an entire sentence.

Donna can hear birds singing outside and the sound of her heart thudding in her ears. But other than that, there is quiet. She can't believe she is here. In her mother's house. Except her mother isn't here and the house has an eerie feel to it, a sense of having been recently abandoned.

'I'm right, aren't I?' Connie says suddenly, turning to Donna and unexpectedly placing a hand on her knee. Donna nearly flinches, surprised by the warm gesture from someone who has seemed so bristly up until this point. The older woman's voice seems softer now too. 'You *are* Eleanor's daughter, aren't you?'

Connie has tears in her eyes and Donna finds herself blinking rapidly too.

'I am,' she replies eventually, her voice shaking slightly. 'Although I only found out very recently. I spent my whole life up until a couple of weeks ago not knowing I was adopted.'

'Ahh,' Connie says, leaning back slightly and nodding, wiping quickly at her eyes and composing herself again, her hands settling in her lap.

Donna glances at Lou, who gives a weak but reassuring smile, watching them both intently but saying nothing.

Connie lets out a long sigh. 'I should explain. I said I'm Eleanor's friend, but that doesn't quite do it justice. We're best friends, have been for over fifty years. Although I've always thought "best friend" doesn't quite express it – it sounds like we're little girls in elementary school. Which I'm clearly not.'

She pauses then, giving them a wry smile, the lines around

254

her eyes deepening. Donna says nothing in response, hanging on to every word.

Connie clears her throat before continuing.

'We met back when we were both young women working in the same department store in New York City. I grew up in this very town but moved to the big city when I was young. I wanted to be where everything was happening, even if in reality that ended up meaning an apartment the size of a closet in Manhattan that some distant relative hooked me up with. I loved it though, at the time. I'd been working at Bloomingdale's for nearly a year when my manager put me in charge of training a new member of staff. She was British, about my age and her name was Eleanor. There was just something about her that I loved straight away. She didn't let anyone walk over her, and let me tell you, back then in New York City there were plenty of people – and when I say people, I mean men – wanting to stomp right over you. She was good at her job – she told me she'd worked at department stores in London. There was a steeliness to her that I admired. I might have been training her, but I ended up learning a lot from her.

'I always got the sense that there was some sadness there behind her confident exterior, though, like she'd been through something. But whatever it was, she clearly didn't want to talk about it. We became friends. When we weren't working, we went for drinks together after our shifts, or to the movies, or just walked together around the city, exploring. She lived in this boarding house in Brooklyn full of lots of other young women, which I knew she hated. So I asked her to move in with me. There was barely enough room for one person, let alone two, but somehow, we managed.

'One day, I came home from work, knowing Eleanor would be waiting for me. I'd worked a later shift than her that day. When I came in, I found her sitting in the middle of the apartment on the floor, hunched over a paper bag crying her eyes out. She was sobbing so hard I couldn't get much out of her at first, but eventually she opened up and told me it was her daughter's first birthday. Inside the paper bag was a cake that she'd bought from our favourite bakery down the street and the saddest little candle I've ever seen in my life.'

Connie shakes her head, wiping her eyes again. Donna feels as though she can barely breathe. Connie glances at her and Donna nods wordlessly, willing her to continue.

'She'd been distant all day,' Connie remembers. 'At work, I'd noticed her drifting off a few times, her eyes glazing over when she was supposed to be serving customers. I'd stepped in to help out but had no idea what was wrong. And now suddenly I did. Eleanor told me everything then, about this older man who had seduced her back in London and persuaded her to come to America with him, promising her a glamorous life. He was married, which I think caused a rift with her family back home in England. She arrived in the city knowing no one apart from this man. At first, things had been good, she told me. But then she got unexpectedly pregnant and everything started to unravel after that. He eventually left her for another woman when their baby was only weeks old. He left them with nothing.'

Connie reaches for Donna again, this time placing a hand on top of hers.

'I'm sorry, I'm talking about "the baby", but, of course, it was you. I can't quite believe it.'

'Neither can I,' admits Donna, taking in everything Connie has told her, the story of a mother she never knew existed until recently. She tries to picture the Eleanor of the photographs she has, living in an apartment with a much younger Connie in the centre of Manhattan. How often did she think of her?

As though hearing Donna's thoughts, Connie squeezes her hand.

'You have to know that she never forgot about you. I think she tried to put that part of her life behind her in order to cope. But once she had finally opened up to me, she talked about you often over the years, imagining what you might have been doing. I don't think she ever would have given you up if she felt there had been another choice. She thought it was the right thing to do. And maybe it was also the only thing, given the situation she had found herself in. Oh, I still can't believe you're here. Eleanor's daughter. Do you mind ... Do you mind if I hug you?'

The older woman feels thin as she wraps her arms around Donna, but she still squeezes so tightly she nearly takes Donna's breath away. A stifled sob makes Donna pull away and look over to Lou. She had almost forgotten that she was there. But now, as she looks at her wiping her face with her sleeve, a rush of sympathy washes over her. Eleanor wasn't just her birth mother, after all. She was part of a family once.

'I'm sorry, I should have introduced you properly, Connie,' Donna says. 'This is Eleanor's niece.'

Connie's eyebrows rise in surprise. 'You're Dotty's daughter?'

Lou's eyes brighten. 'So Eleanor talked about my mum with you?'

'Of course she did! She missed her sister terribly. I'm part of a big family and I think she was always quite envious of that, although we always tried to make her feel welcome – she became part of the family in a way, not having anyone else in America.'

'Mum wrote to her,' Lou says, reaching into the rucksack at her feet and pulling out the box of letters to show Connie. As she does, Connie sits up a little straighter.

'Dotty wrote to Eleanor?'

Lou nods. 'Although she never sent them. She didn't have her address. Mum wondered whether her sister forgot about her once she arrived in America.'

Connie pushes herself slowly and silently from the sofa and heads to the pile of boxes in the corner. After a few moments rummaging, she comes back with a small box, which she rests on her lap.

'I'm still sorting through Eleanor's things. A lot has been given away by now, but I've been storing up the more personal things. I found these just yesterday.'

She hands the box over to Lou, and Donna stands up to join her so she can see too. Carefully, Lou lifts out letter after letter. Each envelope has 'Dorothy Morris' written on the front in curling writing and an address in London. And stamped over each one in black letters is a postmark that reads, 'Returned to sender. Recipient no longer at this address.'

30 July 1955

Dear Dotty,

We made it! We are finally here, in New York City. The crossing was long and I've never felt so sick, but it was worth it when we arrived. It is even bigger and brighter than I imagined – buildings taller than anything in London.

We are living in a place called Brooklyn – the address is here so you can write back. It is a very bustling sort of a place, with not just Americans but people from all over the world. You would not believe the kinds of food and music and all the languages you hear. The one thing that unites everyone is the Dodgers. That is the team that everyone here supports. I know nothing about baseball, but I think I will have to learn quickly because it's like a religion here.

I haven't been to see the Empire State Building yet but have seen it from afar and Sydney promises we will go soon. He says he has some leads about a modelling job for me too. It's all going to happen for me, I can feel it.

I do miss you so, though. Sometimes at night, I wake up and expect to see you there. It is a little strange getting used to living with a man and learning how to wash and sort all his things – it has been a long time since we had shirts and trousers to clean and men's shoes to shine at home. I try to get it right for him, but I do sometimes burn the dinner – I'm nothing like as good a cook as Mother. But it is a relief not to have to hide any more and to be able to walk down the street holding one another's hand. I know you might not understand that, Dotty, but I hope one day you will.

*Are you taking care of my yellow dress? And how is
Mother? I didn't know whether to write to her too. I didn't
know if she would want to hear from me. But tell her I love
her. And I love you too, of course.*

Write soon, I long to hear from you.

Your sister,

Eleanor

26 October 1955

Dear Dotty,

I wonder whether my last letter never reached you? It's the
only reason I can think of for you not writing back, unless
Mother has decided to turn you against me. I can't let myself
think that, so instead I am writing again.

Autumn has arrived in Brooklyn, although they call
it 'fall' here. Which makes sense, I suppose, for the way
the leaves have started to drop off the trees around the
neighbourhood. Thankfully, it is cooler now. My neighbours
warn me that the winters here are beastly, but I can't help
but think they must be better than the heavy heat of the
summer.

Sydney has got a new job in the city. It is a junior role in
an insurance company, but he thinks it has good prospects.
It means he is rather busy now, what with working and
travelling to and from Manhattan. He often has to work
late, so I find myself on my own quite a lot of the time.
Apart from keeping on top of the housework, I use the time

while he is gone to go walking. I must have walked around most of Brooklyn by now, Dotty, and the things I have seen! I wish I could show them to you, but I will try to describe them instead.

As I walk, I pass through different neighbourhoods occupied by different nationalities. On one street you might hear Irish accents surrounding you and then you turn another street and it's all Italians. There are wonderful street vendors everywhere and I've been trying as much as possible – all the walking makes me starving! There are hot dogs and pretzels, of course, but my favourite is the man who sells paper bags filled with roasted chickpeas (they are not at all like our garden peas) tossed in the most delicious spices, unlike anything I have ever tasted before.

While I walk I also look in at all the department stores. When we first arrived, I thought I might try for a job in one of them while waiting for things with the modelling to take off. But now it looks like I won't be doing either for a while …

Oh Dotty, I have left the most important thing for last! I haven't quite worked out how to put it down on paper as it still doesn't feel real to me yet. I haven't even told Sydney yet – I have decided to do it straight after this. I am using this letter as practice to find the nerve to say the words aloud.

I am going to have a baby.

It took me a while to realise it. I thought I was just tired from all the walking and getting heavier from all the pretzels. But I found out today from the doctor. I still can't quite believe it. At first, I was frightened – I wasn't sure that I was ready to be a mother – but the idea is growing on me. I know it's not something we planned to happen so soon, but I think Sydney will be happy with the news. I hope he will be happy.

I can't stand the thought of having a baby, though, and being so far away from you and Mother. We are settled here now, what with Sydney's job, but I wonder if you and Mother would consider coming here? There's an apartment in our building which I know is up for rent – a family moved out just this week. I can ask Sydney to help with the cost of the boat fare – now he is working, hopefully we can stretch to it. I thought of writing to Mother, but I don't know if she would respond, or how she would react to my idea. Perhaps you can talk to her? If you tell her how much you want to come, maybe she will give in and do it for you, if not for me. Then we can be together again. I can show you Coney Island and you can try all the foods here for yourself and see the view across to the city. We can even go in to Manhattan together and visit the Empire State Building. And then you can get to know your niece or nephew when they arrive. How funny, Dotty, that you are going to be an aunt!

I do so hope to hear from you soon. I love you. I miss you.

Yours,
Eleanor

12 April 1956

Dear Dotty,

It has been a long time since my last letter. I must admit I was hurt when you didn't reply, so I put off writing again. And then, after that, I just didn't feel much like putting pen to paper. I haven't felt much like doing anything. This pregnancy has felt insufferably long. It hasn't helped that the winter has been just as ghastly as everyone warned me it would be. Sydney put a stop to my long walks – he thought it was too dangerous, what with all the ice and snow. I hated being cooped up inside, especially as I am on my own so much of the time.

But now it is spring and she is nearly here (I just feel certain she will be a girl) and I have decided I can't be cross with you any more. How are you, Dotty?

Do you remember that evening when I wore my yellow dress for the first time? When you watched me get ready and I made you laugh by practising my poses in the mirror and my catwalk walk along the floorboards? I think about moments like that often, about laughing together so hard that Mother told us to be quiet, but neither of us cared. Do you still laugh like that? I haven't laughed that hard in a long time.

But the baby will be here soon and then things will be different. It will be a new start for me and for Sydney too. When he sees his daughter, I feel certain that he will remember he loves me.

I miss you, Dotty.

Your sister,
Eleanor

1 May 1956

Dear Dotty,

This letter will only be short as I don't have much time, but I wanted to let you and Mother know that she's here. My girl is here. She arrived safely two days ago and she's perfect. I want to show her off to everyone, to the whole city if I could. Most of all, I want to show her to you.

I'll write again soon. I can't believe that I'm a mother.

Eleanor

25 June 1956

Dear Dotty,

I don't know where to start. Everything has gone wrong. I thought that the baby arriving had changed things with Sydney. He seemed more attentive at first and I really thought it could be the sign of a new start. But then he slipped into his old habits – coming back late and smelling of alcohol and a smell like violets that I've tried to ignore for months. One night he didn't come back at all. I must admit that when he showed up the next evening, I exploded. He called me hysterical and I know I should have tried to calm down, but that just made me angrier. How come when he shouts or kicks the table in frustration during one of our arguments, it's anger, not hysteria? And how come he is the one who gets to leave when our baby is made up of equal parts of us?

Because he's left. He finally admitted the truth – that he has been seeing some woman in the city. He said she makes him feel young again. I used to feel young. I can't remember what that feels like any more. Sometimes I have to remind myself that I'm only twenty.

I have been such a fool, Dotty. To think that I used to see good old Percy as boring. I long for boring now. I can't believe that I fell for Sydney's lies and was dazzled by his promise of a bigger life. I would give anything for my small life back.

I don't know what we're going to do. Sydney has paid for the apartment until the end of the month, but after that we're on our own. I have been looking at boarding houses, but none of them will take a woman with a baby. We have nowhere to go. If you get this letter, please, would you ask Mother to send money for a fare so that I can come home? I hate to ask, but I am desperate. We are desperate.

Please write back, Dotty. I need you. We need you.

Eleanor

DOTTY

Dotty didn't want to leave their London home behind. But her mother insisted that they couldn't stay there, not with gossip following them everywhere they went and with a house that felt too big now that it was just the two of them.

'I have some news,' she said to Dotty one afternoon. 'I've managed to find a job as a cleaner and house helper. With both your father and sister gone, there's really no choice. The job is in Essex. We're moving next week.'

'But ...' was all Dotty could manage, her mouth hanging open and her heart beating fast inside her chest. 'But what about Eleanor? We have to wait for her letter, otherwise she won't know where we've gone. She won't know how to write to us.'

Her mother turned away for a moment. As she frowned, Dotty thought she saw tears forming in her eyes, but when she turned back, her expression was hard again.

'You think your sister cares about us now? She made her

choice and she chose that man. Eleanor is gone and you'd better get used to the idea because she is never coming back.'

Dotty started to cry then, fat tears dripping down her cheeks. She thought of what Eleanor said to her when she left her with her favourite yellow dress. 'You can keep it safe for me until I see you next.' She wouldn't have said that if she intended to leave and never see Dotty again, would she?

'She has her man and she has New York,' her mother said. 'We can't compete with that. It's been months since she left. If she really cared about us, she would have written by now, wouldn't she?'

And Dotty couldn't answer that.

The day after Dotty and her mother leave London, Dotty wakes in her new bedroom, the Essex street outside eerily quiet to her city ears. At the same moment, a letter lands on the doormat of the Islington apartment with an airmail sticker attached to the front and a New York stamp in the corner. 'Dorothy Morris' is written in curling handwriting on the front. But with no one there to receive it, the letter remains on the doormat unopened. The letter is stamped again when the new tenants move in, this time with dusty footprints as a new family's furniture is carried through the front door.

A week later, the letter is found, half-torn and crumpled in the corner. The woman who discovers it, a young mother with a baby attached to her hip, examines it, noticing the postmark with interest. She doesn't know anyone who's ever been to America. But then the baby begins to cry and her curiosity disappears, pushed down like so much about herself at the insistent sound of her child's wails. She drops the letter in the bin, bouncing the baby on her hip and wondering if she should ever have had children at all.

And across the sea in a small apartment in Brooklyn, Eleanor waits for her sister's reply. But the waiting does no good. No letter ever arrives.

DONNA

In the near-empty house, the air feels heavy, the words from the letters still playing out before Donna's eyes. She pictures Eleanor sitting in an apartment in Brooklyn writing that final letter, a baby sleeping in a cot beside her as she wrote those panicked, desperate words. It feels impossible to imagine that she was that baby.

'It's so sad,' Lou says, sniffing and wiping her face. 'To think what might have happened if Mum had received Eleanor's letters …'

Connie nods, her own eyes damp too.

Donna's mind spins with it all. Eleanor never wanted to give her up. There's a sort of bittersweet satisfaction to knowing that she wasn't unwanted. Lou is right that the situation is so sad, so haunted by what could have been. But it's also hard for Donna to imagine a different kind of life for herself. If Dotty's mother *had* sent the money and Eleanor had returned to England, Donna would never have been to Cold Spring, the place where she feels so at home. She would never have met John. Brooke and Chloe would not exist. How can she wish away all those parts of her life? And yet it pains her to think that the life she has lived has been at the cost of the woman who brought her into the world.

Not knowing how to put any of this into words, she returns instead to the facts of the story.

'So how did you both end up here?' she asks Connie.

Connie looks around her as though remembering where she is.

'I never thought I'd want to come back to this town,' she admits, 'especially not after loving the city so much. But one day it just didn't feel as fun any more and I felt this urge to come home. I couldn't stand the thought of leaving Eleanor though. So I asked her if she would consider moving with me. I didn't think she would say yes, but she did. She said she'd grown tired of the city too. I think after everything she'd been through she had come to crave a quieter, simpler life. So we left Manhattan. Our apartment was so tiny that we managed to carry all our belongings with us on the train. We stayed with my family for a while until we sorted our own place – a cottage we lived in together until I got married.'

Connie smiles then, glancing down at her weathered wedding ring.

'I married my childhood sweetheart. A total cliché, I know. We hadn't seen each other in years – not since I left for New York City. But when we moved back, we reconnected. He loved Eleanor too. The three of us hung out a lot and somehow it was never awkward. We were all such good friends. She's godmother to our eldest, Sharon.'

'So Eleanor never married herself, then?' Lou asks.

'No. There were men, of course. She was Eleanor, after all. She was a total beauty when we were young – I always wished I could have her looks and figure. But nothing was ever serious. She said she preferred it that way. That way, she was in control of things.'

'I can understand that,' nods Donna.

'Her real love was our shop.'

'Your shop?' Lou asks eagerly, leaning a little closer.

Connie nods, a smile spreading across her face.

'Yes. With our experience at Bloomingdale's and Eleanor's skills with a sewing machine, we decided to open a dress shop in town together. Eleanor made most of the dresses herself and I handled sourcing things from other local seamstresses. It's changed a lot over the years, but it's still there today. My daughters run it now. It was Eleanor who taught them to sew.'

'I can't believe Eleanor had a shop too!' Lou says excitedly, a wide smile filling her face. 'Sorry, Connie, I should explain – I have my own shop selling vintage clothes. I got my love of fashion from Mum. She was a seamstress. Perhaps it was her sister who taught *her*.'

'Really?' asks Connie, her eyes wide. 'Well, isn't that something. I sure bet Eleanor would love that.'

A silence descends. Donna glances around the room. The sun filters in weakly through the branches of the trees outside, casting dappled patterns on the floorboards. She tries to picture Eleanor walking across the floor, perhaps pulling a book from the now-empty bookcases built into the far wall and curling up on this very sofa. What did she like to read? Did she wake early each morning, like Donna, or prefer to sleep in? What did she eat for breakfast every day? Thanks to Connie, she knows so much more about her birth mother now and feels she can picture her more clearly. But there is still so much she wishes she knew, all the tiny details that make up a person. And then there is the big question that remains unanswered.

'So where is Eleanor now?' asks Lou quietly, voicing the words that Donna has been too afraid to ask, the question that has been hovering unspoken in the air above them since they arrived. 'Are we … Are we too late?'

Connie looks down at her lap and then up again.

'Maybe, in a way … It's not what you think, though. You see, she moved a couple of weeks ago. To Maple Manor, just north from here. It's a nursing home.'

Donna's pulse quickens and as she catches Lou's eye, she sees the mirror of her own emotions in her expression: a hint of relief mixed with disappointment.

'She's not been herself for the past few years. It started with small things – forgetting a dinner we had invited her to or arriving on the wrong day. Once, my husband found her in the middle of town, standing by the bandstand. He said hello and asked what she was doing and she said she was waiting for the bus to take her to work at Bloomingdale's. He told me about it and we made sure to keep a closer eye on her after that. We'd check in on her all the time, trying to pretend it was just a normal visit, but secretly checking the cupboards and

272

the fridge and filling them if they were bare. I didn't want to offend her, you know?

'I think she tried to ignore the changes – all the moments of forgetfulness or confusion – but eventually I persuaded her to go to the doctor. I think even she knew something was wrong by then. When he gave her the diagnosis, she told me she wanted to give me power of attorney.

'I tried to keep her here for as long as was possible. She loves this house. She's always said how calm she feels here. But recently it became just too much for any of us. She knew that too, despite it all. She was the one who suggested moving, in the end, in one of her more lucid moments when it felt like I had my old friend back. I've been checking in on the place for her since she moved, sorting it all out to go on the market. Once it's sold, that will cover the cost of her care, at least.'

Connie shakes her head, her pale grey eyes glancing out the window.

'You just never expect it to happen to *you*, you know? Getting old. It's something I always thought would happen to other people, but not me. Not Eleanor.'

The sound of a truck rumbles in the distance, the first traffic noise Donna has noticed since arriving. It is so peaceful here, the kind of place Donna can imagine herself living if she were ever to retire completely from the inn. Not that she can see that happening. But as Connie's story shows, you just never know what is going to happen.

'Can we go and visit her?' she asks.

There's a brief pause.

'Of course,' Connie replies. 'I can drive you there myself.

273

But I should warn you … She gets confused easily. She doesn't always recognise me any more.'

Connie's eyes shine. And Donna suddenly thinks that she was right: 'best friend' doesn't feel a fitting term for a friendship that has lasted almost an entire lifetime. She hasn't experienced anything like that herself; the closest she has is her marriage to John. But maybe it's not too late to make friendship a priority in her life, to put in the effort she hasn't always in the past. She thinks of Maggy and her offer to come and visit one day. She will make it happen, perhaps next spring when the town is in bloom and the air is starting to grow warm. She will invite Lou too and show them her home in the spring. Now that these women are in her life, she doesn't want to let them slip away like so many connections that have fizzled out over the years. Life is too short.

'Before we go, I have to ask you something,' Connie says, turning to Donna. 'Are they nice, your adoptive parents? Have you had a good life?'

The question catches Donna off guard. She still hasn't spoken to her parents since they dropped the bombshell news of her adoption and after listening to Connie's story, it saddens Donna to think she didn't have the opportunity to meet Eleanor sooner. But as she thinks of her parents, she is overwhelmed by countless happy memories – of growing up with them in the Sycamore Inn and how they always made her feel so accepted, never pushing her to be more social than she was, but instead encouraging her interests, her love of books and numbers and lists. She thinks of her mother teaching her to cook, something that has brought Donna so much solace and calm over the years. She remembers them both consoling her countless times as a child when she struggled to fit in at school. Every single time, her parents would tell her that the problem was the other children, not her.

Her parents always made her feel as safe and secure as she feels in Cold Spring itself, the town she has never wanted to leave. And maybe that's why, she thinks now. Perhaps it isn't about the town itself but about them. They're the reason she has always felt such a strong sense of home. Her mom and dad.

'Yes,' she replies now. 'Yes, I have had a good life. And they're good people. I've never doubted how much they love me.'

Connie's eyes water again, but she nods, satisfied.

'Good. I'm glad. And I know Eleanor would be too. That's all she wanted for you.'

The three of them stand to leave. Before they go, Connie pauses.

'She called you Dorothy, you know.' Donna looks at Lou, their eyes meeting as Connie adds, 'Eleanor told me she named you after her sister.'

LOU

Maple Manor is just a twenty-minute drive from Eleanor's house, but it feels as though it is in the middle of nowhere.

'I researched a lot of places,' says Connie as she drives, Donna sitting in the front and Lou in the back, staring out the window, which is rolled down slightly, a breeze filling the car. 'I thought somewhere with lots of trees would make her feel at home. Well … you know, at least feel some sense of homeyness.'

Connie indicates and they turn off the highway and down a long drive, a large wooden sign telling them they have arrived. There are young trees lining the track and a patch of woodland in the distance behind the large cream building and series of smaller buildings behind that make up the care home. A lawn spreads out to one side, where Lou can see small groups of people on benches or walking around a bed of rose bushes, the nurses instantly spotted by their brightly coloured scrubs and the residents by their walking aids and the stoop of their shoulders. As they pull up, Lou watches them, thinking of her mum. Moving back home to become a full-time carer might not have been part of her life plan, but Lou will always be grateful that she was able to do it and that her mum was able to stay at home right until the end. They talked about it a lot and she knew it was what her mother wanted more than anything. But of course, not everyone has that choice.

She thinks back to what Connie told them back at the house and braces herself for how the meeting with Eleanor might go. Lou had been relieved to hear from Connie that she was at least still alive, but the relief had been followed by a wave of disappointment. If only she'd known about Eleanor before. If only they'd found her sooner.

Now, as Connie pulls up in the parking area and turns off the engine, Lou tries her best to calm her nerves. She knows how big this moment must be for Donna; she doesn't want her own emotions to overshadow that. And yet her skin feels hot, her heart jumping beneath her dress. This is why they are here, after all, the reason why she travelled all this way.

'Aren't you coming?' Donna asks Connie as she unbelts herself and opens the door. Lou does the same, reaching for her rucksack and slipping it over one shoulder. But Connie shakes her head, her lined hands resting on the steering wheel.

'I'll be here when you come out. I think it might be confusing for her if we all go in together. I'll be back to visit tomorrow. I've called ahead though, to let them know you're coming. They'll be expecting you at reception.'

'Are sure you don't mind waiting for us?' Lou asks.

Connie pulls a folded newspaper out from the compartment in the driver-side door. 'I'll be fine.'

Lou glances at Donna, trying to read her expression, but after a second's pause she simply nods, her lips set in a firm line.

'OK,' she replies. 'Well, we'll see you soon.'

'Thanks for bringing us, Connie,' Lou says. She smiles warmly at her aunt's friend, trying to communicate what she knows her mother would want her to say. 'And for everything else,' she adds. 'Eleanor is lucky to have a friend like you.'

Connie nods silently and unfolds her newspaper. Sensing that she needs some space, Lou steps out of the car and shuts the door softly behind her. Gripping her rucksack tightly under one arm, she joins Donna, the pair of them looking ahead at the 'Reception' sign that hangs above a set of doors, hanging baskets filled with past-their-best flowers on either side.

'Shall we?' she asks, placing a hand on Donna's elbow.

'Just give me a minute.'

A nurse passes by, pushing an elderly woman with thin white hair and half-moon glasses, her chin slumped slightly on her chest. Could she be Eleanor? Lou searches the woman's face, trying to see any similarity to her own mother. The nurse catches her eye and nods.

'OK, I'm ready now,' says Donna.

The warmth hits Lou as soon as they step inside, followed immediately by the smell – a mix of an antiseptic hospital smell and something softer and more floral. She spots a bowl of potpourri on a coffee table by the reception desk, magazines fanned out on the surface.

Donna steps up to the desk, Lou sticking close at her side.

The young woman behind the desk is looking down at her phone but looks up as Donna clears her throat.

'Hi there, how are you today?'

Donna ignores the greeting and gets straight to the point.

'We're here to see Eleanor Morris. Our names are Donna Greenwood and Louise Jackson.'

To Lou's surprise, the woman doesn't need to consult her computer or look at any notes before answering.

'Oh yes,' she replies brightly. 'Connie called earlier to say you'd be coming instead of her today. Eleanor is in her room right now, I think, but I can get someone to go and bring her down to the living room if you'd prefer? I think there's an art class going on in there right now, but there's plenty of space.'

Donna frowns. 'Can we visit her in her room instead?'

'Of course,' the young woman replies. Lou looks for a name badge and finds one pinned near the collar of her navy uniform. Mandy. She stands up, pressing a button on the desk. 'Let me just get someone to take over here and I can show you up myself.'

'Thanks, Mandy,' Lou says.

When they first pulled up to the drive, Lou had thought there was something soulless about the imposing cream building, but now she is actually inside she can see that the people here are just trying to make the best of what no one would consider an ideal situation. As Mandy leads them down a long corridor, Lou spots noticeboards covered with flyers advertising activities – a piano recital from a local musician, bridge nights, an arts and crafts club and details of a visiting hairdresser – as well as framed photos of smiling members of staff, their names and bits of information about them printed beneath.

A few doors are closed, but most are open, giving glimpses inside to near-identical rooms, most empty but some with quiet men and women lying in beds or sitting in armchairs by the window. In several rooms, televisions are playing, snippets of soap operas and documentaries leaking out into the corridor. There are a few other visitors in some of the rooms: a middle-aged woman in an armchair, while a young boy perches on the edge of a bed enthusiastically showing an old man in bright blue pyjamas a toy car. As they pass this door, the woman looks up and Lou catches her eye, a smile of understanding passing briefly between them before Lou, Donna and Mandy find themselves at the very end of the corridor.

'This is one of our woodland view rooms,' she says, pausing outside the final closed door. 'Your friend Connie was pretty insistent that Eleanor have a room facing the woods and luckily one had just become available.'

Her cheeks colour slightly then. Lucky for Eleanor, maybe, but not for the room's previous inhabitant, Lou thinks.

Coughing slightly, Mandy knocks lightly on the door and reaches for the handle.

'Eleanor, you have visitors,' she says as she pushes open the door.

The room is brighter than the others they have walked past, light shining in through a large window. Lou can make out the outline of trees through the glass, the leaves a vibrant wash of orange and red. Facing the window is a high-backed armchair, a pale cloud of white hair visible over the headrest, a hand resting on the armrest.

Mandy opens the door wider and points to a button on the wall. 'Just press this if you need anything and someone will come and help you.'

Lou has a sudden urge to reach for her arm and tell her not to leave. But Mandy smiles, nods at them both and turns away down the corridor.

Donna and Lou pause at the entrance to the room. It is similar to the other rooms, with its single bed, an armchair and a door which Lou assumes leads to an en suite, but she casts her eyes around quickly, taking in the tiny details that make this room Eleanor's. The bed is neatly made, a green-and-white crocheted blanket spread over the covers. Lou wonders who made it; perhaps Connie or one of Connie's daughters. Or did Eleanor herself choose the colours and spend hours working on the neat squares? There is a stack of books piled on the bedside table and Lou's heart jumps when she spots the familiar spine of an Agatha Christie, one of her mother's favourites. Also on the bedside table is a framed black-and-white photograph of two young women, their arms around one another as they smile at the camera from what looks like a beach, their hair blowing in their faces. Connie and Eleanor. Although Lou might only have met Connie as an old woman, her smile is still recognisable in the photograph, her eyes the same, apart from the lines that have appeared around them over the years. Lou wants to step closer and pick up the photograph to better examine the picture of Eleanor, but she suddenly realises that neither she nor Donna have said anything and are still standing dead still by the open door. She turns to Donna, who is staring ahead, her eyes fixed on the back of the armchair. Lou gives her a little nudge and together they step further into the room.

'Eleanor?' Lou says softly, edging round the chair, Donna following behind until they are standing with their backs to the window, facing the woman they have both come so far to see.

The old woman in the chair is slim but tall, dressed in a pair of navy trousers and a lilac sweater, a checked blanket over her knees. Her white hair is set in neat curls as though she has only recently been to the hairdresser, making Lou recall the flyer she saw on the noticeboard in the corridor. Her eyes are lightly closed, her hands resting on the armrests of the chair. She doesn't wear any jewellery apart from an oval locket on a thin gold chain that sits at her neck. The autumn sun shines on her face, illuminating her pale skin and making her white hair look almost as though it is glowing.

There is nowhere else to sit, so Lou perches on the end of the bed, Donna pausing before sitting down beside her. It feels strange to be sitting where Eleanor sleeps every night, but standing over her had felt awkward too; Lou remembers what Connie said about Eleanor often getting confused. She doesn't want to startle her.

'Eleanor?' Donna says now, slightly louder.

The woman in the chair blinks her eyes open, a hand darting to the locket around her neck before falling into her lap. Her eyes are a pale blue. *Just like Donna's, just like Mum's*, Lou thinks as she watches her glancing momentarily around the room and then back and forth between both.

'Hello. Is it time for dinner?' Her voice is soft, a faint English accent still discernible beneath a layer of American. She looks up at them both expectantly, her expression calm but enquiring.

Lou glances at Donna. But Donna doesn't meet her eye, instead she stares straight ahead, her hands clasped tightly in her lap.

'No,' replies Lou hesitantly, 'but I'm sure we can get you something if you're hungry?'

Eleanor tilts her head to one side and then shakes it.

'You know, I don't think I am.'

She smiles placidly, smoothing the blanket on her lap and adjusting it so the pattern is straight in a gesture that reminds Lou of Donna.

'Is it time for my haircut then?' she asks, patting her curls.

Lou feels the bed shudder slightly and turns to Donna whose shoulders are rising and falling rapidly, one hand covering her mouth.

Eleanor's expression changes then, a frown deepening between her eyebrows. 'Oh, have I done something wrong? Have I forgotten something?' A note of panic rises in her voice and she looks around the room, twisting the locket on her neck between her fingers as she does.

'Everything's OK,' Lou says, leaning forward and placing a hand on Eleanor's. Her skin is warm but papery, reminding her of what it felt like to hold her mother's hand as she sat by her bed reading to her on the particularly bad days. She was younger than Eleanor, but her hands grew old, somehow, over that last year. Even when the pain she was in didn't show on her face, Lou could feel it there in her mother's hands.

283

She blinks back tears and squeezes Eleanor's hand, trying to reassure her. But Eleanor isn't looking at her any more, instead she stares over her shoulder, the panic disappearing from her face, replaced with a wide-eyed expression.

'It's you,' she says suddenly, pointing at Donna, who stops shaking and looks up, wiping her face. 'It's you,' Eleanor repeats, blinking slowly. 'They kept telling me you weren't coming. I've been asking again and again when I could see you.'

She reaches for the locket again, rubbing it between her thumb and forefinger.

'Do you know who I am?' Donna asks in a strained voice.

'Of course I know who you are! They wouldn't let me keep you. They told me you couldn't come and visit. But you came. I knew you would come. I kept telling them – my daughter is coming to visit me today. But they didn't believe me. But here you are. Here you are.'

Lou steps back as Donna steps forward. This is their moment, not hers. She edges closer to the window, the sun warm on her back as she watches Donna crouch down, reaching out for Eleanor, who is stretching out her arms. They might both be adults, one in the winter of her life and the other in autumn, but as Lou watches them, she doesn't see any of that. All she sees is a mother and daughter holding each other tightly.

ELEANOR

For several weeks after Sydney leaves, Eleanor and Dorothy struggle along together. Eleanor leaves the apartment even less than before. When she does have to venture out for food, using what little is left of the housekeeping money Sydney used to give her each month, she walks quickly, not meeting the eye of any of her neighbours. She knows they will have noticed Sydney's absence and even though she doesn't believe it to be her fault, she still fears their judgement or, perhaps worse, their advice on how she might have got him to stay. When her daughter cries, she rocks her and holds her close, telling her she loves her and that everything is going to be OK. But as the end of the month approaches, she knows she has to make a decision. She cannot go on living like this – neither of them can. She is running out of money, the lease on the apartment is about to end and she has nowhere to go. No letter has arrived from England. There is nothing left for her there.

One Saturday, she heads out of the apartment for some fresh air, pushing Dorothy in her pram. It is just a few days until they will be forced to leave the apartment and she still doesn't know where they will go. She has spent all day (like every day since Sydney left) trying to come up with a solution and was getting so panicked and so desperate that she needed suddenly to be walking.

The pram bounces along the sidewalk, Dorothy drifting off to sleep with the movement. Eleanor brushes hot tears away from her eyes, trying not to make eye contact with anyone.

She turns onto one of the nearby streets where, instead of tenement buildings like hers, there are tall brownstone houses, inhabited by one or perhaps two families. The street is lined with magnolia trees. Ahead, she spots a family walking towards her on the sidewalk: a husband and wife holding the hands of a small child between them. They are smiling and as they pass by, Eleanor notices how clean the little boy's clothes are, how plump his cheeks look and how happily he glances up at his parents. She looks down at her own sleeping daughter and knows in that moment what she wants for her child. She wants that. Even more than she wants to hold her forever in her arms, she wants a good life for her daughter. Whatever it takes.

The next day, she packs up the apartment, filling her suitcase with her own clothes and a smaller bag with Dorothy's things. As she locks the door behind her and pushes the key under the door, she knows that one part of her life is ending and that she will never again be the same person she was when she arrived in this city.

She finds the adoption agency through an advert in the paper.

The office is brightly lit and filled with pictures of smiling families; it is clearly geared to the new parents, not the old. She blinks, wide-eyed, as an agent talks her through what will happen next, explaining the forms she must complete and the legality of what is about to happen. Dorothy sleeps against Eleanor's shoulder as she tells the agent that, yes, she understands what she is doing and signs her name on the required lines. From her handbag, she pulls out a couple of photographs that she carried with her from England and passes them to the agent.

'So she knows what her mother looked like,' she tells her. The agent nods and slips them inside an envelope.

'You're doing the right thing. We'll find a home where she can be properly cared for.'

Eleanor nods, kissing the top of her daughter's head. A better life. Her daughter deserves the best life. Even if it's at the cost of her own.

Too soon, it is time to say goodbye. The agent steps outside, leaving Eleanor and Dorothy alone together. For once, the baby sleeps soundly, a fist curled against her cheek, her chest rising and falling, her cheeks rosy and soft. Eleanor leans down and breathes deeply, taking in the smell of her daughter's head, her skin, her clothes washed with the very last of the soap powder that Eleanor owns. She holds her gently, slightly away from herself so that she can look at her properly, taking in her long eyelashes, her fingernails, the soft fuzz of her eyebrows, the ears that are so delicate and pink, like tiny shells, her softly pursed lips and closed eyelids.

'I'm only doing this because I love you,' Eleanor whispers into her daughter's ear. 'Don't you ever think it's because I didn't love you.'

Then the agent returns and gives Eleanor a little nod, holding out her hands. Dorothy doesn't wake as Eleanor passes her over, her arms suddenly strangely empty and light. After months of feeling exhausted, feeling weighed down, suddenly she longs for that ache in her arms. It was an ache that made her feel whole, even when it exhausted her. Part of her wishes Dorothy would open her eyes so that Eleanor could look into them one last time, but another part is glad that she doesn't, knowing it would break her.

Eleanor takes one last look at her daughter and then forces herself to turn out of the room and out of the building. Her feet feel heavy, but she makes herself pick them up, one in front of another. She steps out into the bright sunshine of a Brooklyn morning, her body intact but her heart left behind, held in the arms of a stranger.

LOU

'I'll be back in a minute,' Lou says suddenly, making her way around the armchair. But neither Donna nor Eleanor seems to notice her leaving.

'My baby,' Lou hears Eleanor mumble softly into Donna's hair as Lou's tears start to fall and she races along the corridor, shoulders stooped and head bent. She hurries past the reception desk, ignoring Mandy, and steps out into the fresh air, taking a deep breath.

She checks her watch, still set to England time. It is 9 p.m. back at home – is that too late to call? Fumbling with her phone in her pocket, she strides across the car park to the lawn, cutting a path away from the residents and their entourage of nurses and towards the quiet of the trees. With her back to the nursing home, she leans against the sturdy trunk of a maple tree and dials Maggy's number.

It rings for a little while before connecting.

'Lou! How nice to hear from you. How's it going over there?'

Maggy's voice is slightly muffled by a background noise of voices and laughter.

'Oh I'm sorry, Maggy,' Lou says quickly, 'I didn't mean to disturb you. I just …'

'You're not disturbing me, love. I'm just at the pub, which is why it's a bit noisy, but hold on one second, I'm just going to move somewhere quieter, you stay there …'

With her free hand, Lou runs her fingers lightly over the tough bark of the tree.

'There we go, that's better,' says Maggy, her voice clearer now and the background noise dulled to a mumble. 'So, tell me, how are things? How's Donna? And have you visited Eleanor yet?'

Lou tilts her head, looking up through the golden canopy of maple leaves. She is aware of the building behind her and that if she turned and looked hard enough she might be able to spot Eleanor's room and the figures of Donna and Eleanor, perhaps still held in a tight embrace, an embrace Eleanor has been waiting for for a long time.

'Donna's good – it's been nice to meet her husband and see her hometown. And we are actually with Eleanor now. Well, Donna is, I just needed some air …'

Lou explains everything that has happened, about the visit to the cottage and Connie and everything else.

'Wow,' says Maggy once Lou has finished. 'What a story. Connie sounds like a good woman. And you found Eleanor! You did what you set out to do, Lou. Your mum would be proud of you, I'm sure. But did something happen? Why are you not in there with them both?'

'I guess I just thought they could do with some space,' Lou replies, wrapping a strand of hair around one finger. 'They didn't need me there.'

'That's not true, Lou. You're part of their family too.'

'I suppose ... I guess all of this has made me miss Mum even more too. I wish she was here.'

She bites her lip hard, squeezing her eyes shut.

'I know you do,' Maggy replies gently.

Lou takes a deep breath, opening her eyes.

'I'm sorry if I sounded like I was giving up before, by the way. With the shop and everything. You've been so helpful and so kind. I don't want you to think I don't appreciate everything you've done for me.'

'Of course not. You've been through such a rough time.'

'I think I need to stop feeling sorry for myself though. I'm always going to miss Mum and Dad, but I've got my own life to live. I need to move on and start truly living it, just like Mum wanted. Like *I* want. And I *do* want to try to make the shop a success. I love it and I feel proud of it. I don't want to give up on it.'

'That's very good to hear, Lou.'

The branches of the tree rustle above her and Lou feels a sense of energy rush through her body.

'I should go back up there,' she says, turning to look back at the building. 'Thanks for listening to me, Maggy. I'll let you get back to your evening now – I hope you're having a nice time?'

'I am,' Maggy says, and Lou can hear the smile in her voice.

'You'll have to tell me all about it when I get back. See you soon, Maggy. And thank you. For everything.'

MAGGY

'Sorry about that,' says Maggy, slipping back into the seat opposite Robert, smoothing her dress as she sits down. They are at a table in the corner of the pub, near enough to the bar to enjoy the buzzing sense of atmosphere, but far enough away to be able to talk. But when Lou called, the line had been patchy, so Maggy apologised and headed out into the quieter room at the back. As she'd crossed back through the pub after saying goodbye, it had given her an unexpected thrill to spot Robert waiting for her. At the tables surrounding him, groups of young friends scrolled on their phones, but Robert sat with a cider in his hand, looking around the room with a content and self-assured expression on his face that Maggy found surprisingly sexy. Her cheeks colour as she raises her glass of wine again and looks up at him, meeting his blue eyes.

'No worries,' he says with a smile. 'Was that your lodger? How's she doing over in America?'

Over the course of the evening and several glasses of wine, Maggy had told Robert all about Lou, the vintage shop and about how much her own life had changed over the past few weeks. In turn, she learned more about Robert's grandchildren, about his secret love of musicals and how he had worked as a lawyer years ago before retraining in horticulture.

'A lawyer!' Maggy had said with raised eyebrows. 'Sorry, I don't mean to sound so surprised.'

Robert had laughed then, the sound as rich and warm as the pub's surprisingly good house red that Maggy had been enjoying.

'It surprises me too, to be honest. It was such a long time ago. I did it because I was young and it's what my parents wanted for me. But I was a terrible lawyer. I believed everyone was innocent. Plants are much easier. They might need coaxing and coddling sometimes, but at least they don't tell lies.'

They smile at each other, Maggy feeling both deeply comfortable in his presence while also experiencing a sense of excitement she hasn't felt in a long time.

'I'm having a good time,' she says suddenly, the wine loosening her. 'I'll be honest, I wasn't sure if I would. I haven't been on a date in a very, very long time.'

She had been nervous all afternoon, busying herself with errands and checking in with Beth and Pete about their plans, but feeling constantly distracted. It took her over an hour to decide what to wear, settling on one of the dresses from Lou's shop that Lou had helped her choose. The deep purple shade is a colour Maggy would never have picked for herself, but Lou promised her it would suit her and, to Maggy's surprise, she thinks she was right.

'So, this is a date, then?' Robert asks. He raises an eyebrow and something passes between them as quick as an electric shock. The hairs on her arms stand on end and she is suddenly grateful for the long sleeves on her dress.

'Well, I put on perfume and a dress and you aren't in your usual overalls, and we've nearly polished off a bottle of wine between us. So yes, I'd say it's a date.'

He smiles, his eyes sparkling. 'Good.'

Her cheeks grow warm again and she can't tell whether it's because of the wine she's just finished or that smile.

'I must admit, I wasn't sure,' Robert adds, looking down at his hands for a moment. They are the cleanest Maggy has ever seen them, the usual soil from the garden gone. She thinks about him scrubbing them in preparation for this evening and feels another rush of warmth. It also strikes her that he isn't wearing his wedding ring. 'I didn't know what the situation was with the American who was at the garden yesterday,' he adds.

'Simon is an old friend,' Maggy replies. 'Nothing more.' Perhaps when she headed to the garden yesterday, there had been part of her that hoped they might rekindle something of the spark she thought they once shared. But instead they found something better – honesty. They have messaged each other a few times since saying goodbye and Maggy has the sense that theirs is a friendship that will grow and last. Maybe she really will take up his offer of going to visit him and his husband in New York one day.

'Glad to hear it,' says Robert, clearing his voice. 'I could never compete with all that hair.'

Maggy laughs and Robert smiles even wider at the sound.

'Oh, I don't know,' she says, 'you've got a few things going for you.'

It's his turn for his cheeks to flush now. They hold each other's gaze and it feels as though the rest of the pub disappears, the sounds of laughter and conversation dimming and the figures around them growing blurry. Maggy looks at the man who she has known for years, feeling as though tonight she is properly seeing him for the first time. It feels unexpected, like opening a door in your own home and finding a totally new room behind it.

She knows that it might partly have to do with the wine, but she feels bolder than she has in a long time, cut free from her usual sense of responsibility. She thinks back to the phone conversation with Lou. It's not just Lou who needs to start living her own life.

'I suppose we should call it a ...' says Robert at the same time that Maggy opens her mouth and asks, 'Would you like to come back to mine?'

She doesn't look away as she waits for his answer. She doesn't have to wait very long.

'Yes. Yes, I'd like that very much.'

LOU

When Lou returns to Eleanor's room, Donna is sitting on the bed again, holding a photo album. Donna looks up as Lou steps inside and mouths, 'OK?' Lou nods.

She had needed a moment, but the fresh air and the call with Maggy have calmed her. She remembers her mother's final letter, the letter that she re-read on the plane while Donna slept and that asked her to do whatever she could to find her mother's sister. It might have thrown her to see Eleanor in the flesh and to be confronted by the emotion that flowed between mother and daughter as she and Donna reunited after so many years. But Maggy was right – Eleanor is her family too. There is space for her here.

'Eleanor was just showing me some photographs,' says Donna. 'There are some brilliant ones here of her and Connie.'

Eleanor looks up then, turning to Lou with a smile.

'Is it time for dinner?' she asks brightly.

A pained expression appears on Donna's face.

Lou shakes her head, forcing herself to take a steadying breath.

'I don't actually work here, Eleanor. I'm Lou, your sister Dotty's daughter.'

A cloud passes across Eleanor's eyes, her lips squeezing together.

'My sister? I don't have a sister.'

Lou and Donna look at one another, Donna placing the photo album down on the bed.

'Your younger sister, Dotty Morris,' prompts Donna. 'She stayed behind in England when you moved to New York, remember?'

'I used to live in New York. Have you ever been?'

'Yes, I have,' Donna says and Lou can hear how hard she is trying to remain calm and soothing. 'But what about Dotty Morris, do you remember her?'

Eleanor looks out the window, shaking her head from side to side. Donna tilts her head slightly and gives Lou a concerned look. But Lou is busy reaching down for her rucksack at her feet. Unzipping it, she pulls out a cloth bag that has travelled with her all the way from Somerset, staying close at her side at all times. She opens the bag and carefully pulls out a bundle of yellow fabric. In a smooth motion, she shakes out the skirt of the yellow dress, sunlight catching in its folds, and holds it up in front of Eleanor. As the fabric swishes, the multicoloured flowers shining in the light, Eleanor's expression changes again. Her eyes widen and she reaches out, her fingers grasping for the fabric.

'My dress. You kept it.'

Tentatively, she strokes the hem of the yellow dress, a look of wonder on her face.

'I …' Lou is about to correct Eleanor again, but then she hesitates. *What good would it really do?* So instead she nods and smiles. 'I did. I kept it safe for you, just like you asked me to.'

Eleanor beams at Lou, her eyes sparkling.

'I knew you would. You were always such a good girl.'

She reaches out a hand then and Lou takes it and squeezes.

'Here,' says Lou once Eleanor has let her hand fall again. Lou lays the dress gently in Eleanor's lap, her knees covered in yellow. As she does, she spots tears filling the edges of the old woman's eyes.

'You didn't write to me though,' she says now, her voice shaking. 'I wrote to you, but you never wrote back. I waited for such a long time.' As she speaks, she runs her hands over the dress on her lap, tracing the outline of the embroidered flowers with her fingers.

Lou thinks about everything she has learned about Eleanor and Dotty's story since first discovering her aunt's existence: the missed letters, the missed opportunities at reconnection.

'I never received your letters, Eleanor. Maybe some got lost in the post and then we moved house. I didn't know where you were, otherwise I would have contacted you.'

Eleanor frowns, looking up from the dress, her eyes and cheeks damp. 'So, you didn't forget about me?'

Lou swallows hard. She thinks of her mother spending her whole life waiting for a reply that never arrived. Of the secret

298

she carried alone of a lost sister, a sister she loved and thought about every time she put on her yellow dress. The yellow dress that was there at every key moment in her life, almost as though Eleanor were there too. It hits her that the yellow dress that her mother loved is also responsible for Maggy and Donna coming into Lou's life – Maggy drawn into Lou's shop one grey day by the bright beacon of it shining in the window and Donna finding the dress online, the dress that was one of the only things she knew about her mother.

'No, I never forgot about you. I did write to you though. I just was never able to send them, as I didn't know where you were. I wrote you so many letters. Would you like to hear some of them?'

And she reaches into the rucksack again, this time pulling out the old biscuit tin that she found among her mother's things, filled with dozens and dozens of unsent letters.

Lou settles herself on the edge of the bed, Donna so close beside her that Lou can feel the warmth of her cousin's body. In the armchair, Eleanor looks up at Lou with an expectant expression on her face, the sun falling on her cheeks as Lou begins to read.

Dear Eleanor ...

For a while the three of them sit comfortably together, Lou reading her mother's words, with Donna beside her and Eleanor in the chair, nodding every now and then, her eyelashes damp. The sun is beginning to dip outside now, the light turning the colour of golden syrup as it floods the room through the large window. Eventually, Eleanor's eyelids begin to droop and Lou pauses, a letter held aloft in one hand. As Eleanor's chin sinks onto her chest, Lou carefully folds the letter and places it back with the others. The yellow dress, which had been held tightly in Eleanor's hands, slips from her fingers as her body slackens with sleep.

Lou bends and picks it up, folding it and replacing the dress and the letters in her rucksack. She glances at Donna, who is watching her birth mother as the small hum of a snore escapes her lips.

'Are you OK?' Lou whispers.

Donna nods. 'Are you?'

'Yes, I am. I'm glad we came.'

She wishes her mother could be here and that they had arrived sooner, before the fog began to swoop into Eleanor's mind. But she is glad that she met her and that she was able to finally deliver the letters to their intended recipient. On second thoughts, she reaches back into her rucksack and removes the biscuit tin, placing it gently on the table beside Eleanor's bed.

'Don't you want to keep them?' Donna says quietly. 'They were your mother's after all.'

But Lou shakes her head.

'They were meant for Eleanor. Perhaps reading them will remind her of Mum.'

As Donna stands too, the bed creaks and Eleanor's eyes snap open. She looks around her, disorientated.

'Hello. Are you here to do my hair?'

Donna smiles weakly and leans down to kiss the top of Eleanor's head. Then she steps away towards the door.

'Not today,' says Lou, 'your hair looks perfect.' She crouches down and when Eleanor doesn't seem alarmed, Lou leans forward and hugs her tightly. 'That's for Mum,' she says quietly, but Eleanor doesn't seem to hear.

'Is it nearly dinner time?' she asks.

Lou steps away and shakes her head. 'I don't think so.'

'Good,' replies Eleanor, settling herself in the chair, leaning her head back against the headrest. 'I might close my eyes for a bit then.'

She shuts her eyes and Lou takes one last look inside the room. As she follows Donna out into the corridor, she hears Eleanor's quiet voice, muffled with the onset of sleep.

'Goodbye, Dotty.'

DONNA

Connie is asleep in the car, her head resting against the window and her newspaper abandoned across her lap. As Donna and Lou approach, the sound of the crunching gravel beneath their feet wakes her. Donna opens the front passenger door, Lou climbing in the back.

'Sorry to disturb you, Connie,' Donna says.

Connie shifts in her seat and stretches her arms out to the steering wheel.

'I must have nodded off. How did it go?'

Donna thinks back to the feel of Eleanor's thin body as she held her, the way she squeezed Donna close and muttered in her ear, 'My baby, my baby.' A lump forms in her throat.

'It was good. I'm so glad I've met her. Thank you for waiting for us.'

'That's OK. I got to catch up on some news and some sleep. How was she? Did she know who you were?'

'I think so, yes,' replies Donna. She doesn't mention the moments of confusion where she could sense a cloud rolling over Eleanor's mind, obscuring her memories and sense of what was happening around her. Lou says nothing in the back, so Donna doesn't mention that Eleanor thought Lou was her sister. She wonders if it really matters. Lou got to meet her aunt and Eleanor learned that her sister always remembered her.

'Did she show you her locket?' asks Connie, starting the engine.

'I noticed her playing with it,' says Lou from the back. 'It caught my eye – it was pretty.'

'But no,' adds Donna, 'we didn't see what was inside.'

'She's had it as long as I've known her. When I first met her, I wondered if there was a photograph in there, maybe some secret romance. But once we'd been friends awhile and she'd told me the truth about her past she opened it to show me the tiny lock of baby hair in there. Maybe she'll show you next time. Will there be a next time?'

'I'd like to come back, yes,' replies Donna. If Donna is honest with herself, the meeting didn't go exactly how she'd originally hoped. She had wanted to ask her birth mother endless questions about herself, to find out everything about her and discover similarities that would help her to understand herself better. How can she really think she knows herself if she doesn't know all the details of where she came from? But when she hugged Eleanor, none of that seemed to matter. She didn't have all the facts that she usually arms herself with to feel settled and secure, but she had something simpler and deeper than that. Eleanor might have been a stranger, but when Donna held her, she felt an unmistakable sense of connection.

Connie nods and smiles.

'That's good. The doctors have warned me that things are likely to go downhill quite quickly. But they said there may always be occasional moments of clarity. I guess that's why I keep coming – for those few moments when she does seem pleased to see me. And because I'd never leave her.'

She backs the car out of the space and turns it round swiftly and neatly.

'Right, I'll take you back to the cottage then.'

'Actually,' says Lou, leaning forward slightly, 'do you mind if we make a stop on the way? I'd love to see your and Eleanor's shop.'

Connie smiles in the rear-view mirror. 'Of course. I don't know why I didn't think of that myself.'

The shop is situated just off Main Street in the centre of Connie and Eleanor's town, down a tree-lined street that they didn't drive along on their way from the cottage to Maple Manor. Connie pulls up in a space opposite and steps out, Donna and Lou following behind. Wedged between two antiques shops, the shop has a red-and-white striped awning, buckets of flowers standing invitingly outside the front door, an 'Open' sign gleaming behind the glass. In the windows are several mannequins wearing brightly coloured dresses that remind Donna of Lou's outfits, but in slightly more muted shades and prints.

Connie pushes on the door and a bell tinkles as the three of them step inside. A middle-aged woman with a dark bob, dressed in a delphinium-blue fifties-style dress looks up from the counter.

'Mom! I didn't expect to see you today,' says the woman.

Connie introduces them both to her daughter Sharon, explaining Donna and Lou's story and why they are here.

'Wow, I have to give you both a hug,' says Sharon, coming out from behind the counter. 'Eleanor was like a second mom to me. Of course, my own mom is great,' she adds, smiling at Connie, 'but you know what I mean. Eleanor has always been there for me and my sister.'

'And I'm glad that she was,' says Connie. 'Especially when you were young. You know what teenagers can be like sometimes – they never want to talk to their own mom, but at least you had Eleanor to confide in.'

Donna smiles silently. It feels strange to think of her birth mother having been so involved in another woman's life. But she reminds herself of what she learned from Connie: Eleanor didn't want to give her up – she didn't have a choice. Whatever hint of abandonment she might feel is overshadowed by how glad she feels that Eleanor found Connie.

'The shop is beautiful,' says Lou, looking around. There are a couple of customers browsing quietly, the rails neatly colour co-ordinated, hung mostly with dresses, but with some other items and a few accessories mixed in too.

'Thank you,' says Sharon with a wide smile. 'My sister and I make most of the things ourselves. She's got the day off today, she'll be sad to have missed you. We updated it a little bit when we took over from Mom and Eleanor, but we kept most of the main features, like all of Eleanor's pictures.'

305

'Pictures?' Donna asks.

Sharon smiles and leads them to the changing room in the corner. It is currently unoccupied and she pulls the curtain back to reveal a large mirror and, surrounding it, dozens of framed pictures – ink sketches of dresses filled in with water-colours.

'Look, Donna!' says Lou, pointing at one particular picture in the middle of the wall.

Donna's eyes rest on a sketch in a gold frame of a dress with a nipped-in waist and a full skirt. The dress is bright yellow and covered in flowers.

'It's the yellow dress!' Lou says. 'I can't believe it!'

Sharon looks on inquisitively and Donna gives a neat account of the significance of the yellow dress.

'Oh wow, I'd love to see it,' says Sharon. 'That's always been one of my favourite pictures.'

'I've got it with me!' Lou replies, reaching into her bag.

Sharon and Connie gather round as for the second time that day Lou shakes out the sunshine-yellow dress that Eleanor made and that her sister kept safe. Sharon insists on taking a photograph of Donna and Lou holding the dress up in front of the matching drawing.

'Will you send me a copy?' asks Lou. They exchange details, Lou telling Sharon a little about her own shop.

'It sounds fantastic,' Sharon says.

'Thanks,' replies Lou. 'I think it will be.'

So, does that mean that Lou has changed her mind about leaving Somerset? Donna catches her eye and Lou's smile seems to confirm it. Donna smiles back. Good. Lou didn't seem like the type to give up and Donna hates being wrong about people.

Exhaustion suddenly washes over her, the events of the day catching up with her. It abruptly feels too much to be here with these people. She wants to be at home with her husband and her dog and to sit quietly for a while, taking time to process everything that has happened. The voices of Connie, Sharon and Lou blur into a buzz around her as she steadies herself against the wall. Lou looks up at her and seems to somehow know exactly how she is feeling because she folds the dress away again and zips up her rucksack.

'Thanks for everything, Connie, but we should probably make a move. It's been a long day and my jet lag is starting to kick in.'

'Of course, I'll get you back to your car.'

They say their goodbyes in the shop and make promises to keep in touch, Donna's head spinning.

'Oh, before you go I want to show you something,' says Connie.

Donna almost tells her that she doesn't care, that she's tired and wants to get back to Cold Spring right this minute. But Connie is twisting a handle at the side of the door, the red-and-white awning rolling back to reveal the shop's sign that had previously been hidden.

'I let Eleanor choose the name,' says Connie.

There, in swirling letters, is one word. *Dotty's*.

MAGGY

When Maggy wakes, it takes her a moment to register that for the first time in a long time she is not waking up alone.

'Morning,' says Robert a little sheepishly, smiling at her from the other side of the bed.

'Good morning,' she replies, suddenly panicking about the state of her hair and the lines on her chest and all the countless other ways her body has changed over the years. But then she looks at him again, propping himself up against the cushions now, the duvet draped over his well-padded stomach. He seems at ease and it makes Maggy relax too. Yes, she's a seventy-one-year-old grandmother and looks like one. But he didn't seem to mind last night. The opposite, in fact, she thinks, as a particular moment flashes back into her mind of him kissing the side of her neck and telling her he thought she was gorgeous.

She coughs slightly at the memory and takes in the room around her, their clothes lying haphazardly around the floor. *We're like a pair of teenagers*, she thinks, but then corrects herself. In all her years with Alan, even when they were both young and looking the best they ever had (something she wishes she had realised at the time), she can honestly say it had never once been like *that*. It had taken her totally by surprise last night with Robert, that spark, that sense of connection and how much they had both *laughed* together. Alan always took their encounters in their marital bed as seriously as he did filing his company accounts.

They had stayed up late talking too, covering everything from loss and parenting to their favourite music, the best holidays they've ever been on (Maggy: a trip with her children to a cottage by the sea when Alan was too busy with work one year to go on their usual trip to his favourite resort in Majorca; Robert: a hiking trip in Scotland a few years ago with his son) and their go-to meals to cook. It turns out that as well as having an affinity with plants, Robert is a confident cook, something he promises to show her one day soon. Maggy glances at the alarm clock on her side of the bed and sits up with a jolt.

'I can't believe the time. I haven't slept in that late for years.'

A memory suddenly enters her mind of all the times when her children were teenagers that she spent shouting up the stairs at them to hurry up or they would be late for school. What would they say if they saw her now, she thinks, her skin growing warm at the thought. She expects they prefer to think of their mother as some sort of aged nun. And up until recently it wouldn't have been too far from the truth. When Alan left, she thought that part of her life was over too and it actually came as something of a relief. But now …

'I've got to go,' she says, pulling herself up as hurriedly as her knees will allow, fishing about for her dress on the floor. 'I completely forgot that there's something I have to do this morning. But I won't be too long if you'd like to stay. We could have brunch together?'

A look of relief spreads over Robert's face.

'I thought you were about to kick me out and tell me you'd never be coming to visit the garden again. But yes, if you are not totally filled with regret about last night, then I'll stick around. It's my day off today, actually. I can make us something to eat.'

'Great.'

She kisses him on the cheek and then carries her clothes off to the bathroom to get dressed.

As she leaves the house later, hair neatly brushed and a new lipstick applied, it gives her a thrill to think that he will still be there when she gets back.

Beth is waiting for her in the café. She looks up with a smile when Maggy steps inside. At her side, her partner Danie prepares a coffee order for a man waiting by the door.

'Am I late?' Maggy had walked quickly across the park and into town and is a little out of breath. But Beth shakes her head.

'Not at all, you're bang on time. Let's go through to the back where it's quiet. Are you OK to take over here, Danie?'

'Yes, of course,' replies the redheaded woman with a smile. 'I've got it covered. Good luck!'

Beth and Maggy sit down at a table in the back of the café. It's still early, so most customers are ordering takeaways, the tables around them empty.

310

'So, remind me of how it's going to work?' Maggy asks, nerves suddenly creeping in.

'The host's name is Kirsty,' Beth says, taking her phone out and placing it on the table. 'They're doing a segment about small businesses and one of their researchers is local and suggested they do a spotlight on the town's independent market.'

When Beth had told Maggy about the opportunity, she could hardly believe it. The radio show was a programme that she regularly listens to herself, the noise filling the kitchen on days when she needs the company of voices in the background. As the head of the town's independent business network, Beth was approached about the interview and thought they should talk to Lou too – she thought it could be a well-needed boost for her after the break-in. But then she left for America before Beth had a chance to ask her about it. Beth told Maggy all of this when she popped into the café after Lou and Donna left and told her about her own plans to help Lou. Maggy had considered calling Lou about it then but decided against it. She had been so despondent about her business when she left and had enough on her plate with the journey and the visit to Eleanor. Maggy hoped the trip might be a chance for Lou to step away from it all and come back feeling refreshed. So Beth had asked if Maggy would consider doing the interview with her instead.

'You've lived here for most of your life,' she had said, 'you've seen the changes the town has gone through. And maybe you can find a way to talk about Lou's shop too.'

Now, Beth unlocks her phone and checks the time.

'They're going to call any minute,' she explains to Maggy, 'and then we'll be on air. Have you ever been on radio before?'

Maggy almost laughs. 'No!'

'I've done a couple of local things with the business network. Just be yourself and you'll be fine.'

The phone rings and they both look at each other. Then Beth gives a reassuring smile and picks up. She is a natural, Maggy thinks, as she listens to her talk enthusiastically about the independent market and how it came about and about the town's small business network and how they support one another. Then it's suddenly Maggy's turn to talk.

'So, Maggy, I hear you're a local resident who has lived there for over fifty years. What do you make of this all? There's a lot of talk about the death of the high street at the moment. Do you see that happening in your own town? And with so much choice online, does it even matter?'

Maggy takes a deep breath, picturing the first time she visited Lou's shop, drawn in by a yellow dress on a day when she felt anything but yellow. And she thinks about everything that has happened since and about her friend who has put so much into making the shop a success.

'I'm pleased to say that our high street is alive and well. But I think that we have to do whatever we can to support small businesses in towns like mine. We can't afford to take them for granted. Browsing a website just isn't the same as going into a shop or a café and being among other people. I'll be honest that I have had times over the past year where I've felt lonely – I think we all have those moments, whether we admit to them or not – but the community in my town has helped to pull me out of that. And when we talk about small businesses, I think we tend to forget that what we are really talking about is

312

people. People who have taken a risk and worked hard to make something of themselves. People like Beth and like my friend Lou Jackson.'

Her name comes out before Maggy can stop herself.

'My friend Lou runs the most wonderful vintage shop here in Frome. She has poured her heart and soul into the place and it's so much more than a shop. I've seen first-hand the joy the place brings to its customers and the memories and stories that are sparked when people come in and run their hands over the rails of beautiful clothes. I could talk all day about how wonderful the shop is and how much it's come to mean to me, but what I really think people should do is come and see it for themselves – to put their talk of supporting small business into action and come and support *all* of the great businesses in our town this Sunday at the independent market.'

'Well, you've certainly convinced me, Maggy,' says the host at the end of the line. 'Thanks to both of you for dialling in. And now ...'

Maggy zones out as her adrenaline kicks in and she realises it's over. Beth says goodbye and thank you to the producer, who chips in now over the background noise of the broadcast continuing, and then hangs up.

'That was great!' Beth says enthusiastically. 'That's definitely going to give the market a boost.'

'I hope so,' Maggy replies. She thinks about how much she has come to care – how Lou and her shop have reignited a love for her hometown and sense of passion that she lost somehow over the years. And she just hopes that everything she is doing to help is going to be enough to make a difference.

LOU

It is time to say goodbye.

'I can't believe how quickly these few days have gone,' Lou says, her suitcase at her side as she and Donna stand facing each other in the airport car park. Behind them comes the buzz of traffic as taxis pull up outside the airport terminal, accompanied by the constant roar of planes taking off and landing. John and Brooke are there too, both of them having insisted on coming to wave Lou off. Over the past few days, she has enjoyed getting to know both of them, feeling a particular closeness with Brooke, who is around the same age as her and as no-nonsense as her mother, but with her father's more extroverted nature. They have exchanged numbers and have promised to keep in touch.

Lou and Donna went to visit Connie again yesterday, this time meeting her husband and their other daughter Gill. Together, the family shared more stories about Eleanor. Lou hadn't suggested another trip to Maple Manor – she feels as though she said everything she needed to when she was there – but she knows that Donna has arranged to visit again next week. Knowing Donna, Lou expects that the visits will become a regular part of her week, happening on exactly the same day and at the same time. But Lou has the sense that Donna feels ready to shake up her usual routines too; last night over dinner she mentioned that she would like to take a step back from the inn and go travelling with John, something that seemed to delight him.

'About time!' he had said. 'I've been ready to retire for years. But I didn't think you would want to.'

'I didn't think I wanted to either,' Donna had replied. 'But I think maybe I was just too scared to try something different. But after everything that has happened recently and the adventure I've been on, I think it's time to embrace doing things a bit differently. Life is short and I want to make the most of it. Cold Spring will always be here to come back to.'

Lou is excited for her cousin's plans and inspired by her determination to push herself outside of her comfort zone.

'It's been so nice to get to know you,' Brooke says now, giving Lou a tight hug.

'You're welcome at the Sycamore Inn any time,' adds John, his arms warm around her too.

'Thank you both, that means a lot. Oh, before I go, I can't forget ...'

She reaches into her rucksack for the final time that trip, pulling out the cloth bag containing the yellow dress, the dress that brought them all together.

'I'd like you both to have this,' she says, holding the bag towards Donna and Brooke.

'But it's yours, Lou,' says Donna, 'it belonged to your mother.'

Swallowing hard, Lou shakes her head.

'Not really. It always belonged to Eleanor – my mum was just holding on to it for her. It feels right that it should go back to you. And although my mum loved wearing it, I've never been able to bring myself to even try it on.'

There might be many of her mother's things that have found their way into her own wardrobe, but somehow the yellow dress is the one thing Lou could never wear.

'I think it would suit you, though, Brooke. If I keep it, the dress will just stay hanging above my shop counter. And that's no life for a dress. A dress is meant to be worn.'

If the dress stays pinned to a hanger, it is as though its story – the sisters' story – has ended. And Lou realises now that isn't true. Her mother might be gone and the sisters may never have had the chance to meet again, but it doesn't mean the story is over. Lou is still here. Even if parts of her memory are fading, Eleanor is here. Donna and Brooke are here. And so too are all the others who form part of their story – Connie and her family and Maggy, who was there when Lou and Donna met. Their lives will all forever be linked together now like tangled threads.

Brooke frowns slightly, reaching a hand out towards the bag but then hesitating.

'It is a beautiful dress. I just love the colour … But it's not just a dress though, is it? It's so much more than that. It's all your memories of your mother wearing it too. Are you sure you can part with that?'

Lou's mind floods with the sound of her mother's voice and the softness of her hand in hers when she was young. She sees her dancing with her father in their kitchen, a flash of yellow shining brightly as she twirls. Lou bites her lip and a faint smile spreads over her face.

'I don't need a dress to remember my mother. I have a whole lifetime of memories.'

Donna and her family walk with Lou to the departures terminal, helping her with her bags and checking the flight is running on time. As they prepare to say their final goodbyes, Donna hands Lou a paper bag.

'Just a few things for the journey,' she says.

Lou reaches inside and pulls out a neck pillow, a silk eye mask and a pair of earplugs.

'Thank you, Donna,' Lou says, reaching out and pulling her into a tight hug. She doesn't know quite how to express everything they have been through together over the past week. It has been a whirlwind, a moment in her life that she will never forget. Donna hugs her back with so much more warmth than their first embrace when they had only just met and Donna was stiff and awkward in Lou's arms. Maybe they don't need to say anything after all.

'Cold Spring is really lovely in the spring,' says Donna once they have parted.

'Is that an official invitation?' asks Lou with a smile.

'Only if you wanted to … I know how busy your life is. You

might not want to waste your holiday coming to visit an old woman like me.'

Lou's mind fills with everything that is waiting for her back in Somerset, all the unknowns that she needs to work her way through. But then she tucks her pillow, eye mask and earplugs into her rucksack and slips it back on her shoulders. She is not on her own. She has people to help her. Maybe it will all be OK.

'I'd absolutely love that,' she replies.

Donna, John and Brooke wave goodbye as she passes through security and then they are gone, Lou on her way back to a life that she thought was over, back to a life she feels ready to embrace again, this time without giving up.

As she walks through the bright lights of duty-free, her mind is filled with a vision of her small town and the people that are waiting there for her. 'I'm going home,' she says quietly to herself.

DONNA

'It's OK, Mom, she'll be back soon,' says Brooke, wrapping an arm around Donna's shaking shoulders.

'I don't know what you're talking about,' says Donna with a loud sniff. 'It's just my allergies.' But she doesn't pull away as Brooke squeezes her again, tighter this time.

It had surprised her, the wave of emotion that hit her when she said goodbye to Lou. They only met just over a week ago, but in such a short space of time, Donna has come to feel closer to her than to some people she's known for years. Their shared story binds them together; Donna feels confident that her cousin will always be part of her life. So will Connie and her family. Connie has made it clear that she thinks of Donna as part of her family now. Donna will be able to ask Connie as many questions as she likes about her birth mother, even as Eleanor's own memories continue to fade. In that way, Eleanor will live on, kept alive by the people who knew her.

'Let's go home,' Donna says, looping her arm through her husband's, her daughter close by her side. She will be glad to get back to Cold Spring and feel settled for a while after the upheaval of her trip to England and the journey to find Eleanor. But she already feels excited instead of nervous at the thought of doing something else in the future that will take her outside of her day-to-day routine. Now that she's had a taste of adventure, she wonders what she was always so worried about. *It's only taken me sixty years*, she thinks as she walks with her family out of the airport, *but I'm ready to live a different kind of life.*

As the car pulls up outside the Sycamore Inn, Donna looks up at the familiar frontage of the building where she has lived her whole life. There's just one thing missing to make her feel as though she is truly home.

'I'll join you inside in a bit,' she says. 'There's something I need to do first.'

John and Brooke look at each other and share a smile.

'Of course,' says John. 'I'll make us a coffee when you get back.' Brooke kisses her on the cheek and then they both head inside the inn.

Donna sets off down the street, walking slowly and taking in the autumn colours and the displays in the shop windows which have changed over the past weeks to reflect the change of seasons. She nods at a few people as she walks, and they nod back. When she reaches the blue house by the river, she pauses, taking in the swing seat on the porch and the two pairs of boots tucked neatly in the corner, and then she knocks on the door.

Her father opens it, his mouth falling open in surprise.

'Oh,' is all he manages.

'Hi, Dad,' she says and then she steps forward and gives him a hug. She can feel his shoulders sinking beneath her arms as he lets out a long breath.

'We've missed you,' he says.

'I've missed you too.'

'I'm sorry …' he begins, but she shakes her head.

'You don't have to be sorry. I'm sorry for not being in touch. I just needed a bit of space.'

They stand in the doorway, both smiling tentatively at one another.

'Is she …'

'She's in the living room,' he replies. 'The doctor seems happy with her progress. I know she'll be happy to see you. Shall I leave you to it?'

Donna nods, stepping inside and hanging her coat on its hook.

'Thanks, Dad.'

He smiles and squeezes her hand and then disappears into the kitchen, leaving Donna to walk alone through to the back of the house.

Her mother is sitting in an armchair facing the window and as Donna steps inside, she turns round, a momentary frown appearing on her face before it spreads into a wide smile.

'Donna!'

She leans forward, but Donna lifts up a hand.

'Don't get up.' She sits down in the armchair next to Shirley's, the chair her father usually sits in when they have their morning cup of coffee. They sit side by side, both looking out at the river that is washed in gold as the sun sets over the hills.

'Not long until the leaves drop,' says Shirley.

Donna takes in the red and orange trees on the other side of the water.

'Yes. It will be Halloween before we know it.'

'You always used to hate Halloween when you were little, do you remember? You thought dressing in costumes was a type of lying.'

Donna smiles. 'Yes, although I didn't mind the candy. You let me be the official distributor of candy when kids came to the inn trick-or-treating. You never made me dress up and you kept a special bowl of candy just for me.'

'Of course. Just because trick-or-treating wasn't your thing didn't mean you should miss out.'

Their eyes meet now and Donna properly takes in her mother. She is still pale, but looks better than when she last saw her. A wave of guilt courses through her.

'How are you feeling? I'm so sorry I reacted so badly and haven't been in touch.'

Shirley shakes her head, a pained expression appearing on her face. 'No, you had every right to be angry. *I'm* sorry that I wasn't brave enough to tell you the truth years and years ago.'

'I went to see Eleanor.'

Donna's mother raises her eyebrows, her mouth forming an 'o'.

'You found her, then?'

'I did. It took a while and I'll tell you all about it later, but yes, I found her.'

322

Shirley sniffs and clears her throat.

'I'm glad. And? How was it?'

Outside, a riverboat passes slowly by, the sun glinting off its windows and lazy ripples spreading out in its wake across the water.

'I'm glad I got to meet her and to hear that she didn't give me up because she didn't want me, but because she couldn't look after me. She did the right thing based on the situation. I think when I found out about her, though, I got so caught up in this need to know everything about her in order to know who I am. And it's true that without her I wouldn't exist. She's an important part of my story. But I wouldn't be me without you and Dad either. I think I lost sight of that. But nothing's ever going to change that.'

Donna can see the tears filling her mother's eyes.

'I know I'm an old woman now,' she says in reply, 'and that you don't exactly need me any more. You've got your own family and have been independent for years and years. But you'll still always be my daughter.'

'And you'll always be my mom,' replies Donna.

Shirley lets out a breath and places her hand on top of Donna's.

'You don't know how happy it makes me to hear that.' She squeezes Donna's fingers and Donna squeezes back.

As Donna sits beside Shirley, she thinks about her two mothers and the different roles they have played in her life. Eleanor, who gave birth to her and cared for her for a short time before doing what she felt was the only thing she could to protect her and secure her future. And Shirley, who might never have carried her inside her body, but was there for all the childhood scrapes and illnesses and who gave her a home and a life that made her feel safe and accepted. Both types of mothering required huge sacrifice and love. She will always be grateful to both women and feels proud to be their daughter.

'Can we start again?' Donna says and beside her Shirley nods. 'I love you, Mom,' she adds.

'I love you too.'

The two women sit side by side as the sun sets over the river.

LOU

This time, Lou sleeps through the entire flight. She arrives back in England feeling surprisingly refreshed. A taxi she booked before leaving is waiting for her, ready to take her back to Maggy's. They messaged regularly throughout Lou's trip and Lou sent one when she landed to tell her how much she was looking forward to seeing her again but is yet to receive a reply.

As the car travels further from the airport, the view turns to green, orange and brown as fields and autumn trees roll by the windows. Lou lets out a small sigh, happy to see the familiar countryside again. By the time the taxi has pulled up on Maggy's street, she is eager to catch up with her friend in person. But when Lou drags her suitcase up to the front door, she is greeted instead by a note tucked beneath the knocker.

'Lou,' reads the note, 'Hope you had a good flight. I have popped down to the independent market for a look around.

I will be at Beth's having a coffee – please come and join me when you're back. There's something I need to talk to you about. Maggy x.'

Lou had completely forgotten that today was the day of the town's independent market. After the break-in, she cancelled the swing band she had hired and all other plans she'd been making for the relaunch of the shop. She doesn't feel much like going in to town and thinking about what might have been, but she reminds herself of the resolve she found on her trip to pick herself up and carry on. And besides, she wants to see Maggy and to support the other businesses – her new friends. It will be nice to see Beth and Danie again and maybe looking around the market will give her some good ideas for a potential event once the repairs are finished at the shop and she is ready to open again.

She pops inside briefly to drop her bags and change out of her travel clothes into a fresh outfit – a bright red dress and matching shoes – then throws on her coat, locks up again and heads straight out, walking briskly across the park, where leaves drift to the ground like snowflakes. It is a perfect October day, the air cool, but a lingering warmth still in the sun, the sky above a pale blue.

As she draws closer to the centre of town, she starts to hear the buzzing sounds of voices and music. There are people walking ahead of her, some heading down the hill into town chatting and laughing in groups, others walking back up holding paper bags and takeaway cups. Everyone seems to be smiling and Lou finds herself smiling too. *This is my town*, she thinks as she joins the steady flow of people coming and going.

As she nears the top of Catherine Hill, the movement of people seems to stop, a crowd gathering in the street. The music has grown louder now, the cheerful sound of a band reaching her above the background noise of all the people. She spots colourful bunting hung high between the buildings and as she looks back down at the street in front of her, she realises that the crowd of people she noticed are standing right in front of *her shop*. Except it doesn't look anything like how her shop looked when she left for America. She stops on the pavement, staring in disbelief at a view she hardly recognises.

The broken glass in the door has been fixed and the 'Closed until further notice' sign is gone from the window. In its place are mannequins dressed in brightly coloured outfits, some that are her favourites from those that were left behind after the break-in, but some that she has never seen before but immediately recognises as vintage Biba. Each item looks pristine, as though it has been freshly steamed and pressed. Also in the window is a display made up of jugs of autumnal flowers and silk scarves somehow arranged into the shape of birds mid-flight.

Lou blinks back tears, unable to comprehend what she is seeing. She can't believe it's really her shop. She thinks back to how the place was when she left, glass and debris scattered across the floor that she felt too overwhelmed to deal with. Back then, it felt sad and broken. But now it looks totally alive.

She spots the swing band stationed opposite the shop, the music adding to the joyful atmosphere in the air. As she looks closer, Lou recognises them as the same musicians she originally booked to perform today but cancelled after the break-in.

The guitarist notices her and smiles. A few couples are dancing in the street in front of them, laughing as they do.

Lou suddenly notices Beth and Danie, serving coffees and an array of cakes from a table set up outside between their café and the shop. Beth looks up and waves, a huge smile on her face. As Lou returns the wave, her mouth still open in shock, she finally sees Maggy.

She is standing just by the entrance to the shop and she looks the most beautiful Lou has ever seen her. Her hair has been freshly cut, her waves bouncing at her chin in a style that suits her perfectly. Her lips are traced in a deep shade of red and spread into an enthusiastic smile as she talks to someone on the street. She is wearing one of the dresses she bought from Lou, a forest-green shirt dress that she has accessorised with a brighter green belt. As she notices Lou too, she stops talking, the smile slipping slightly from her face. She suddenly looks nervous.

Lou takes a step closer and Maggy says something Lou can't hear to the person she had been talking to and then steps off the pavement towards Lou until the two of them are standing facing one another in the street.

'Lou, it's so nice to see you. What do you think?' Maggy looks around her and then returns her attention to Lou, raising a hand to her face anxiously.

'Was all of this you?' Lou asks, finally finding her voice.

'Not all of it,' replies Maggy, shaking her head, Lou spotting sparkly earrings glinting in the sun. 'I had lots of help from Beth and the others. Zara provided the flowers for the window. Gemma at the bookshop has loaned us an old till to keep you going until you can replace yours. Oh, and I can't forget your lovely builder, Pete, who repaired the door free of charge. But today was my idea, yes, so if you think we've totally overstepped the line, then I am the one who is entirely to blame. I just wanted to do something nice for you – we all did. You worked so hard on your shop and you've had such a rough year. We wanted to help and to show you that you're not alone.'

Lou puts a hand over her mouth and starts to cry.

'Oh no, I knew it was too much,' says Maggy, her face falling. 'I should have asked you first, shouldn't I? I didn't want to interrupt your trip and wanted it to be a surprise, but I can see now that I've made a huge mistake, I'm so sorry.'

'Maggy,' Lou says, composing herself enough to reach out for her hand. 'Stop. This is the nicest thing anyone's ever done for me. I can't believe it. Thank you.'

She lets her tears fall as she pulls Maggy into a hug, the older woman's shoulders relaxing in relief.

'Oh,' Maggy replies. 'Oh, I'm so pleased.' They hold each other tightly as the swing music plays and the cheerful sounds of the busy street swirl around them.

'I do want to know how you managed it all, though,' Lou says once they've stepped apart, both women wiping their eyes and sniffing slightly. 'The place looks incredible. And I swear those Biba pieces aren't mine.'

'No, they're mine,' replies Maggy.

'What?' But before Lou can ask any more questions, Maggy explains.

'They're things I collected when I worked there in the sixties.

But they have been gathering dust in my attic all this time. I had boxes and boxes full of them. I'm never going to wear them again and they're not my daughter's style. I thought they would be much better off in your shop and could replace the items that were stolen.'

'That's so kind, Maggy, but your collection must be worth a fortune.'

Maggy waves a hand through the air. 'We can talk about all that later,' she says. 'But there's still more for you to see. There's someone waiting for you upstairs. Here.'

Maggy takes a shiny key out of her pocket, strung on a bright red ribbon, and passes it to Lou, whose eyes flick up to the windows of the flat above the shop.

Maggy nods at her. 'Go on, we can chat about everything later. I'll mind the shop – I've already made a few sales this morning.'

After another hug with Maggy and another with Beth and Danie, Lou climbs the stairs that lead to the upper floors above the shop. She pauses outside the front door – her front door – before slipping the key in the lock and stepping inside.

The room has been completely transformed since her last visit. Sunlight pours in through the sparkling windows, shining on the floorboards, which have been cleaned up and painted a bright white. The walls are freshly plastered and painted a matching white, ready for the vibrant colours that Lou has already picked in her mind. From the ceiling hang the retro light fittings that she picked out and through the living-room door she can spot the finished kitchen, the bright yellow units a pop of colour against the white surfaces and shiny stainless-steel cooker. And there on the far side of the living room by the windows is Pete, dressed in his work clothes and smiling at her.

'Welcome to your new home, Lou.'

'Oh my God,' she exclaims, 'it's finished! I thought you still had a couple of weeks to go!'

'I thought so too, but I managed to rearrange some other work I had lined up. I felt so angry about what happened in the shop – it was so unfair. Your friend Maggy spoke to me about doing the repairs in there too and I decided my other jobs could wait. I nearly thought I wouldn't get it done in time, but luckily I had a few helpers. Gemma at the bookshop is pretty handy with power tools – all those bookshelves – and Beth got a whole group together to help with the painting.'

'I'll have to thank them all – I can't believe how kind everyone has been. And it looks *amazing*, Pete. You've done such a brilliant job. I can't believe I get to live here.'

In her excitement, she can't stop herself. She rushes forward and flings her arms around him.

'Thank you. Thank you so much.'

'I'm glad you like it,' he mumbles into her hair. And then somehow their arms are wrapping even more tightly around one another and she is tilting her chin up as he leans down, their lips meeting in a kiss.

After a few moments, she steps back.

'God, I'm sorry about that.'

'Don't be,' he says, grinning and reaching gently for her waist again. 'I always fancied you when we were at school together, you know.'

'You did?'

He nods. 'Big time.'

She kisses him again, closing her eyes slightly against the slanting sun that pours in through the windows. She can't believe that she is really here, standing inside the flat that will become her new home, her shop and her friends waiting for her downstairs. Just a few months ago, she couldn't imagine the sadness ever lifting, let alone feeling happy. But now a sense of warmth fills her whole body.

Once she and Pete have parted just enough for Lou to speak again, she lifts her eyes to meet his with a smile.

'You know what you just said about when we were at school?'

'Mhhmm?' he replies.

She pulls him a little closer.

'I always fancied you too.'

MAGGY

The shop has been heaving since opening that morning. Some of the customers are regulars, but many have never visited before, drawn either by the music and buzz outside or by the radio interview; several people tell Maggy how much they enjoyed what she had to say. To her relief, Lou seemed amused – pleased even – when she heard about it.

'I'll have to listen to it online,' she'd said. 'And thank you again for everything, this is just amazing.'

The local friends who helped out have all popped in quickly to say hello and Lou thanked each of them warmly and enthusiastically. She promised to return Gemma's old till as soon as she has bought a new one and secretly made a pact to buy all future birthday and Christmas presents from Gemma's bookshop for the rest of her life. She thanked Zara for the flowers for the window display and told both women that they had to come in and pick something from the shop as a thank-you when they weren't so busy themselves – both of them having to head back to their shops thanks to the crowds the market has attracted today.

Maggy's group of girlfriends have been in to visit too, each leaving with a hefty paper bag.

Now, Maggy and Lou work side by side behind the till serving a small line of customers, Maggy carefully wrapping each purchase while Lou deals with the payments, both of them chatting to the customers. It might have been decades since Maggy had her job in the Biba store, but it has all come back to her. She loves seeing the happy expressions of customers who have found exactly what they were looking for or something they never expected to buy but that captured their heart.

'I can't believe how similar this is to a cardigan my mum used to wear,' a woman says as Maggy gently folds a 1950s cropped cardigan in Easter pink and slips it into a bag for her. 'I always thought it was such a "mum" cardigan. I loved hugging her when she wore it – it was so soft. Now that I have my own baby, I want him to feel the same way when I wear this one.'

The rush of customers dies down for a while, a few happily browsing, and Maggy and Lou both let out a sigh, enjoying the brief moment of calm.

'I can't believe how well it's going,' says Lou. 'This is definitely going to be our best day since opening. It's amazing. I'm going to have to source some new stock – but that's a brilliant problem to have. Maybe you can help me, Maggy? Only if you want to, that is. You have such a great eye, I could really use your input.'

Maggy beams, relief rushing through her. If Lou is asking her to help out, then maybe she will be open to Maggy's plan, the plan she still has to talk to her about …

Before Maggy can reply, a small voice makes her look up.

'Granny!'

Fleur is standing in the doorway, looking around the shop with wide eyes. Just behind her, Maggy spots her grandsons Luke and Otis, followed by her son Nick and daughter-in-law Sam, as well as Charlotte and Séb.

'This place is amazing!' exclaims Fleur.

'I think these are your customers,' Lou says with a smile. 'We can talk later.'

Maggy steps out from behind the counter and into the wide arms of her granddaughter. Her grandsons are less enthusiastic, looking around as though they'd rather be anywhere else, but they do at least give in and let Maggy kiss them.

'How wonderful to see you all!' She looks over Fleur's head, catching Charlotte and then Nick's eyes. 'Thank you for coming.'

'We were intrigued when you sent the invites,' says Charlotte. 'I had no idea you'd become involved in the shop. You look amazing, Mum,' she says, taking in Maggy's new hair and outfit.

'Thank you,' Maggy replies warmly. 'Actually, do you both have a moment to talk outside?' Her skin grows warm as she says it. It's a conversation that has needed to happen for a long time and that she's been thinking about more and more over the past few days.

'Of course,' replies Nick.

'We'll have a look around in here, won't we, kids?' says Sam, and seeming to get the hint, Séb stays behind too, letting Maggy step outside with her two children.

It is still lively in the street, people coming and going up and down the hill. By now, it's nearly lunchtime and many of them are carrying cardboard containers of steaming food bought from the stands down in the market square. The smell of melted cheese makes Maggy's stomach rumble.

'Mum, the shop looks amazing,' says Charlotte once they have found a seat on a bench opposite the shop, Maggy in the middle and Charlotte and Nick either side of her. 'I can't believe you did all of this – helping get it up and running again for today. I didn't even know you'd been helping out here.'

'Well, it's been fairly recent,' Maggy acknowledges. And yet it feels as though so much in her life has changed over the past few weeks. She feels as though *she* has changed.

'I should have asked, though,' Charlotte replies, shaking her head slightly. 'I'm sorry, I know I can get caught up in my own stuff sometimes. It's just so busy with work and everything.'

'That's OK,' replies Maggy. 'But I do want to talk to you both about something.'

She takes a deep breath. It's a hard conversation to have, but she knows she needs to do it.

'It's been a difficult year, what with your dad leaving and now getting remarried. But it's also been an opportunity to have a good think about my life and how I want to live it. And you know how much I adore you and my grandchildren, but I think I need to find a better balance in my life. I need to have

336

more time for me and to do things outside of just being your mum and the children's grandmother. And for quite a while that balance has been off. I've got lots that I want to do now, and it means I'm going to have less time for the last-minute babysitting.'

Once the words are out, Maggy feels lighter, dizzy with having stood her corner.

Charlotte and Nick glance at each other, exchanging a furtive look. Charlotte is the first to speak.

'You know, Mum, Nick and I have been talking about this recently too. We both know that we've been relying on you too much. It's not fair and we're sorry.'

'Sam and I are getting a nanny,' adds Nick. 'Finally!'

'And I know I'm the worst for last-minute meetings and for being late to pick Fleur up when she's with you. I need to work harder to get a better balance, too.'

'I do still want to see plenty of my grandchildren!' Maggy replies. 'And you two, of course.' Her head turns to take in the two of them – the proudest achievement of her life. 'But I want to try to have my own adventures too.'

'And we want that for you too, Mum,' says Charlotte, resting a hand on top of Maggy's. 'You have to live your own life. And I don't think we've checked in enough with you since the divorce, either. It must have been a massive thing for you – you and Dad were married for so long. But you've just always seemed so capable, Mum, that I guess we forget to ask how you are. I'm really sorry. We're really sorry.'

Nick nods. 'Yes, Mum. I'm sorry we've been so useless.'

'Oh darlings,' says Maggy, shaking her head. 'You're far

from useless. But I do appreciate you saying all of that. And I'll be honest, the divorce has been hard. Really hard. But actually, I'm doing OK now. Better than OK. I feel good.'

'You look it, Mum,' says Charlotte. 'Honestly, you look amazing. There's something different about you and I don't just mean the hair and the clothes ...'

'I feel happy,' Maggy replies, realising that until recently she hadn't felt truly happy in quite a long time, well before Alan left her. Her mind races with all her plans for the future – dates she wants to go on with Robert, her plan to get more involved with Lou's shop and that trip to America she promised Donna that she would make. And for a second she remembers the moment when her divorce papers landed on her doormat and she thought that her life was over. *How wrong I was*, she thinks with a smile.

'We're so proud of you. And we love you, Mum,' says Charlotte, squeezing Maggy's hand. Maggy squeezes back, tilting her head to rest on Nick's shoulder. The three of them sit like that, still and content as the crowds move up and down the hill around them.

LOU

Later, once the town has finally cleared and the only signs left of the day's market are the bunting still hanging in the street and the odd dropped chip waiting to be snaffled by a lucky small creature, Lou and Maggy settle on the sofa at Maggy's house, sharing a bottle of Prosecco that Lou picked up on her way home.

'I think we've earned this after the day we've had,' Lou says, topping up both their glasses.

She had been right in her prediction: it had been the shop's busiest day by far. On Maggy's suggestion, she had put an email sign-up sheet on the counter and by the end of the day had a long list of addresses to add to her new database and a plan to start a newsletter talking about the shop but also sharing stories about her vintage collection and how it came about, as well as tips on how to care for and mend old clothes. She might start a blog too and has decided to invest in a decent camera in order to take better pictures of her stock and the shop. Her idea is to better recreate the feel of the shop online in order to attract customers from further afield, as well as building a loyal local customer base. But all of that can wait until another day. For now, she raises her glass to Maggy's, tapping them together with a satisfying 'ding'.

'I can't thank you enough, Maggy, for everything you have done for me. Not just for today, but for everything. You have no idea how much you have helped me. You've helped to turn my life around.'

Her voice is a little unsteady, but she is smiling. She thinks about the many kisses she shared with Pete earlier and their plans to go out for dinner tomorrow night and her smile grows even wider.

Beside her, Maggy is smiling too.

'But, Lou,' she says, 'you've done the same for me.'

Lou watches as Maggy glances around the living room before returning her attention to Lou.

'I felt so lost and directionless when we first met. But having you here has brought colour back into my life. I've just loved having you here.'

'And I've loved living with you too, Maggy. But now I'll be leaving …' Lou says sadly. 'I mean, I am really excited that my flat is ready,' she adds, 'but I'm going to miss seeing you every day.'

Maggy shuffles slightly on the sofa and clears her throat. Her face suddenly looks serious, and a flash of worry rushes through Lou.

'About that …' Maggy says. 'There's something I've been

wanting to talk to you about. It's an idea I had just before you left and have been thinking about ever since.'

Lou nods at her to continue, taking a nervous sip of her drink.

'Spending time in your shop with you has reminded me of how much I used to love working in retail. And, well, it's made me think that I'd like to get back to work. I know that's probably the opposite of what most people my age are doing, but I've never really had a career. I don't want to say I've missed out exactly, because I loved the time I spent with my children. But now I feel ready for a new chapter. I want to have a new sense of purpose. I have decided to put this house on the market and move somewhere smaller. It's much too big for me and it's time for a change – somewhere that's just mine. It's going to free up a decent amount of capital, and if you are interested, I would like to invest in your business.'

Lou's mouth drops open. 'Oh my God, Maggy, this is too generous.'

'This isn't a favour,' she insists, 'it's a business proposal. I see great potential for your business. You are such an expert in your field, but you can't do everything by yourself. You need time to source new stock and build your online presence – and I can manage the shop while you do that. I wouldn't want to take over – it would still be your business – but I'd be there to help.'

It feels to Lou as though a huge weight has just been lifted from her shoulders. Today might have been a good day, but there is still so much work to do on growing her business, work that she would struggle to do on her own. And now she doesn't have to.

'You can take time to think about it, of course,' says Maggy. 'I don't want to pressure you.'

But Lou shakes her head quickly. 'I don't need time to think about it. Yes. Yes, let's do it!'

'Really?' replies Maggy, letting out a small sigh of relief. 'Are you sure?'

Lou lifts her glass again.

'Absolutely,' she replies. 'There's no one I'd rather work with. To business partners.'

Maggy lifts her glass too, a wide smile spreading across her face and making her eyes twinkle.

'To business partners.'

ELEANOR

It's only been six months since Eleanor left New York City, but already she feels at home in her new quiet town, Connie's town. She never pictured herself living somewhere like this, somewhere where she has already learnt so many of her neighbour's names, where the staff at the local café know her order and where the town seems to fall asleep after the sun goes down. But when Connie had confessed how much she had grown to miss her home, Eleanor realised that without Connie there was nothing keeping her in New York any more.

They moved in to their cottage a few months ago, the place feeling enormous, with its two separate bedrooms and its kitchen and living room, after their tiny apartment in Manhattan. It has a small patch of garden where Eleanor has started growing flowers and vegetables in neat rows, finding an unexpected comfort in the feel of soil beneath her fingernails. Eleanor expects that the cottage will feel even bigger before long; Connie has been spending more and more time with Ralph, her rekindled childhood romance, and Eleanor can see a proposal in the not-too-distant future. She doesn't mind though. She likes Ralph, and however much she might miss Connie, the thought of living alone doesn't scare her like it might have done once. She has grown comfortable in her own company, confident in her ability to look after herself.

Every now and then, she thinks of Sydney, wondering for a moment where he might be now. She hopes that he is alone and that he hasn't tricked another girl with his empty promises. Because looking back on it all now, she can see that she was just a girl. It has taken her a long time to realise that and to acknowledge that what happened wasn't her fault.

But right now, Sydney couldn't be further from her thoughts. Because today is the day that she and Connie finally open their shop. For months, they have been working hard, Eleanor making the dresses and Connie finding the premises and decorating the space to perfection. Now, they stand together inside their building, the door still locked and the sign on the door turned to 'Closed', but the place ready at last for its first customers.

Eleanor looks around, pride rushing through her as she takes in the sight of all the neatly hanging dresses, each one carefully designed and made with her own hands and a sewing machine given to her by Connie's mother. She loves everything about the shop, from the shiny bell hanging above the door to the bright new till and the large mirror in the changing room surrounded by the pictures she created, finding calm in the act of sweeping ink and watercolour across a page.

Her new role as a shop owner might be a little different to

the dream she once had of becoming a model, but as Eleanor stands in the bright, tidy space after months of preparation, it feels better than that old dream. Because this one is real and was built with hard work and alongside her best friend.

'It looks good, doesn't it?' says Connie beside her, nervously adjusting the collar of her knee-length dress. They are wearing matching ones for the occasion, Connie's a pale blue and Eleanor's a bright yellow.

'It does,' Eleanor replies, her eyes starting to water.

'The sign looks great,' Connie says. 'It really catches your eye as you walk by.'

Connie had let Eleanor choose the name of the shop. There was only one thing that came to mind.

'They'd be proud of you, you know,' Connie adds, and Eleanor nods in reply, not able to speak, but thankful for the kindness of her friend, the friend who over the years has learnt every part of her story.

Eleanor will never forget her past and everything that she has been through. There will always be an ache, a hole in her life where a sister and a baby once fitted. But for the first time in a long time, she feels hopeful about her future.

'Do you want to open the door?' says Connie, reaching for Eleanor's hand, holding a key out in front of her with the other. Out of habit, Eleanor's fingers rise to the locket that hangs at her neck, a locket filled with a tiny curl of the softest hair. Then she reaches for the key, keeping Connie's hand held tightly in hers. Eleanor turns to her friend with a smile.

'Let's do it together,' she says. It's time for both of them to open the door on a new life. And it might have taken her a long *time, but finally Eleanor has come to believe that she deserves that. It's time for a second chance at happiness.*

EPILOGUE

At the top of the cobbled hill in Frome stands a vintage shop. The rails are filled with colourful clothes that entice customers in when viewed through the large windows. It's a place where memories are sparked by the rustle of fabric, run by two friends who love their shop almost as much as they love each other.

Behind the counter, the space where a yellow dress once hung is now taken up by four photographs in burnished gold frames. Two are black-and-white and show two sisters, their photos hung side by side and close to one another, the way they always should have been.

The third photo shows two women holding up a yellow dress in a shop in America, a shop that the Frome women will soon visit together on a trip that they are classing as 'work' because they plan to source new stock while they are there. They will also pay a visit to their friend in a small town called Cold Spring.

The final image on the wall was taken on the day the vintage shop came back to life. It shows its two owners standing behind the counter, their eyes meeting and their mouths open in laughter, a brief moment that neither of them can exactly remember from the whirlwind of that day but that is captured forever in a photograph.

Beside the photos is one final frame, this one holding a handwritten letter. Without this letter, the vintage shop might not exist. Every now and then while she works, the youngest of the two shop owners glances up at the letter, her eyes settling on one particular phrase. *'Live life colourfully.'* As she looks around the shop, her shop, she thinks that the woman who wrote the letter would like the place that she has built. She thinks that she would be proud.

ACKNOWLEDGEMENTS

As this is my fourth book, I feel as though I should have perfected a succinct acknowledgements page, but the truth is, writing books doesn't get easier – if anything, this one was harder than ever, because life simply got harder too.

This book is about starting a new chapter, and while writing it I began a new one of my own, when I moved, while heavily pregnant, to Frome in Somerset (also the setting of this story!). I'd like to thank everyone who has made me feel at home here in Somerset, in particular Harriet, Joe and Hannah, and my mum friends who have helped me navigate the whirlwind of both a relocation and becoming a parent. Bex, the two Lucys, Em, Fi, Trina, Lizzie and Victoria: it's been a privilege to share this wild ride with you all. And to my friends further afield, who have visited and provided kindness and love from afar: you are the reason why I want to keep writing books with female friendship at their heart.

Independent businesses like Lou's vintage shop really are places that bring people together, and I feel so lucky to live somewhere with such a thriving independent scene. A particular thank you to Tina at my lovely local indie bookshop, Hunting Raven, for welcoming me so warmly to her hometown. And a special mention to Rye Bakery and the River House for all the coffees and pastries over the past year, and for always making my son and I feel so welcome, however many croissant crumbs he leaves in his wake.

As ever, thank you to my wonderful agent, Robert Caskie, and to the whole team at Orion. In particular, thank you to Sarah Benton, Lucy Brem, Britt Sankey, Virginia Woolstencroft and Ellen Turner.

A big thank you to all the readers, reviewers, booksellers, librarians and authors who have supported my previous books. It is an absolute thrill that the 'Also by Libby Page' section at the front of this novel now has three titles underneath it, and that wouldn't be possible were it not for you.

A final thank you to my family. Alex, Mum and Sally and Michael, for everything, but in particular for supporting me through the massive life change of becoming a parent. And to Bruno and our Somerset son, for being my home and my two favourite people. Robin, you fill my life with every colour of the rainbow.

CREDITS

Libby Page and Orion Fiction would like to thank everyone at Orion who worked on the publication of *The Vintage Shop* in the UK.

Editorial
Sarah Benton
Charlotte Mursell
Lucy Brem
Rhea Kurien
Sahil Javed

Copy editor
Francine Brody

Proofreader
Jade Craddock

Contracts
Alyx Hurst
Dan Herron
Ellie Bowker

Audio
Paul Stark
Jake Alderson

Finance
Jasdip Nandra
Sue Baker

THE SUNDAY TIMES **TOP TEN BESTSELLER**

Meet Rosemary, 86, and Kate, 26. Dreamers, campaigners, outdoor swimmers.

Rosemary has lived in Brixton all her life, but everything she knows is changing. Only the local lido, where she swims every day, remains a constant reminder of the past and her beloved husband George.

Kate has just moved to London and feels adrift in the city. She's on the bottom rung of her career as a local journalist, and is determined to make something of it.

So when the lido is threatened with closure, Kate knows this story could be her chance to shine. But for Rosemary, it could be the end of everything. Together they are determined to make a stand, and to prove that the pool is more than just a place to swim - it is the heart of the community.

WELCOME TO THE CAFÉ THAT NEVER SLEEPS …

Day and night, Stella's Café opens its doors to the lonely and the lost, the morning people and the night owls. It's a place where everyone is always welcome, where life can wait at the door.

Meet Hannah and Mona: best friends, waitresses, dreamers. They love working at Stella's – the different people they meet, the small kindnesses exchanged. But is it time to step outside and make their own way in life?

Come inside and spend twenty-four hours at Stella's Café, where one day might just be enough to change your life . . .

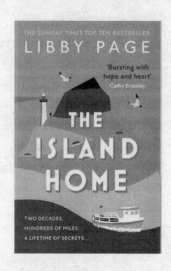

LORNA'S WORLD IS SMALL BUT SAFE.

She loves her daughter and the two of them are all that matter.
But after nearly twenty years, she and Ella are suddenly leaving
London for the Isle of Kip, the tiny remote Scottish island where
Lorna grew up.

ALICE'S WORLD IS TINY BUT FULL.

She loves the community on Kip and how her yoga classes draw
women across the tiny island together. Now Lorna's arrival might
help their family finally mend itself – even if forgiveness means
returning to the past . . .

CAN COMING HOME MEAN STARTING AGAIN?